The smallest thing

Lisa Manterfield

Steel Rose Press
REDONDO BEACH, CA

Published by Steel Rose Press, Redondo Beach, CA

Publisher's Note: This is a work of fiction. Names, characters, places, and incidents are a product of the author's imagination. Locales and public names are sometimes used for atmospheric purposes. Any resemblance to actual people, living or dead, or to businesses, companies, events, institutions, or locales is completely coincidental.

The Smallest Thing/ Lisa Manterfield. — 1st ed.
ISBN 978-0-9986969-2-8

Also by Lisa Manterfield

Fiction
A Strange Companion

Non-Fiction
*I'm Taking My Eggs and Going Home: How One
Woman Dared to Say No to Motherhood*

*Life Without Baby: Surviving and Thriving
When Motherhood Doesn't Happen*

This book is dedicated to the humanitarian aid workers who risk their lives in service to others.

Chapter One

Sunday, July 17

IT'S CLOSE TO MIDNIGHT BEFORE the house falls silent and I'm sure Dad is asleep. I roll out of bed and dig out the clothes I've stashed under my "Keep Calm and Carry On" pillow. Slipping out of my pajamas, I feel the sting of the cool night air against my skin. I pull on jeans and a cami, then cover up with a baggy sweatshirt, knowing I won't be wearing it for long. Holding my breath, I ease up the handle of my window and feel the locks slide from their slots. With a sharp press against the wooden frame, the seals break like the pop of a champagne cork muffled inside a tea towel. I freeze, listening for any sign of disturbance from down the hall. Mum and my little sister Alice are the light sleepers, but I doubt they'd hear me tonight from three hundred miles away. Dad sleeps like the dead. I push open the window and peer at the garden below. In the long, violet midsummer half-light, Dad's potting bench is just visible. It looks a long way down.

I know that climbing out of the window is a childish thing to do. I'm almost eighteen, for pity's sake, close to official adulthood. I should be able to leave by the front door, like a normal person. But if Dad had any inkling of where I was going, or why—or, most especially, with whom—he'd nail the front door shut. If he insists on treating me like a child, then a child he gets. Out the window I go.

I dangle a foot over the ledge until it meets the roof of the sunroom. Swinging myself over the edge, I drop soundlessly onto the potting bench, feeling the weathered timber lurch beneath me. I do a quick check that the coast is clear and scurry across the garden, over the low back wall, and out into the village. My heart thuds in my throat, pumping euphoria through my veins. I am free.

Flashing across the open village green, I duck into the shadow of the war memorial and check for gimlet-eyed neighbors. An upstairs light is on in Dr. Spencer's cottage. If he's about to leave for a house call, he's bound to spot me. News travels faster than the plague around here and if I'm seen, my dad will know about it in ten seconds flat. But I have to risk it. I have to see Ro.

I sprint for the edge of the churchyard and hunker down below the wall, out of sight, trying to catch my breath. The air is warm tonight and the breeze picks up the scent of freshly turned earth from the other side of the mossy limestone wall. I've had to borrow one of Mum's black dresses twice this week to attend the funerals of elderly neighbors, a rare occurrence even in a village with as many oldies as ours. At both services, everyone talked about good people, solid members of the community, their quiet lives well-lived. In other words, two perfectly good lives wasted away in the dullest corner of the British Isles.

Alongside the churchyard's newest residents are the sunken graves of ten traceable generations of my ancestors—the Dead Syddalls, as I call them—person after person who never had the guts or the wherewithal to leave the village of Eyam. It boggles my mind to think that most of them never even saw London, never had the urge to uproot and try a different life. When I think of all the invaders who traveled from far-off lands to conquer our little island—the Vikings, the Romans, the Normans—and all the adventurers who sailed the uncharted seas in search of new worlds, I can't believe I ended up descended from people who never aspired to anything more than the simple country life. Well, that family tradition ends with me. I'm moving to our capital, no matter who tries to stop me, and I swear I am never coming back.

At the crest of the hill I clamber through a rocky entrance, shining the light from my phone onto the damp rock walls around me. A few uneven steps and I burst out into Cucklett Delf, an open, grassy bowl rimmed with trees. At the bottom, a narrow path crosses the stream that marks the Eyam village boundary and meets a rough track coming from Ro's farm on the hillside opposite. The tingle of adventure prickles my skin, and my breath becomes shallow with anticipation. Only now that I am no longer in danger of being caught am I suddenly afraid. Ro and I have talked and dreamed about this possibility for months, since the first night we met, but now I've made it real and my doubts about his resolve come creeping in.

From the darkness, the sound of boots crunching against the stony path moves my way. I tuck my hair behind one ear and lean against the rock beside me, trying to look casual, willing my heart to be quiet. I feel Ro's presence coming closer and closer until I can hear his breath and see his dark, rangy silhouette. His arms wrap around my waist and pull me toward him. When his lips slip against mine, I finally relax.

"Well, this is an unexpected treat," he mumbles at last, his mouth brushing against the top of my head, softening his voice.

"I needed to see you."

His fingers touch the purple streak in my pale hair. "Sneaking out at night? You're turning into a right rebel, aren't you?"

I don't answer at first. I'm not a rebel, not really. I'm just a girl who's ready to start her real life. But if I want to be the person I know I am, and less like the girl my parents think I should be, I'm going to have to make some waves.

"I got the job," I blurt, getting straight to the point.

"Really?" he asks, and I'm not sure if his tone is excitement or shock.

"She rang me today. It's only three nights a week to start, but she says the tips are good and I can probably pick up extra shifts, plus that will leave my days free to work on my mosaics and take them around the markets. And... you're not going to believe this... she said she'd listen to your demo and think about bringing you in."

"You're kidding," he says. This time he's definitely excited.

"Yep. And look at this." I pull out my phone and show Ro the room I found for rent. I pause on the picture that shows the window facing a tiny courtyard and not the one facing a faded brick wall. I definitely don't show him the kitchen the size of a shoe box or the avocado-colored bathroom with a wall decoration that looks alarmingly like toxic mold. "I've got enough saved for the deposit and two months' rent, plus whatever you have. I think we can do it. We can finally get out of here."

I can barely contain my excitement, but I sense Ro's hesitation through the darkness.

"When do you start?" he asks.

"She wants me August first." It's all happened so fast, much faster than I'd imagined, and I'm scrambling to put the pieces of my plan together. It will be a lot easier if Ro doesn't put up a fight.

He pulls back and peers at me in the dim light. "That's only two weeks away. What do your folks think?"

I let out a long sigh that feels like it's been trapped inside my whole life. It's all Ro needs to understand that my rebel streak has yet to extend to telling my dad any of this.

"This is stupid, Em. All this sneaking around. I should be able to pick up my girlfriend at her front door and take her out, not always have to meet her where we won't be seen. And now you're escaping through the window like bloody Rapunzel?"

Technically, the prince snuck *in* to see Rapunzel, but now's not the time to quibble over details. "I'm not the greatest fan of risking my life, either. But you know what my dad's like."

"And you think he's going to let you go to London? Why do you even need his approval?" Until I turn eighteen there's a long list of things I can't do without an adult to vouch for me, including renting a mold-infested room in a flat with three strangers and a boyfriend voted least likely for parental approval. And, technically, I can only work as a bar back until I'm legal to serve drinks, but I won't bore Ro with that hitch just yet, either. If the job offer had come a month later, I wouldn't be in this pickle, but it didn't and so I am.

"Then, let's just go," I tell him. "We can put the flat in your name and my parents can approve or not. Who cares? We might not get another chance like this, and as long as we have each other, we can work out the rest when we get there."

Ro's gaze roams across my face, and for the smallest of

moments I think he's going to say no. And then he throws back his head, his long, dark hair flying around his face, and howls like a wolf on the prowl. "Emmott Syddall, you've got balls," he yelps.

"Oh no, I don't," I say. "I'll prove it." I grab his hand, pulling him off the path and into the soft grass, peeling off my sweatshirt as I go. Ro shucks his jacket and fumbles with the button on my jeans, sending up the scent of coconut from his hair and a whiff of rugged leather. As he kisses me down into the grass, I'm enveloped in the primal scent of moist earth and fresh bracken, its spores warmed by the summer sun and primed for release. With the babble of the stream for background music, I fantasize about a lumpy bed in a damp room with a window that faces a wall. And finally, I feel alive.

Ro slings his arm around my shoulder as he walks me back to the village. We press together down the narrow path, so close we look like a three-legged monster. But neither of us speaks. As a bank of clouds rolls across the moor, blotting out the last of the moon light, the temperature drops and he pulls away from me. "You know I love you, don't you?" he says.

"Of course," I say back, but something prickles just underneath my skin, a sense that he wants to say more, that there's a "but" to this declaration. I don't press him because I don't want to hear it, and he doesn't continue, so we walk in a silence that I fill with plans.

"How are you going to get back in the house?" he asks as we reach the edge of the churchyard.

My London daydreams lurch to a halt. *Oh, bugger. I haven't thought about that.* My plan to get out was flawless; my plan to get back in is nonexistent. There's no way I can climb back up to the window. I have seriously cocked up, and when my dad finds out, the days I'm counting down until I move out will feel more like a lifetime.

As we round the corner, a trio of bright blue flashing lights illuminates the village green.

"Oh, bugger me," I hiss, pulling away from Ro. If my empty room has been discovered and my dad has wigged out and called the police, I'm a dead woman. If he catches me with Ro, I'm buried as well. If Dad ever actually met Ro in person and gave him even a sliver of a chance, he'd see he wasn't so bad. But Ro's dad's farm once belonged to a Syddall, and although the feud was buried over a century ago, the Torre name will forever be synonymous with land thieves and charlatans. And people wonder why I want to leave.

Ro takes a step backward, no doubt having similar thoughts. But as we skim the churchyard wall, I can see that the lights come not from a police car, but an ambulance. Several villagers have gathered around, and there's no way I could get by without being seen.

"Something bad's happened," I say. "You should go."

He pulls me into the church's lych-gate and gives me a long, hard kiss. "Don't get caught," he whispers, then scoots off into the darkness.

Slipping around the edge of the village green, I pat down my swollen lips and flushed face, trying to look as if I've just stepped outside to see what's going on. I glance back at Ro for a last snatch of moral support, but he's long gone. I have no option now but to get out of this mess alone.

A small group, fleece jackets and fluffy dressing gowns wrapped hurriedly over their nightwear, has gathered near the gate of Dr. Spencer's cottage. At the center, our neighbor, Mrs. Glover, holds court, her hands waving excitedly. An ambulance in the village could be the highlight of her year, a guaranteed source of gossip for the nosey old bat. I inch into the periphery of the cluster, but before I can glean what's going on, the front door of Dr. Spencer's cottage opens and a paramedic backs out, jockeying one end of a stretcher. A second paramedic has the other end, and between them, under a white blanket, lies the stocky form of the young doctor who confirmed I was "healthy as a horse" at my checkup just last week. He had seemed completely fine. Even through the semi-darkness and flash of blue lights, I can see his handsome face is pale and glossy, as if this is a wax version of the compassionate man who always warms his stethoscope. An oxygen mask is secured across his face, and his eyes are glazed. Down one side of his cheek is a dark rivulet that appears to have come from his nose. My mouth goes dry. I am fairly certain the rivulet is blood.

The chatter among the group stills as Dr. Spencer is carried by. Each of us shrinks back, as if hounded by a fog-like sense of doom. Whatever has happened to Dr. Spencer is serious. I pull away, leaning out of the fog's reach. As the solemn procession moves past, Dr. Spencer's unfocused eyes suddenly seem to clarify, his stare connecting with mine. In that wild-eyed glance, I see fear. I hold his gaze, the blood chilling in my veins, finding myself in the disconcerting position of offering our family doctor my silent reassurance that he will be okay. And then the paramedics load him into the ambulance and pull away.

"What's going on?" an all-too-familiar voice says behind me.

I keep my eyes forward, praying my dad won't recognize me, won't sense the presence of his own flesh and blood.

"Emmott?" he says. Truly, I have no luck.

I'm ready with a lie about being woken by the commotion, but Mrs. Glover (God love her) saves me by pouncing on the opportunity to share valuable information with my dad. "It was just the flu is all," she gushes. "But he took a terrible turn. I heard the fuss next door, and then the ambulance arrived. Poor lad looks awful."

My dad nods gravely. "Where's Louise?" he asks.

His question is answered when Dr. Spencer's wife steps out of the house, closing the door behind her. In her loose sweatshirt pulled over pink polka dot pajamas, Louise looks like a little girl who's woken up from a bad dream. Pale, disoriented, and frightened, she's a barely-recognizable remnant of the energetic leader of our village conservation group. It's the change in Louise that shocks me into realizing how serious the situation is.

For a second, Dad looks torn between the panicked old lady and the vulnerable young woman, his wayward daughter temporarily forgotten.

"I'll drive you to the hospital," he tells Louise, taking her by the elbow and guiding her to his car. He's only gone a few steps before he turns to me and narrows his eyes. I think for certain he's going to come down on me like a ton of bricks. I prepare for a public humiliation of epic proportions, but instead, he says, "Make yourself useful and make Mrs. Glover a cup of tea. And then get yourself home."

As I watch his receding back, a flicker of anger flares inside me. Is my father really so consumed with the welfare of our neighbors that he's oblivious to his daughter's covert activities? Or does he simply not care? As his car pulls away and my neighbors disperse back to their beds, I wonder if I've just been handed the freedom I've been fighting so hard to win. If Dad has given up trying to control me, my victory feels far less sweet than I'd expected.

"I don't know what we'd do around here without your dad," Mrs. Glover says, shuffling her slippered feet back toward her house.

It's meant as a compliment, but beneath her words I hear the sting of comparison, the suggestion that she finds me lacking. A knot of fury unravels inside me, and I'm reminded of why I hate it here. No matter what I do, no matter where I go, no matter what I accomplish in my life, I will always be measured against the standard of my dad: a man who never left the village he was born in, who is proud to descend from similarly unambitious blood. She's right that I am nothing like him—but I will always be judged as something less.

I step toward the old woman, determined to set her straight, but then I remember: I'm leaving. I don't have to be nice, and I don't have to live up to my dad's standards anymore.

"Make your own cup of tea," I say. And with that, I march home to bed.

I don't go back to sleep, though. I toss and turn for hours, planning my escape to London one minute and feeling bad for telling off Mrs. Glover the next. I barely feel I've slept when, sometime around dawn, I get a text from Dad.

Dr. Spencer is dead.

Chapter Two

Monday, July 18

I STARE AT DAD'S TEXT, BUT it takes ages for the words to make sense. I see them—*passed away in the early hours*—but I can't get a grasp on what they really mean. I know people die every day, several every second even, but my mind can't seem to reconcile the sudden end of my neighbor, how he could be laughing and talking with me a few days ago and then suddenly be gone, like someone hit the "off" button on his remote control and threw away the batteries. It doesn't add up. He was young—younger than my parents by a long way—and healthy. He was a doctor, for goodness sake! I force my mind to picture him dead, lying in hospital, the life gone out of him, but each time he sits up and grins as if he's just pulled the best prank ever. What scares me most of all is, if this could happen to Dr. Spencer, it could happen to anyone. We're all just a flick of a switch from oblivion, every single one of us. I feel as if someone has performed one of those tricks where they yank away a tablecloth, leaving the plates and cups in place. From a distance, it looks as if only the cloth has been moved, but everything on the table has felt the silent friction of its departure.

I brush my hands across my face to rub away these shaky thoughts. I need something solid and logical to grasp onto, something that makes some sort of sense. I text Deb.

You hear about Dr Spencer?

I wait an unacceptable length of time before Deb responds. I love my best friend, but she is stuck in the Dark Ages when it comes to electronic communication. *No*, she replies, at last. *What?*

I fill her in on what I know about Dr. Spencer's illness and unexpected demise. *Flu*, I write. *How do you die of flu?*

A second later, Deb FaceTimes me. Even at this early hour, she is dressed in black. Black isn't a statement for Deb, it's a matter of practicality. "My brain has more important things to think about than what to wear," she likes to say.

"Are you sure it was the flu?" Deb asks.

"That's what I heard, but people don't usually die of the flu, do they?"

"Not from the common strains, no," Deb says, switching to her talking encyclopedia voice. "Maybe the very old and very young, people with compromised immune systems."

"Doesn't sound like him."

"But then there was the Spanish flu. Completely different animal. I won't bore you with the details, but basically it killed off the young and strong."

"Oh, great," I say, trying to ignore the creeping fingers of worry that ripple across my stomach. "That's us."

"Well, it's *you*. That particular strain had a thing for strong immune systems, so for once, I'd be among the least likely to get it."

Deb is notorious for getting every cold and bug that comes around, and coupled with her asthma, they wreak havoc. I blame it on the fact that she spends way too much time in her room, hunched over her books. On the other hand, that's the reason she'll be heading off to Oxford after the summer and why someday my best friend will insist I call her "Dr. Elliot."

"Do you think that's what he had?" I ask, not sure I want to hear the answer. A chill sense of dread flares up inside me. "What if it's not the flu? What if it's something worse, like Zika or Ebola or some new thing and we're the first to get it?"

The look Deb gives me will come in handy for telling her patients in a kind, comforting, but no-nonsense way not to get their knickers in a twist over nothing. "It's too cold for those kinds of mosquitos here, and I can't think of a single person in this village who's been anywhere near Africa lately. Can you?"

I shake my head.

"Most likely he had something else going on that hadn't been diagnosed."

"Are you telling me I shouldn't worry?"

"I am. But keep your hands washed, don't touch your face, and don't go around kissing too many people, just in case."

My face flushes as thoughts of Ro and last night come rushing in. "It's a bit late for that," I say.

"Oh, Salty," Deb sighs, my nickname rolling off her tongue. "No need to ask who the lucky recipient was, I suppose."

Deb—Pepper because some bright spark thought my blond and her dark hair made us look like salt and pepper pots—listens as I relay my adventures from the night before. I tell her about my daring descent from the window, about noticing the light on at Dr. Spencer's, but not knowing then what it meant. I tell her about the ambulance and the terrible look on Dr. Spencer's face, and about Dad all but ignoring the fact that I was there. And I tell her about my decision to go to London, with or without my parents' consent.

"You never want to do anything the easy way, do you?" she says with an admiring smile. "If you're adamant about going, why not wait another month until you can get a job that could actually support you?"

I love my friend, but sometimes we are more like chalk and cheese than salt and pepper. Even though it was our differences that brought us together in the first place, it's still hard to explain to someone on a trajectory to a brilliant career in medicine that I'd rather take my chances and risk living on the edge of poverty than bury my dreams for the sake of security.

"I'm tired of waiting for something to happen. I can't stand to be stuck here for one more month."

"You don't have to explain that to me," she says.

During the first nine years of her life, Deb lived in Canada... and Brazil and Malaysia and Saudi Arabia. When her dad finally got sick of trailing his family around after his wife's career, he moved Deb and her brother here, to (and I quote) "a nice quiet place to raise kids." A newcomer to our school was a rare novelty, and Deb's exotic background made her a flashing red target for the mean kids. But to me, she was like a precious jewel in a heap of dull gray pebbles, and I immediately felt protective of her. Her defense cost me a torn uniform and a trip to the headmistress, but our friendship was cemented. And even though we're now on different paths, we share a common goal: To live our lives anywhere but here.

"But why the rush?" she says. "You've got your whole life ahead of you."

"Dr. Spencer probably thought the same thing."

Deb nods that she knows I'm right. "And what does Ro think about all this?"

I answer with a coy smile.

Deb sighs and twists her mouth across to one side of her face, a sure sign she's contemplating something profound. "If anybody can pull off an insane plan like this, it's you," she says. "But not everyone has the stomach for risk. Go with Ro, if you must, but make sure you can support yourself if you have to. That's all I'm saying."

I could protest her suggestion that Ro might get cold feet, but I know she has my best interests at heart. She isn't saying I shouldn't trust Ro, only that I should hang my own safety net first. A niggling feeling I don't want to voice tells me my friend has good advice.

Building a safety net means keeping my summer job for two more weeks, which means keeping my boss happy. Unfortunately, my boss is also my dad, and with Mum off at Auntie Margie's with my little sister for another ten days, I'm Dad's right-hand woman. In an attempt to get—and stay—on his good side, I button my army-green work shirt up to the neck before slipping into the brown sleeveless jacket that makes me look as if I'm heading out on safari instead of guiding old ladies around the historical highlights of Eyam. Everything about my uniform screams "boring" and "safe," just as Dad likes it. I tuck my purple hair streak out of sight, pinning it with a girlie clip, and trade my trusty pink special edition Doc Martens—the ones that make me feel like I can kick any of life's obstacles aside—for sensible brown walking shoes. I look like a drab, middle-aged version of myself. I look like my dad.

Dad still isn't home by the time I'm ready, so I use the spare hour or so before work to dash off an email accepting the job, put in an application for the room, and fill Ro in on the events of the previous night and my close call with Dad. I don't press him about London. I'll wait until he brings it up. But, with Deb's warning to remain independent pinging around in my brain, I search around a website, inappropriately named A Bit on the Side, listing hundreds of gigs in the city. I add lunch delivery person, bicycle courier, and even human billboard to my list of possible ways to make some extra cash. On the next page, I spot a listing for part-time tour guides. *Over my dead body*, I think, and turn my attention instead to packing.

I'm almost ready to leave the house when Dad phones. "You'll have to manage on your own today. I need to stay with Louise until her folks can get here."

This is my dad in a nutshell. He always has to have his nose in everybody else's business. This is exactly the sort of thing I want to get away from. But as he seems to have forgotten about me being out last night, I opt not to poke the tiger.

"Dad," I say, gathering my resolve to break my own news about leaving. "I've got something I need to talk to you about."

"Do you feel ill?" he asks.

"What?" His question shocks me into temporary silence. Does he know something he's not telling me? "No. Why?"

"Then if it's not urgent, it will have to wait until tonight."

With that, he goes back to his business, leaving me feeling as if I've walked into a freshly washed window and wondering why I didn't see it.

At the village green, the same cluster of neighbors has regrouped to tittle-tattle about Dr. Spencer's untimely departure. I consider slipping in to see if I can glean more information about this flu thing, but a familiar rumble stops me. Seconds later, a red minibus with "Oldfield View Residential Facility" emblazoned on the side trundles around the hairpin bend by the stone "Welcome to Eyam" sign and disgorges a haphazard clump of elderly ladies. I force a welcoming smile, and the ladies fall in line like waddling ducklings, their collapsible metal walking sticks clicking in a syncopated beat beneath a twitter of excitable chatter. It's a slow procession to the churchyard, the ladies stopping every ten steps to fumble with cameras and snap photos. I wish they'd hurry up so I can get this over with, although now that the rain has stopped, leaving a pristine blue sky in its wake, even I have to admit that the village is postcard perfect. The flowers have pushed through in tubs and hanging baskets around the doors of our neighbors' cottages, adding a sunny charm that the tourists flock to enjoy. Every square of front garden is ready to burst with blooms—hollyhocks, roses, fuchsia, and sunflowers, rambling Scarlet Runners, and brilliant displays of petunias and chrysanthemums. It's all too jolly and sunny, and in complete contrast to the gray cloud of unease that hangs over me.

The tour gets off to a rocky start. I know the spiel by heart, but I can't focus on the story I'm supposed to tell. My thoughts flit from the Dead Syddalls to Dr. Spencer to my troubling conversation with Deb until finally landing on my exodus to London and the big talk I still have to have with Dad. The old ladies don't seem to notice my stammering. They cluck and ooh with every tidbit of history, and a small, round woman gushes, "Aren't you lucky living in a lovely place like this? No wonder your family's never wanted to leave."

I hold my smile in place for her benefit, but inside I'm thinking, *Lady, you are wronger than wrong.*

As the troupe waddles off to the tea rooms for refreshments, I have a vision of myself years from now, no longer seventeen, but middle-aged, like my dad. I'm standing right here, proudly spouting about the dullness of my family tree. The enormity of that fate hits me, my alternate future staring me in the face. In keeping my dreams of moving to London to myself, my parents have assumed I will stay. If I don't pluck up the courage to tell Dad about my plans, I may as well join the Dead Syddalls and rot away for all eternity in the only place I've ever called home.

My thoughts lurch to a halt when a bright yellow ambulance swings around the village green and pulls up outside the Coopers' house, next door to the Spencers'. A new uneasiness grows as, minutes later, the paramedics emerge carrying Karen Cooper, who moved here with her husband a few months ago. She is sitting up and talking, but her face has the same yellowish pallor as Dr. Spencer's.

Deb assured me I shouldn't worry just yet, but three deaths in the space of two weeks isn't exactly normal. If Karen has the same thing, it means it's catching, and there is no way I'm waiting around to find out if it's coming for me.

As the ambulance pulls away, I race home, taking the stairs to my room two at a time. I hammer out a resignation letter to Dad, leaving it on the kitchen table for whenever he gets home. Then I type up everything I must do to get to London. I save the file as "The Beginning of the Rest of My Life."

Chapter Three

Sunday, July 24

ON THE MORNING OF MY third funeral in as many weeks, a crowd gathers outside our small stone church, filling the forecourt and spilling out through the lych-gate and into the street. The mood is quiet and respectful, but underneath is an air of worry. I don't know anyone who didn't like Dr. Spencer—there was nothing to dislike about him—and ordinarily, almost everyone in Eyam would turn out to pay their respects. But this flu thing has people in a flap, and almost half have stayed away.

Dad has no such qualms. He immediately steps through the gate and circulates among our neighbors, shaking hands and offering supportive words. I hold back, staying out of his way. Since I handed him my notice last week, he's been more distant than ever. "Why in God's name would you want to move there?" was his first response, before he remembered he was supposed to put his foot down and forbid me. Mum didn't seem surprised by my news or Dad's response when I rang to tell her. "He'll live," she said, confirming my fear that he had hung all his hopes on my staying, not just to keep me close to home, but to set me on a track that follows in his footsteps. His plans couldn't have been any further from mine if he'd decided to send me on a homemade rocket ship to Mars.

I have not mentioned Ro's part to either of them. Why rock an already unstable boat?

Finally, I spot Deb trailing alongside her family. As usual, she's dressed head to toe in black. For once, she blends in with everyone else. Except for one small detail. "Hiya, Salty," she says, her voice muffled inside the blue surgical mask covering her face.

"What's the disguise in aid of?" I ask.

Deb indicates with a twitch of her head that we should move out of earshot to talk. For a horrible moment I think she's going to tell me she's got the flu, and I hurry after her to hear her news.

"Helena's freaking out," Deb says, referring to her step-mother by first name, as she always does.

"About what? Are you okay?"

"Fine," Deb sighs, as if the explanation is too wearisome. "We went to this exhibition of medieval medicine in Manchester yesterday. Really fascinating. But now she's all wigged out about epidemics."

Deb reaches into her pocket and hands me a small plastic bottle. I glance down at the label. Hand sanitizer. If we weren't at a funeral, I'd laugh from relief.

"I certainly appreciate modern medicine and the importance of basic sanitation," she says, squeezing a blob of clear gel into my hands, "but Helena has gone seriously off the deep end. She's talking about sending Tom and me to our grandparents."

"What?" I say. "She can't do that."

"I know. I'd rather die from the flu than boredom. And Mum's off in Russia again, building pipelines to China, so we can't stay with her. But don't worry, I'll work my magic and talk Helena out of it. That said, I wouldn't shake too many hands if I were you. Don't want you spending your last days here in bed."

"I wish," I say, my mind flitting to Ro. Since I gave Dad my notice, I swear he's tried to wring every last minute of work out of me before I leave. I've barely had a chance to be with Ro.

Deb is about to say more when a line of black cars pulls up in front of the church. We sober instantly, pressing against the chilly stone wall and bowing our heads as Louise is helped out of the car by her family. I wait for a team of pallbearers to lift Dr. Spencer's coffin from the hearse, but instead a lone man in a frock coat and top hat carries a small wooden chest through the lych-gate, up the stone path, and into the church.

"Bloody Nora. Is that him?" I whisper to Deb.

She nods. "They cremated him. Coroner's orders."

"Why?" I hiss as the congregation funnels into the church in silence.

"The post-mortem was inconclusive," she says.

"So they don't even know if it was the flu?"

"Right," she says.

"So why the mask?"

"Well," Deb lowers her voice to a whisper, "something killed him, and until we know what, Helena thinks it's wise to be cautious."

At the door of the church, I hesitate, glancing around at all the bodies in this enclosed space. Deb and her family aren't the only ones being cautious. In the back rows and around the edges of the congregation, small pods of masked people huddle away from the others, leaving gaps like missing teeth in the normally orderly rows of pews. Beneath the subdued murmur of voices, the tension is palpable, causing the hairs on the backs of my hands to prickle. Perhaps Helena isn't overreacting at all. I fumble for a tissue in my pocket and press it over my mouth and nose, pretending to stifle my grief.

Taking a quick glance around the congregation, I'm surprised to see Ro sitting with his parents and older brothers, six black-haired Torres in a pew by themselves. That they came all the way into Eyam from their farm says a lot about the impact of Dr. Spencer's death. I'm not surprised to see that none of them wears a mask. Like me, Ro comes from a long line of locals, and people around here are made of tough stuff. Among the masked people, I recognize Mrs. Glover, the world's biggest hypochondriac, and Millie Talbot's family, who never mingle because they think they're better than the rest of us. And Deb will be the first to admit that Helena tends to err on the overprotective side with her stepchildren. None of these people are good judges of danger, and if our bug were anything more serious than the flu, we'd have heard about it by now. I wish I could sit by Ro, feel the comfort of his arm around me and his body pressed close. *Soon*, I think. I shoot him a quick, seductive look from behind my tissue, checking to make sure no one else has seen, and hurry to the front of the church where Dad has secured a pew for us, right behind Louise. He clearly isn't worried about a bout of summer flu.

The Reverend Mompesson gives what the old folks will later refer to as "a nice service." He talks about Dr. Spencer's place in the community, his service to its residents, and how he always had a kind word and a smile for everyone. He reminds us all, as if we could forget, that life is short. He acknowledges Louise and their families and asks them to find strength now that the doctor has been "called back to God's side." It's an odd phrase, and I drift away for a moment, visualizing God looking down on his flock and realizing he hasn't had a good chat with Dr. Spencer for a while. *I think I'll call him back*, thinks God, and the next minute the doctor is struck down with the flu and transported up to God's couch, all because the Almighty was lonely? I don't mean to be sacrilegious, but I hate the randomness of death. I hate that a person who wasn't even that old could suddenly be gone. I try to imagine not being here anymore. I can't picture what it would feel like to be dead. That's stupid, it wouldn't feel like anything, of course, but when I try to imagine me, Emmott, suddenly no longer existing, I just can't get my head around it.

From nowhere, a knot of emotion forms in my chest, making it hard to breathe. I don't know what this is. I've been sad about Dr. Spencer's death, of course, but this fresh grief is unexpected. It's like the sadness over losing Dr. Spencer has magnetized every bit of sadness and fear I've ever felt, drawing them close until they've collected inside me as an enormous clump of loss. I had no idea I'd be so affected.

Dad glares at me sideways, and I blink away my tears before he can see them. I wait for him to put his arm around me, like Mum would, or give my shoulder a squeeze, or pass me his hanky. I can almost feel him deciding which to do, and I will him to do something. But when I look up at him again, his eyes are focused squarely on the altar. I suck back my tears, pulling my sadness back inside, where I know it will be safe.

The vicar keeps the service short and everyone seems grateful, but as he wraps up his eulogy to Dr. Spencer, he asks that we keep those not present in our thoughts. I think he's talking about our own dearly departed, but then he mentions Andy Hawksworth, with whom Dad sometimes plays darts, and who was most definitely alive and well a week ago. Only now he isn't well enough to pay his respects today. And the Wainwrights, who've stayed at home with their two sick boys. Then he breaks the news that Karen Cooper passed away this morning after a short illness. A ripple of shock makes its way around the congregation. I pivot to find Deb and gauge her reaction, but she's not there anymore.

As we file out of the church, Dad's face is grim.

"Dad," I whisper. "This isn't good."

He looks at me as if I've just said the most moronic thing ever. "No," he says. "In fact, I'd say that, for the Coopers, it's absolutely tragic."

"Deb's parents are really worried," I say, telling him about their plans to send Deb away. "Do you think we should leave?"

"Leave?" Dad stops so abruptly that we almost cause a pile-up with the people behind us. "And go where, exactly?"

"I don't know. Auntie Margie's with Mum and Alice?"

Dad shakes his head and I think he's going to say something sarcastic about me leaving soon anyway, but instead he fixes me with a look that makes me feel about an inch tall. "If ever there was a time for us all to stick together, it's now. Yes, we need to try our best not to catch this flu, but you can't just run away whenever things get difficult, Emmott. Especially when people need you."

And with that, he strides away, leaving *me* at the exact moment I need him most.

Slowly, the mourners disperse, heading to Louise's for strong tea and slices of pork pie. Deb and her family have already gone home, hopefully not to pack their suitcases. Standing in the church forecourt, I have no idea what to do next. I don't want to go to Louise's and be around all this sadness and worry anymore, especially now I know this flu is going around fast, and I definitely don't want to be around my dad and his pathetic lectures. But I don't want to be alone either.

I step off the path into the freshly mown grass and scuff my way toward the part of the churchyard where the newer granite and marble headstones sit. My great-grandparents are buried here, along with Dad's dad, who died before I was born, and Grandma Syddall, whom we lost a couple of years ago. Next to my grandparents is a small, white stone—a memorial, not a grave. The grass is trimmed neatly all around it and the stone washed clean so the inscription can be clearly read.

"Sandra Ellen Syddall" is part of the reason Dad is so opposed to my leaving. Years ago, before I was born, even before my parents met, Dad's younger sister—my wild Auntie Sandra—went off backpacking around Europe and never came back. He doesn't talk about it much, doesn't talk about it at all, actually, but Mum told me once, after I pressed her for the story, that a fellow backpacker, part of a group Auntie Sandra had met up with, had been charged with her disappearance. Nothing was ever proved, he was later released, and the mystery was forgotten. But not by Dad. The short leash on which he tries to keep me is thanks to a woman I never even met. It's another reminder that death isn't selective, that neither youth, innocence, nor good behavior will buy you a free pass. The thought gives me little comfort.

Just then, I spot Ro breaking away from the crowd and making his way to the bottom end of the churchyard. He waves, inviting me to follow. His long, lean figure ambles over the crest of the hill and drops out of sight. I know what I'm supposed to do; I should go to Louise's, offer my condolences, share my sadness with my friends and neighbors. But the tug of my other life pulls at me again. "Life is short" is no longer just an expression for Dr. Spencer, and I'm painfully aware that I can no longer fritter my short life away on other people's expectations. I need to go where I am wanted, and I need to get the hell out of this village before I become generation number eleven of the Dead Syddalls.

Turning away from the village, no longer caring who sees me go, I brush through the damp grass and pick my way through the headstones to where Ro, and my future, are waiting.

Chapter Four

THE FOLLOWING MORNING, I THROW back the sheets, ready to finish my last week of work in the Syddall family tour business. A list of tasks bounces through my mind like the Bingo balls Mr. Glover pulls for the Tuesday night games in the village hall. Last night, Ro agreed to come with me to London. Now we have to decide what to pack and what to store, given the small amount of space we will have. I need to transfer some savings to pay the deposit on the room and see if I can scrounge a set of old sheets or if I'll need to buy new ones. We text back and forth as I dart between getting dressed, packing up my art supplies, throwing books into boxes, and fielding texts from Alice about whether she can take over my room when I'm gone. I'm so excited by the prospect of leaving, I can barely keep my thoughts in order. But as I pull on my uniform, I'm aware that something else feels different today. In my gut is a lump of regret that I didn't go to Louise's to pay my last respects to Dr. Spencer. Beside it is a nugget of sadness for the distance that's grown between Dad and me and a small ball of worry that Deb might have left. And burgeoning underneath all that is a niggling feeling that something is on the brink of going wrong.

All this is mixed together inside me, and yet none of it is exactly the thing that feels wrong.

Outside, the atmosphere feels like a Bank Holiday, one of those bustling, sunny Mondays when the tour buses rumble through one after the other, and parked cars squeeze into nonexistent spaces, backing onto grass verges and littering the streets until the village looks more like a car park than a scenic spot. The bustle outside makes it feel like something big is happening, but it doesn't feel like something good. I pad to the landing window and pull back the curtain. A line of cars snakes through the village, just as I'd expected, but it takes me a moment to see what's wrong with the picture. The cars are facing the wrong way. It's not until I recognize Deb's parents' Mercedes that I understand what I'm looking at. These aren't tourists trying to get *into* Eyam; these are residents trying to get out.

I pull on the rest of my clothes, run my fingers through the knots in my hair, and head downstairs to find out what's going on. The house is empty, which means Dad is undoubtedly out in the village in the thick of the melee. I jog out the front door and into the street, trying to see where everyone is going.

At the bottom of the village, right by the welcome sign, is gathered a cluster of people wearing fluorescent yellow jackets. Each has "Police" emblazoned on the back. That curve in the road is notorious for accidents—people taking the bend too fast—and the stone sign has been rebuilt several times. Judging by the number of police, this must be a bad one. I have a fleeting thought about today's visiting ladies and venture a little closer. I want to know what's happening, but I'm afraid of what I might see. After the way Dr. Spencer looked at me the night he was carried away, I don't want to be among the nosey parkers gawking at someone on the worst—or even last—day of her life. Plus, if I really want to see what happened, I have no doubt I'll be able to find video online within the hour.

As I turn away, a noise looms overhead. Above the church tower is a large, green helicopter, its rotors making an eerie whooping sound. All around, the leaves on the trees turn their underbellies upwards so that the green becomes silver, as if the color has been blown away. It's a military chopper. Suddenly the holiday atmosphere I've been sensing takes on a different meaning. The energy in the air isn't excitement, it's fear. It washes over my skin, leaving a trail of goose pimples in its wake. I turn back toward the accident scene, and that's when I spot my dad.

He's standing in the middle of the street, talking to someone. But the other person isn't talking back; he's shouting and flailing his arms. His body arches up, and even from this distance I can see fury radiating from him. He looks like he could kill someone—and the nearest target is my dad.

I take off down the street, passing car after car, each one vaguely familiar. The occupants of some of the cars have climbed out and stand in the street looking toward the activity. I recognize some of my neighbors, and someone calls my name, but I don't stop. I keep running toward my dad, and even though I have no idea what I'll do when I get there, my adrenaline keeps pushing me forward.

Dad's attacker is Mr. Wainwright, the math teacher at my old school. I'm not sure I've ever heard him raise his voice before, except the one time when one of the boys in my class threw a pen at me, but hit Millie Talbot instead. I remember Mr. Wainwright losing it that day, but his yelling was a whimper compared to the fury that flushes his face now. Mrs. Wainwright stands by the open car door, and the faces of the Wainwright kids press against the window, their cheeks pale and their eyes rimmed red with tears. I cannot imagine what my dad has done to incur this wrath.

"This is my family we're talking about, John," Mr. Wainwright shouts. "My kids. If your wife were here, you wouldn't think this way. It's more than a bit convenient that she's not, though, isn't it? Did you know this was coming? Did you send her away and leave the rest of us to fend for ourselves?" He pushes my dad in the chest. "Did you?"

Dad takes a step back but keeps his balance. He holds up his hands in a gesture of peace. "I didn't know anything about it, Alan. They didn't give us any warning. If they had, do you think I'd still be here?"

"It's my family," Mr. Wainwright yells, and his voice cracks. "My family."

I don't know what's going on exactly, but I do know I'm missing from this discussion. Yes, Mum and Alice are away visiting Auntie Margie, but I'm not. "Dad?" I say, stepping forward. "What's going on?"

They both turn to look at me, but it's Mr. Wainwright who speaks. "Oh, Emmott," he says, his angry mask falling to reveal a look of anguish. "Oh, no." He seems to deflate at the sight of me, and although I've somehow diffused the tension between him and Dad, his reaction gives me no peace of mind.

"What's happening, Dad?" I ask. My voice is frantic, and I'm scared of something I cannot see. But as I look from Mr. Wainwright to my dad, I see something that freezes me to the core. Behind the line of police officers is a row of armored Land Rovers. They're parked end-to-end across the entire road into the village. On either side is a barricade. It's clear to me this is no traffic accident. "Dad?" I urge. "What is it?"

My dad doesn't answer right away, but in the brief glance that flits between him and Mr. Wainwright, a whole encyclopedia of information is exchanged. And then my dad puts his arm around my shoulder and turns me away. "Take your family home, Alan," he says over his shoulder. "Get them into the house and keep them there until we get more information. I'm going to do the same."

He pulls me next to him and leads me back up the street past the row of cars. It's supposed to be a comforting gesture, but this uncharacteristic PDA is the most terrifying thing of all.

"Dad," I say again, pulling away from him. "Please tell me what's happening."

Dad drags his hand across his face as if wiping away something he doesn't want me to see. Underneath is a face older than I've ever seen before. "They've quarantined the village," he says. "This thing that's going around? It isn't the flu."

Chapter Five

B Y THE AFTERNOON, THE FIRST invaders of our village
have arrived in a caravan of vehicles. They form a camp
inside the barricade, as if the circus has come to town. Heeding
Dad's warning to stay inside, I press against the upstairs
window, gaping as trucks and buses disgorge an army of
aliens—doctors, scientists, investigators, and, for all I know,
assassins, given that they all look the same, sealed inside their
yellow hazmat suits. They spill into Eyam as if someone has
knocked the lid off an ant farm, each ant preprogrammed to
go about its task, as if quarantining innocent people and taking
over their lives is the kind of thing they do every day. They're
robots, not humans, doing their work, oblivious to the fact that
real people's lives have just been upended, that *my* life has been
turned upside-down.

I'm overcome with an urge to run, to make a break for
it and take my chances at the barricades. But something else
has arrived in my village. Guns. They are not the polished,
tended shotguns of hunters. These new guns are brandished
for enforcement, black gashes to keep us in our once-tranquil
village. I have never seen weapons like this before, and the
shock of their threat terrifies me. I am living in a war zone.

I've tried all day to reach Mum, but Auntie Margie says she

had to go up to London for a meeting, and my calls just roll straight to voicemail. When my phone finally pings, it's Ro's name, not Mum's, that flashes on my screen.

You OK? he types. *Where are you?*

I tell him I'm at home.

Quarantined?

Yes.

Fucking hell, is his only response, and yet his shock touches a spot deep in my chest.

I need to see you, I type.

What?

I know we're supposed to stay in, but I just want to see you.

Can't, he writes back. *Won't let anyone near the quarantine zone.*

The room seems to slide away from me as I feel the distance between Ro and me stretch. From the first night we met, when Ro's band played a pop-up gig at the village Bonfire Night last November, everything has been set against us. But we always vowed to be a united front, to not allow anyone or anything to tell us we couldn't be together. But this, this *obstacle*, is the first that feels truly insurmountable. I should be glad that Ro is safe, that his family's farm is well outside the zone. Maybe this means the breakout is isolated, something they can control quickly, something that will be gone as fast as it came. Or perhaps it means that the suspected source is *in* the village, an invisible specter silently touching its victims. How do I know if it's touched me? A brutal reality hits me. I could get sick, and I could die. My stomach twists around inside me, and the room begins to waver. What I want more than anything else right now is the thing I might never have again—to hold Ro and know I have an ally.

You OK? Ro asks.

I steady myself. My heart swells, and my eyes prickle. I had no idea this was what I needed to hear, that someone, one person, cares enough to ask if I'm okay.

I'm scared, I tell him, the admission catching me off guard. But I'm relieved at having someone to tell.

But, are you all right? he responds.

I realize then what he's really asking me. Not whether I am anxious or afraid or confused or lost. He's asking me if I am sick. If I think this thing is infectious. If there's a chance I could have passed it to him. He's not asking if *I* will be okay; he's asking if *he* will be okay.

I square my shoulders, determined not to let this crumble me. Not now. *Fine*, I tell him, to answer his question. But to answer the question I wish he'd asked, I'm no longer sure I am fine at all.

The next time my phone pings, I don't lunge for it right away. If Ro has something else to say, something more reassuring, I'll let him wait. But it's not him; it's Deb.

Nightmare, Deb's text reads. *Total nightmare.*

Where are you? I tap back, half hoping she's left and half hoping she is still close enough to see.

Home. On lockdown. Helena.

I know it's wrong to feel relief that Deb is still here, but I can't imagine going through this without my best friend, even if I can't get to see her.

What have you heard? I ask. I've trawled the news and social media, but no one seems to have actual facts, just speculation about a mysterious breakout, a military operation, an "unfolding situation." It's as if what I can see isn't happening. It's not normal, and the silence scares me.

Not a squeak, Deb types. *They don't know anything yet.*

I'm supposed to leave for London on Saturday.

Not sure that's going to happen IMHO.

The muscles in my jaw knot. This cannot be happening to me. I have plans. I have a future and a job and place to live. *I can't stay here,* I respond.

No choice, she says.

I don't believe there is such a thing as "no other option." *It's a free country,* I type.

Not anymore.

The air sucks in around me, and I can't take a proper breath. Deb has voiced a thought I've been trying to hold at bay: We are prisoners here. My phone slips from my hand, pinging with another message as it falls. I scramble to grab it, hoping for words of reassurance from Deb, but all she has written is: *Don't do anything stupid.*

I don't know if I can promise that. All hell has broken loose around me, and even my brilliant best friend can't change that. And as for not doing anything stupid, that definition has blurred. Nothing here makes sense to me anymore, and I no longer know where the lines between stupidity and self-preservation cross, or if they're now one and the same.

I press my face to the window. From inside my fish bowl, I watch the bizarre story unfold on the stage below me. It's like I'm living in another world, far away from my own, but minute-by-minute that world is closing in until I can't catch a full breath.

I can't stand it another minute. I bolt from the house, out into the village, my ears filling with the unfamiliar sounds of motors running and people shouting. At the yellow barricades, now topped with curls of barbed wire, an angry cluster of my neighbors gathers. I recognize the shapes of their bodies and the contours of their faces, but their violent gestures of hostility are completely foreign. They hurl their objections at the line of riot police on the other side, fighting for the right to be free. From the back of the small but fiery group, something soars over the fence. It appears to be a beer bottle stuffed with a flaming rag, an impromptu Molotov cocktail. I watch in horror as it explodes by the welcome sign. A savage cheer rises from my side of the border, and the line of riot police presses forward, threatening the protesters into retreat. Their presence suggests that this kind of trouble was expected, but it does little to quell the fury of the group.

Something tugs in my gut, just below my ribs, as if an invisible string is pulling me toward the action. It's a feeling of powerlessness, the realization that everything I once believed has been dismantled, and I am drawn to fight, to thrash out against it, even though I know it will be to no avail. I could hurl myself against the barricades and scream to be let out, but when I'm done, I know I will still be trapped here. Fighting my instincts, I drag myself away from the trouble, trying to shake my thoughts into clarity. I have to do something, but going to war with a well-armed enemy isn't the answer.

Away from the front lines, a more subdued cluster of my neighbors gathers in a shocked huddle. Mrs. Glover is in the thick of it, of course, and at the center is my dad, patting arms and bobbing his head in a reassuring manner. I duck my head, praying he won't catch me disobeying his instructions, but I needn't have bothered. He doesn't even notice me as I slip past and make my way to the opposite end of the village. In my rebellion, it's clear I am an army of one.

I hurry past the allotments, the rented gardens where Dad and some of our neighbors grow vegetables, trying to get to a place I can think straight. When I reach the cricket pitch, the sight of a hazmat-suited group stops me. Their suits are white, not yellow, but I don't know yet what makes them different. I can't make out at first what they're doing, until one of them bores a deep hole into the velvet green of the wicket, extracting a slender core of earth. Nearby, another places a silver canister on the ground and steps away. They are taking samples, testing our soil and the air we breathe. Is it possible this thing is seeping up from the very ground on which we live? Tiny footprints of fear travel up my body as the realization hits me: They have no idea what is killing my village. It's this knowledge that suddenly clarifies a plan.

Along the back edge of the cricket pitch, beyond a low stone wall, a narrow path runs through a small wood and out to a rutted lane that provides access to the surrounding fields. The authorities have the main roads into Eyam covered, that much is apparent, but they can't know all the local routes in and out. But I do.

I'm not the only one with this thought, apparently. Up ahead of me, the figures of the five Talbots disappear into the copse of trees by the river. Fellow escapees. I will them to succeed because if they can find a way out, maybe I can too. I hold my breath, wondering where they've gone, trying to guess their escape route. How long before I can be sure they've made it? But I can't wait to find out. If this exit is discovered, the authorities will bump up security in an instant and my chance will have passed. It's now or never. I glance back toward the village with a vain hope that my dad might have seen sense and decided to run too. But no. I'm on my own, and I have to get moving.

The path is overgrown with nettles, now at the peak of their stinging power, but I hold my arms out of range and push through. At the end of the path, I check over my shoulder. No one has seen me. Hope flickers in my chest, and my heartbeat speeds up at the realization that I'm about to make a run for it. I drop down into a copse of trees, scramble over a rotting log across the path, and struggle out back into daylight at the edge of the lane. The Talbots are ahead of me, in the lane. But their backs are no longer facing me. Instead, they are trudging toward me.

Millie Talbot is my age, but has never been a friend. She's the kind of girl who smiles at your face while she's stabbing you in the back. But right now, Millie is not smiling, and aimed at the middle of her back is the barrel of a gun. An open-top Land Rover rumbles behind the family, the armed soldier never taking his eyes off the fugitives marching like prisoners back to their prison. I don't wait to find out what will happen next. I dart back into the trees and don't stop moving until I pass through the honeysuckle-framed door of our cottage, back to the relative safety of home.

Chapter Six

THE TOTAL LACK OF INFORMATION about what's happening to our village is infuriating. Dad has told me nothing, but I'm not sure he has anything yet to tell. All I know is that we're being held prisoner, but our jailers won't say why. Again and again I search social media, frantically scrolling through my apps for a snippet of fact or some hint of reassurance, but every page is filled with unfounded speculation about our village. The more I search, the less I really know. The environmental contingency points to fracking and groundwater pollution. Climate change is blamed for resurrecting Jurassic viruses and dormant toxic spores. The conspiracy theorists shout about botched biological weapons testing and government cover-ups. Another group points its finger at a local excavation project, calling the operations "environmental murder." Food contamination, super bugs, toxic vaccinations. Everyone has an opinion, and every possibility is terrifying. Even worse are the scaremongering "news" reports of the coming of the end of the world, which come accompanied by harebrained hypotheses of what should be done—everything from shutting down the borders of our country to incinerating Eyam and everyone in it.

The idea that someone could consider snuffing out my light to save his own skin causes my temples to throb with fury.

Others post meaningless prayers for the poor souls trapped inside the quarantine, and there is story after personal story of connections to the tragedy. "OMG, I was just in Eyam last month." "My cousin knows someone who lives there." "I woke up feeling ill, and now I'm worried I might have this thing too." It's like The Tragedy Olympics, with everyone competing to prove they are in the most danger or have the most heartbreaking story, without actually being trapped behind the quarantine or dying. My thumbs hover over the screen of my phone, shaking. I want to set these idiots straight, tell them they have no right to fuss unless they're here, but that just puts me in the gold medal spot of the same competition, and I refuse to lower myself to that. Defeated, I slump to my bed and click on the TV.

It's a mistake. I need information, but even the local news has hopped on the terror bandwagon, sending an intrepid reporter into the hinterlands to stand on the safe side of the barricade and speculate about the "Mystery Illness." One channel shows a map of the region, where our village is no more than a pretty dot, no reason to pass through on the way to anywhere else. The roads to other, more important places skirt through the valleys on either side of ours. Our isolation has kept us quaint. Now our isolation is making us famous.

On the screen, the trailers and mobile response units move in, followed by ambulances, more police cars, and armored vehicles. I watch my familiar village morph before my eyes, as if someone has graffitied over a sweet watercolor painting. The camera pans across the rows of stone cottages, the vivid hanging baskets, the church, the bus shelter, the school, and the tea rooms, but slashes of cold, hard metal interrupt the scene with the sterile, invasive colors of Armageddon.

The reporter returns to the screen, her expression grim as she informs her viewers that the two deaths prior to Dr. Spencer's have also been linked to the outbreak. "The death toll now stands at six," she says without emotion. In the background, two suited aliens wheel away a small, white bag. My insides shrink in on themselves because the bag can only contain one thing: a body... a small one.

Before I can fully grasp the horror of what I'm seeing, an infographic pops onto the screen. It's a dark blue silhouette of a man overlain with a bullet-point list of symptoms: body aches, headache, stomach pain, nausea and vomiting, bleeding... I can't watch any longer. It's so clinical and cold compared to the very real bagged body of what must be one of the Wainwright children, the image now seared into my memory.

Finally, Mum FaceTimes me. I click on the video icon, resolving to put on a brave face, or she's going to wig out. My own video comes up first, and I fiddle with the screen until I'm centered. A second later, Mum's face appears. She's off to one side of her screen with a window behind her, but even in the shadowy light, I can see she looks frantic.

"Em," she breathes. "Oh, Em. I just got all your messages. Are you okay?"

"Where were you?" I screech, my false bravado crumbling immediately until all I can manage is a childish, "Mu-um!"

"Oh, Emmott. I'm sorry. I should never have left you. As soon as I heard about this thing with Dr. Spencer, I should have come home. I should have listened to my gut. I..."

"Mum, stop," I say, gathering myself together. "You couldn't have known."

None of us could have known. For the last three years, I've fought epic battles to avoid the annual trip to Auntie Margie's dull seaside town. Ironic that this is the year I won.

Mum takes a breath and settles herself. "Tell me everything. What's going on? Are you and your dad all right?"

I tell her about the barricades and the army of helpers. I leave out the guns and military vehicles. "But we're okay."

"I've only just seen the news reports. They're showing the riots and the medics in space suits carrying out all those bodies." Her voice is squeezed to a high-pitched whine.

"It's not really like that," I say, "Not all the time." I try to tell her about the quiet in the village, how it feels like everyone has left even though they're still here, just hidden inside their houses. We hear word of new cases and deaths through the grapevine, through the hushed, "Have you heard…?" Leave it to the news outlets to replay over and over the footage of the Molotov cocktail incident and the removal of the Wainwright kid's body, adding their own commentaries to the scenes of carnage. I'm not saying being here is a picnic, but it makes me furious that they need to amp up the drama when the quiet, seeping fear of the unknown is terrifying enough.

"Are you sure you're okay?" Mum asks again. "You haven't had any headaches, any muscle aches, fever, anything that feels unusual?"

"Honestly, Mum, I'm fine," I tell her.

"Promise me you'll be careful. Do exactly what they tell you."

"I will."

Mum narrows her eyes at me. "Em?" she says like she doesn't believe me.

"I'll be careful, Mum. I promise."

She gives me an understanding look. "And your dad?"

I'm not sure if she's asking if Dad's okay or if he's being careful, but I don't have an answer to either. I haven't spoken to Dad since he told me to "stay indoors, no matter what." I have no idea where he is now.

"He's fine," I tell Mum, because it's easier this way.

"You and Dad, you have to look after one another."

"I know."

"And don't let him be a hero."

It's probably too late for that, but I don't say that to Mum. Instead I promise her we'll be okay.

"Mum?" I'm trying to find the words to tell her everything I'm feeling, that I'm scared, that I don't know what's going to happen, that I wish Dad were more like her. But I don't know what I wish anymore. In a different time and place, I could have said, "Mum, I need to talk to you," and she'd have made us tea and listened until I'd talked my way to what I really wanted to say. Then she'd give me good advice, and maybe, if I needed it, I'd have a good cry and she'd give me a hug. Such a simple need, but now totally out of my reach.

"What is it, my love?" Her face tightens with the effort of keeping it all together for me. I half wish she'd just let it all out, so I could too.

"Nothing," I tell her. "I'm okay."

"I'll get back as soon as I can," Mum says. "I just feel so helpless."

"And do what, Mum?" She doesn't respond. "You need to stay where you are, and keep Alice as far away as possible, at least until we find out what's going on." I realize what I've said immediately, and I see it register in the way her eyes seem to sink into her face. If Eyam is not safe enough for my little sister, it's not safe enough for me either. But here I am. "There's nothing you can do. Even if you were here, there'd be nothing you could do."

"Well, I can't do nothing. Mark has connections in London. He's trying to find out what he can. If there's any way we can get you out of there, we will."

"Mark who?" I ask.

"Auntie Margie's friend. You remember him."

Right, that Mark, the one with the fancy boat and the year-round tan. I was once in the car when he talked his way out of a speeding ticket. He's one of those people who floats through life, bending the rules with charm and a silver tongue. But I doubt even he could spring us from this mess. "That would be great," I say without enthusiasm. "Is Alice there?"

Mum shakes her head and looks more remorseful than ever. "I'm actually in London at the moment. Alice is with Margie."

I don't think to ask what she's doing there or why she hasn't seen the news until now. All I can think is that she's where I'm supposed to be, and I am trapped here. Everything is upside down.

"I'll ring Margie and have her put Alice on. But I haven't told your sister anything yet. I'm waiting until we find out more."

"I promise you an Oscar-winning performance."

Mum gives a timid nod. "Oh, Em," she moans. She looks as if she's going to fall to pieces again.

"Oh, Mum," I say, mimicking her. "What happened to that brave face? If this is the height of your acting skills, don't give up your day job, okay?"

Mum sniffs and shows me what I assume is her brave face. She looks remorseful and utterly terrified. I tell myself that

Mum is just being Mum-ish, and getting herself all knotted up is her job. But deep down I know that what she showed me *is* her brave face, and we both understand how serious my situation is.

A few minutes later, Auntie Margie's name flashes on my screen, and Alice pops up. We only talk for five minutes, but in that time, she relays every detail that an eight-year-old deems newsworthy of their trip down to the coast. She describes their arrival at Auntie Margie's, the fact that she has her own room with a view of the beach, that they baked cupcakes with real chocolate chips, and that she got to stay up late watching old DVDs because Mum had to stay overnight in London. It takes every gram of my willpower to keep smiling and laughing with her and not to let on that anything is in the slightest bit wrong. I'm glad she's safely away from all this, still I can't help but envy her blissful obliviousness. Physically, Alice is less than three hundred miles away from me, but as she talks, the distance between us grows. Mum's right about it being better that Alice doesn't know about the quarantine. If this thing goes away as fast as it came, she might never need to know. More than almost anything, I wish that for her.

After assuring her that Pandicorn, the favorite stuffed animal she left in my care, isn't missing her too much, and promising to say "hi" to Daddy, we say goodbye. Even as Alice's face fades from my screen, I can't put my phone down. I stare at the spot where her innocent eyes smiled back at me, but all I can see now is the reflection of my own frightened face.

That night Dad and I finally sit across from one another at the kitchen table in our silent house. Between us is a single sheet of paper I found taped to the front door. It gives us all the available information about the quarantine, and it's next to nothing. I am trying to get my mind around what I do and don't know, but I have so many questions, I don't know where to begin. All I know is that our village has been quarantined to contain something bad—not the flu—-and life as I know it has come to an end.

"How long do we have to stay?" I ask Dad, wondering if I'll need to ask the landlord if he'll hold the room in London.

"I don't know yet," he says. "For now, they're just asking us to sit tight."

"Can we go out at all?"

"At the moment, yes. We just can't leave the village."

"But we can talk to other people."

Dad nods. "But they're advising precautions."

"I assume that means you won't be checking in on everyone anymore."

"Of course I will," he says as if I've asked why he insists on taking in oxygen and blowing out carbon dioxide. "It's neighborly, Emmott."

The trouble with being neighborly is that it always seems to result in sticking your nose into other people's business, and while Dad seems to believe it's his job to take care of everyone in the village, I prefer my own business nose-free. "Well, I hope you don't bring anything home with you."

Dad glares at me, but I don't regret my grumpy outburst.

"What about Mum and Alice?" I ask, changing the subject. "What's going to happen to them?"

"No one's allowed in or out until further notice. For the time being, they'll be better off staying there. You should have gone with them."

"So should you."

Dad's lips twitch into a tight grimace as if to say, "Touché." I take no satisfaction in his reaction.

"I don't understand. What good does it do to quarantine us?"

Dad looks uncomfortable with all my questions, but he's my sole source of information, even if he has none. "They're not being very forthcoming, but my guess is that until they know what's causing this, they're erring on the safe side."

"On whose safe side?" I ask, the words quavering in my throat. "Not safe for us, that's for certain."

Dad doesn't say anything, and I wonder if he's thinking the same thing. If the source of the sickness is something in the village, keeping us here is only keeping us closer to danger. If our mystery illness is something contagious, the quarantine isn't for our benefit either. In both cases, we are the proverbial sacrificial lambs.

The edges of the kitchen start to blur, and I close my eyes, feeling as if everything is about to start spinning. "They can't stop us leaving." It comes out as a whimper. "They can't tell us what to do or where we can and can't go. It's a violation of our rights."

"Emmott," Dad says, "I know this isn't easy, and I know it doesn't seem fair, but this quarantine is serious. The best thing we can do for now is to wait and see what happens. We need to trust that this is in our best interests, and we need to do what's asked of us. This isn't like sneaking out of a window."

In all the insanity of the past week, I'd almost forgotten to worry about Dad and Ro. I struggle now to make sense of the fact that he *knew* I was out that night and said nothing until now, but my brain is already overloaded with things I can't fully grasp. I don't even get to react before he adds, "Now's not the time to be a rebel."

I stare at my dad. I want to grab him by the collar and shake him. How can he be so passive? How can he just sit there and allow this to happen to us? And how can I possibly be related to him?

"When *will* it be time to be a rebel?" I ask, barely able to keep the sarcasm out of my voice.

"I don't know," he says. "But if that time comes, I promise I'll let you know."

Of all the platitudes Dad has spouted over the years, this is the one I believe the least.

Chapter Seven

Wednesday, July 27

THE SOUND OF THE DOORBELL drags me from my bed the next morning. Pulling on a hoodie to make myself presentable, I'm halfway down the stairs before I remember that a visitor at the front door is no longer normal. Maybe it's a neighbor bearing a casserole or some homemade bread, which is what usually happens in a crisis. A cup of tea is the standard prescription for just about any ailment or trouble around here, and I'm surprised to realize I hope that's what I'll find. But when I open the door, my view is blocked by a yellow wall. It's a man—as far as I can tell—covered from head to toe in a yellow hazmat suit. Rings of blue tape wrap around his ankles and wrists, sealing him inside. Two strips of red tape have been stuck over his chest to form a cross. Over his hood, he wears a see-through face shield that covers his forehead down to his chest. The edges of the shield are steamed, and droplets of condensation form as he breathes. I can't see his face because a respirator covers his nose and mouth, so that only his eyes show. The narrow strip of skin I can see is pale, and a few boyish freckles creep up over his mask. His eyebrows and lashes are light and his eyes are… I stare through his face shield until his eyes meet mine. They are hazel, with flecks of gold, but as he turns I see greens and browns and yellows. *Tiger eyes*, I think, as the moisture evaporates from my mouth.

He hesitates for a moment, as if he'd expected someone else to open the door, but then a smile flickers in his tiger eyes.

"Mornin'." His overly cheery voice echoes inside the sealed mask and plastic barrier. "Nice jumper. My favorite place in the whole world, that is."

I glance down at my "I love London" hoodie. The red, silky heart reminds me of where I am supposed to be and where I am instead. I try to speak, to say that London is my favorite place too—*was* my favorite place—but my voice has left me. There is nowhere else to look except his eyes, and the intimacy it creates is unnerving. I can't observe and assess his mannerisms, the way you'd normally do with a stranger. I can't see how his lips move, if his nose is big, if it looks as if he's done something with his hair today. All I can see is his eyes, and it forces me toward a deeper knowledge of him than I'm ready for.

I break the connection, dropping my eyes to his feet, overly large in their layers of boot and suit. This quarantine is messing with my mind. It's like that syndrome hostages get when they fall for their captors. Three days without Ro and I'm getting gooey for a guy in a plastic bag.

"Are you the head of household?" he asks.

I snap my eyes back to his and give him a look that I hope conveys what an idiotic question that is.

"Right," he stammers, his cheerful tone dropping. "Um, is he—or she—in?"

"He. It's my dad, and no, he's not in." I stop myself short of adding that I woke to a note on the kitchen table telling me that Dad was out in the village, but that I should stay in the house. Part of me was irked at his double standard, and part was relieved to have an excuse to hide.

The alien shifts inside his suit, like his training didn't cover this situation. I register for the first time that he's nervous, and his awkward shuffling makes him seem younger than I first thought. I bet he's not more than a few years older than me. He hands me a sealed plastic packet. "I've brought you some masks and gloves to use, and some information for you and your family to look at. It's basic protocol and procedures, that sort of thing."

His tone is almost casual, as if he's offering me a catalog of Christmas cards to browse through. But the seriousness of what he's telling me seeps through his friendly demeanor. He's done this before, I can tell.

"There's a map of the quarantine boundary in there as well," he goes on. "Make sure you have a good look at it; you don't want to accidentally cross it."

My mind flits to the armored vehicles barricading access to our village. "Accidentally? Is that possible?"

His eyes dart down to my feet, as if there's something he doesn't want to tell me. "I think they'll be quite strict about enforcing it. Until we know more, we're asking everyone to stay close to home and keep dealings with other people to a minimum. There are instructions in there about registering your mobile number and email so we can keep everyone informed as things change. It's really important that we get everyone in the household, so if you can make sure your dad…"

"What do you mean by 'know more'?" I ask.

He straightens up. This question must have been in his training. "At the moment, we don't have precise details about the illness. We're taking every precaution until we know the cause, how it's transmitted, and how we can contain it. So, for now…"

"You don't even know what's causing it?"

He shakes his head. "Not yet."

"Then how are we supposed to make sure we don't get it?"

"Like I said, we're taking every precaution…"

I take in his fully-sealed suit and his mask and respirator, a high-tech version of the flimsy paper masks he's just handed me. He is in a bubble, completely isolated from our village, safe and protected. But I am not. I am here, exposed to an unknown illness. It could be in the air, in the water, in our food, clinging to the packet he has handed me. The packet full of paper, of bureaucratic information based on nothing. A hazmat suit like his would protect me, but instead I have *protocol*.

"Thanks for the information," I say, closing the door to my house. Inside these four walls I am supposed to feel safe, but I don't. I feel trapped. "A prisoner in my own home" is such a cliché. But that is exactly what I am.

I shuffle through the papers until I find the registration instructions. When they find out what this thing is, I want to be the first to know. I tap in the information, feeling the weight of the electronic handcuff I'm locking onto myself. I'm not normally one for paranoia, but I can't help wondering if this registry is for me to keep track of updates or for the government to keep track of me. As I glance over the sheets outlining protocol and safe practices for everything from preparing food to bodily functions, I spot the map of the zone. The familiar layout of our village, with its winding main street and spider veins of lanes and side roads, has been overlaid with a red, hashed geometric block. It has a long, straight edge at the bottom and shorter edges at the side, so that it looks like the kind of lopsided house that Alice might have drawn when she was small. But along the top edge is a wiggly line, as if someone nervous was asked to close the shape. When I look closer, I see the line follows the course of a stream—the one that runs through the northeast side of the village, behind the cottages and the tourist information office that border the village green. The one that runs through the bottom of Cucklett Delf. My body folds in at the sight of my secret spot: the narrow gap between the rocks where I've stood so many times waiting for Ro; the curve of the grassy hollow where we last made love; the stream in the bottom that provided the soundtrack for our romance. Now it's the boundary that will keep him out and me in.

I stuff the map back in the packet, cramming the hurt down with it. I don't need to see what I already sense… that I may not see Ro, or anything beyond this village, for a very long time.

I spend the rest of the day drifting around the house like a robotic vacuum cleaner, wandering from one window to another, peering out, each time hoping that things will be back to normal. Each time I'm disappointed. I try to focus on a new mosaic, telling myself I can use this unexpected confinement to stockpile a few pieces before I leave for London. When Ro texts, I try to keep our conversation light, not wanting to say anything that might scare him away. He doesn't mention London and so neither do I. I'm supposed to start my new job in five days, and I don't want to risk anyone shooting down the one dream that's keeping me hopeful. Ro always ends our chats by saying he can't wait to see me again. Today, even that isn't enough to keep my chin up.

I text Deb. *Can't talk now. Asthma attack*, she replies.

I ask if she needs anything. She answers with one of her usual droll responses: *Better lungs.* Her familiar gallows humor gives me a morsel of relief.

Unable to suffer any more time with the social media circus, I settle on reading an actual printed book, but I can't concentrate. All I can think about are the walls of my room, this house, this life moving closer and closer, squeezing what's left of my hope from me.

I must have fallen asleep because the next thing I know, I hear voices downstairs and heavy footsteps moving across the hallway. By the time I can shake myself awake and get to the stairs, it's gone quiet again, and all I can hear is Dad clattering around in the kitchen.

As I make my way down the stairs, a faint smell of cooking drifts up. I can't tell what it is, but it doesn't smell good. I find Dad at the stove, poking a fork into a bowl of unidentifiable mush.

"What is *that*?" I ask, wrinkling my nose.

"This is dinner," he says.

"But what *is* it, exactly?"

Dad picks up a foil package and reads the plain, black lettering stamped on one side. "Shepherd's Pie with Mixed Vegetables."

Now that I look again, I can identify a grayish, meaty slop and globs of anemic orange and green that I assume are supposed to be carrots and peas. It's all covered in a thin layer of parched mashed potatoes and about as far removed from Shepherd's Pie as a piece of cardboard is from a forest of pines.

"We're not going to eat that, are we?" I ask.

"I'm not sure we have much choice. Government issue." He nods toward two large cardboard boxes on the kitchen counter.

I peer into them and lift out a series of foil bags and plain cardboard packages, their contents emblazoned on the front: powdered milk, powdered eggs, sugar, flour, and beans. I pull out a large foil envelope stamped "Roast Beef and Yorkshire Pudding," but when I shake it, it sounds more like buttons and sawdust.

"We can't live on this," I say.

"Live?" Dad scoffs. "Not hardly. Survive maybe, but not live."

"Well, I'm not eating it." I fling open the fridge door, determined to make my point by having a giant salad, but I'm almost blinded by the glare of white that greets me. I turn to Dad for an explanation. He wafts another piece of paper in the air.

"They took our food?" I ask.

He nods. "Precautionary."

I pull open the pantry. That's empty too. "What about your allotment?" I ask. "You've got plenty of veggies ready, don't you?"

Dad gives his head the smallest of shakes, and I understand. He doesn't have a garden anymore; they've taken that too.

"I think I'd rather go hungry," I say.

"That is the other option."

Dad and I stare into the box in silence. I don't know what he's thinking, but I'm trying to control a rumble in the pit of my stomach. It's not a hunger rumble, although I'm sure that will come eventually. This rumble feels like a storm cloud rolling through the sky, and if I don't keep it inside, it's going to erupt in a thunderous scream. My life is being stripped away, layer by layer, like decades of wallpaper in an old house. Before long there'll be nothing but bare stone walls left, the shell of a life, but uninhabitable.

"I can't do this," I mumble to myself.

Dad hears me. "It's only for a while," he says. "We just have to get through this as best we can."

"But what if we don't?" My voice cracks.

"We will. We have to. I'm not saying it's going to be easy, but I don't see that we have much choice."

I try to nod, but my head won't move. I can't make myself agree with him to comply, even though I know it's what he needs to hear from me.

"I talked to Mum and Alice," I tell Dad as we poke at our poor excuse for a shepherd's pie.

"Oh, good," he says, but nothing more.

"Mum seems to think Mark might be able to pull some strings."

"Mark?" Dad says.

"You know. He's that friend of Auntie Margie's. The one with the yacht."

"I know who he is," Dad says.

It could be my imagination, but Dad seems to stab at his "potatoes" a lot more aggressively at the mention of Mark. I can see why Dad wouldn't take to him. They're polar opposites—Mark in his crisp, pressed trousers and designer shirts; Dad in his faded jeans and baggy sweatshirts, looking like he's just climbed out of a charity shop donation bag.

"Do you think he could spring us from here?" I ask.

Dad sighs and stops eating mid-potato. He seems lost in

his thoughts, like he's hoping to get inspiration from the pale, floury blob of spud.

"Emmott," he says at last. I wait for him to go on, but he looks as if he's searching for words with no clue where to find them. I watch his face and see a tiny flinch in his cheek, like he's about to say something. It disappears and he's left looking lost, a man who's been marooned on a desert island with a mysterious creature whose language he doesn't speak. In a way, that's exactly what he is.

I'm overcome with an urge to wrap my arms around him and tell him it will all be okay. But Dad isn't a cuddly dad, at least not with me, and while I got away with crawling into his lap and forcing cuddles when I was Alice's age, doing it now would only make him more uncomfortable.

"Em, we're not going to get 'sprung' from here, as you put it, no matter who *Mark* claims to know. All we can do is make the best of a bad situation, do what we're told, and try our damnedest not to get ill."

"In other words, lie down and hope not to die?"

Dad says nothing, and the impact of my own words reverberates in his silence. He sighs, exasperated, and goes back to his shepherd's pie as if he's said only, "If you go outside, try not to get sunburned." I glare at the top of his head, feeling a slow fury building inside me. It sticks in my chest, where it expands until I'm sure it's going to burst through my ribcage. I don't understand how he can be so placid, how he can just sit and accept our fate. I don't understand how we can be related, how he can seem so resigned when I feel as if I'm about to explode.

I push away from the table, leaving the pale slop of my dinner untouched. "I'm going out."

"Oh, no you're not," he says. "It's not safe."

"It's safe enough for you," I say. "But I'm not sure anything is safe anymore, so I might as well do something that makes me at least a bit happy."

Before he can object again, I grab a protective mask and wave it at him on my way to the door, just to prove I'm not completely reckless.

"Don't get too close to anyone. And try not to touch your face. And for goodness sake don't eat anything!" he shouts after me, but I'm already halfway out the front door.

Chapter Eight

I T'S A PERFECT SUMMER EVENING, the kind where the sun
seems to hang above the horizon for hours before it finally
sinks away. It's the kind of night you'd expect to hear sparrows
chirping in the shrubbery and wood pigeons cooing from the
cottage roofs, but instead the village is alive with the whir of
generators and the rumble of heavy vehicles shuttling into
position.

I stomp down to Dad's allotment and peer over the fence.
His vegetable patch is stripped bare, the rich, dark earth turned
over and trampled down. There isn't even a nub of carrot or a
wilted cabbage leaf left behind. Littered across the adjoining
grass are the decapitated bodies of hundreds of flowers. The
purples, yellows, and pinks of freesias, lilies, and begonias are
strewn like confetti across a scattered carpet of muck, splashed
with the fallen heads of brilliant red poppies. Tossed to one
side and cracked in two, half of a large, black boot print visible
on each shattered piece, is the "Dad's Garden" sign Alice and
I once painted. The sight of it presses a fist of sadness into my
chest. I turn and hurry away.

As I pass the village hall, a team of medical personnel
scurries back and forth, rolling temporary beds into the old
stone building along with boxes of supplies and bales of starched

bed sheets and patterned gowns, everything sterile and cold, no comforts of home. They appear to be setting up a makeshift medical center. Ro said that, even though it's miles from here, the hospital where Dr. Spencer was taken has been quarantined too. Does this mean they're no longer accepting our sick? Why would a place dedicated to treating illness refuse to take people who are ill? A wave of fury and fear wells up inside me. Do they know more than they are telling, or is our village hall less a central location to treat the sick than a convenient place to stash the dying?

From an unmarked, white van, two aliens wheel a long, rectangular bubble. It looks like a typical hospital gurney with a see-through plastic tent on top. These aliens' suits appear to be inflated. A low whir as they pass makes me think they have some kind of personal air conditioning system built into their suits. Whatever is in that tent, it's clear they want to keep their distance from it. As I peer into the bubble to see what they're hauling, I recognize the pale, hairless head of Andy Hawksworth. His motionless body shows none of the wry humor and teasing I've come to expect from Dad's oldest friend. His face is a yellowish, expressionless mask, and his eyes stare skywards in a zombie-like trance, just like I saw in Dr. Spencer. Blood crusts around his nose, and purple bruises splash his normally ruddy cheeks, as if he's been in a fight. I want to shout out to them to stop, that they can't take him away like that, but everything I've seen tells me that the Andy I know no longer inhabits that body. He's not dead, not yet; he's existing in some in-between world.

I turn away. I can't watch people I've known my whole life shuttled into a place I'm not sure they'll come back from.

They're rounding up the sick like stray sheep in the hills. I have to get out of here before they start rounding up the healthy too.

I run toward the village green, away from the hall, and I don't stop until I reach the memorial that sits at the narrow end of the triangular patch of grass. It's a stone pillar, about my height, with a carved Celtic cross on top. Engraved around the base are the names of the twenty-two men from Eyam who "gave their lives" during the Great War. I don't like to look at the memorial because it makes me sad. No, actually, it makes me angry about the waste of life, and when I read those names, all I can think about are the young men, most of them not much older than me, who suddenly ceased to exist, who never had the chance to go on and live amazing lives. I think about all the things I want to do with my life—London and my future beyond this village—and the thought that I may never get the chance to do them leaves me paralyzed. My legs seem to dissolve beneath me, and I reach for one of the small stone pillars that holds a painted iron chain around the memorial. I slide to the ground, staring into nothing, my future so blurred and unfocused that I can't seem to make anything appear clear.

Finally, my eyes come to rest on the inscription around the bottom of the memorial. A single letter comes into focus, an *e*, and then another, until finally I register a word: freedom. I blink the surrounding words into focus and read the inscription from top to bottom, something I'm not sure I've ever done before.

"They whom this monument commemorates were among those who at the call of King and Country left all that is dear to them, endured hardness, faced danger, and finally passed out of the sight of men by the path of duty and self-sacrifice, giving up their own lives that others might live in freedom."

There are no Syddalls on the list of dead, even though several branches of our family lived in Eyam at that time. I come from either a long line of self-preservationists or the luckiest family in the world. Maybe we Syddalls display our heroics like my dad, by leading committees and visiting elderly neighbors in a nice, safe, war-free zone. But maybe I wouldn't be standing here reading this if the turn-of-the-century Syddalls had been braver and more dutiful. *There's a lot to be said for self-preservation*, I think.

Every year, our village honors its war dead in a Remembrance Day ceremony, including the families who did have courageous relatives—the Ashtons and the Glovers, and old Mrs. Talbot, whose great-granddaughter, Millie, wheels her down to the green so she can lay a wreath for the brother she barely had the chance to know. "Let those who come after see to it that their names are not forgotten," reads the end of the inscription. A century later, their names live on. A hundred years from now, if I don't make it out of here, will anyone remember me? I doubt it.

They call it the Supreme Sacrifice, giving up your life for the greater good, dying for a cause. I try to imagine those men enlisting in that war, as good as signing their own death warrants. It seems insane to me, and I wonder: Does that make me a coward, or does it just mean I value my own life more? And if I listen to my dad and keep being a good girl, if I sit tight and follow the rules, am I signing up for certain death?

I realize then: I have my dad's genes, his blood in my veins, but I am not like him. I'm not prepared to sit around while life, or in this case, death, happens to me. Dad isn't going to like this one bit, but my life isn't his to squander. As far as I know, we only get one life, and I am going to do whatever I can to preserve mine. All I need is a plan and a little bit of help.

Chapter Nine

B Y THE END OF THE week, word arrives that the air quality and soil tests have come back negative. Whatever is making people sick, it isn't something toxic in the air or the ground.

"They tore up my garden for nothing," Dad says, looking forlorn.

Other news filters through too, but not much of it is good. They're tallying the dead and broadcasting statistics like they're reading off the weekend football results. Barely a week into our quarantine and the score is already: Dead: fourteen, Infected: thirty-two. Every time the news comes on, Mum rings, more panicked than ever. Dad and I take it in turns to reassure her that a) we're fine, and b) she should stay exactly where she is.

What's most worrying is the pattern of victims. It started with the two elderly residents, then hopped to Dr. Spencer and his neighbors, picking its way through two entire families, but leaving Dr. Spencer's wife, Louise, unaffected. But now it's popped up in a house at the other end of the village and a farmhouse just inside the quarantine zone. In both cases, only two people in each house have contracted it, which suggest it's more random than they first told us. If they've spotted a relationship between the victims, they're several steps ahead of me.

I tell Dad I'm going out to look for mosaic pieces, now that the ground is safe to touch again. He's hesitant at first, but doesn't argue. I'm sure he's as sick of me rumbling around the house as I am of being captive. He insists I wear my mask and gloves, reminds me not to get too close to anyone, not to eat anything, and not to touch my face. I start to object, but he makes a good point: Even though air and ground pollution have been eliminated as the culprit, there is still a long list of other possibilities, one of which will prove to be the offender.

"I think you should wear your sunglasses too," he adds. "Can't hurt to protect your eyes."

The sunglasses are a bit much, but I don't argue. My goal now is to keep under Dad's radar while I put my plan in place, which means doing as little as possible to annoy him. I pull up my mask, put on my white gloves, and put on my sunglasses. I catch a glimpse of myself in the hall mirror as I leave. Apart from my blond hair, I look exactly like Michael Jackson. Still, Dad's overprotection will serve as a very handy disguise for the plan I'm beginning to brew.

It's eerily quiet out in the village. Most people are staying in, and the only activity is centered around the temporary medical unit inside the village hall and the school where Quarantine HQ has been set up. On a sunny day like today, Eyam would normally be bustling. The road would be full of cars looking for parking or passing through to a nearby beauty spot. There'd be packs of hikers heading off into the hills with backpacks full of sandwiches and cereal bars and cyclists whizzing around. The tearooms and shops would be buzzing with tourists out for a day of tea, cakes, and trinket-hunting. And the villagers would be out in their gardens, going to war with the endless weeds, stopping now and then to gossip over the wall with a neighbor. On a normal day, Dad would be in his allotment or guiding his ladies on one of his tours, and Mum would be on the back patio, marking her students' homework and trying to get a bit of color on her legs. Alice would be outside playing or down at the park with a friend. And on a spectacular day like today, I'd be out with Deb and our friends on the village green, or maybe up in Cucklett Delf fooling around with Ro. I used to think life in this village was simple and boring, but I'd take simple and boring over complicated and frightening any day.

As soon as I'm out of sight of the house, I text Ro. He's key to my plan, and I need to test his loyalty to my cause. I'll admit I'm surprised when he agrees to come, but I don't kid myself that it's anything but curiosity and daring that drives him. It's the latter I'm counting on most. We both know crossing the quarantine boundary is strictly forbidden—Alien Boy made that quite clear—but the rules don't say anything about standing near the border and *looking* at someone on the other side. Our rendezvous will give me a chance to scope out the territory and test my plan for flaws. To my dad, "don't be a rebel" means "don't break the rules and cause me any trouble." To me, it means "bend the rules as far as you need without getting caught, and if all else fails, snap them in two." My rules are about to get flexible.

As I make my way to the path, a white delivery van rolls up the road toward me. It looks official, so I keep walking, past the gate, as if I have a purpose elsewhere in the village. The van stops outside a row of cottages, and a suited alien hops out. He pulls a stack of boxes from the open loading door, resting them on the step. The boxes have red crosses printed on the side, like the kind you see on the news, handed out in third world countries—disaster relief for the unfortunate and needy. So, that's what's become of us. We're a charity case now.

It seems impossible that any sort of personality can show through those sealed layers of material. (What are those things even made of? Vinyl, Teflon, poly-plasto-super-duper-something? I haven't the first clue.) And yet this alien seems familiar. As it turns my way, I glimpse his eyes and realize it's the same one who brought the information to our door. I'm hoping he won't recognize me, but he raises one hand and parts his fingers in a Vulcan salute. Apparently he has a sense of humor, something that's been sorely lacking around here lately. Cursing my bad luck, I lift my hand and give a cursory wave back, not wanting to make a fool of myself by proving I have zero dexterity, finger-wise. The visible strip of his face crinkles into a smile. Even though I can only see his eyes, I can tell it's a wicked smile, but wicked in a good way, friendly and a bit cheeky. His tiger eyes light up as he hurries toward me.

"All right, London," he says. His voice is raspy and echoes in the chamber of his respirator. "How are you doing?"

"Fine," I say, smiling that he remembered my hoodie. I don't have time to get caught up in a gossip session, though. I have things to do and standing around chit-chatting with a man in a bubble is not on my list.

He glances at my name tag, another item of protocol that's been laid on us. "Emmott?" he asks. "That's an excellent name."

I'm aware that his eyes have not left my name tag, which is clipped to the pocket of my jacket, just over my left breast, and the thought that he might not be looking at the tag at all infuriates me.

"It's a family name," I tell him. "My great-great-grandma's."

I nod toward the churchyard where my namesake has lain for over a century.

"Aiden," he says. He taps the front of his suit, where he's now written his name in black Sharpie, along with a cartoon that I assume is supposed to be him. Clearly, it's an attempt to make himself appear more approachable. The face has spiky hair and a giant smile; small dots that I think are supposed to be freckles decorate a sharp, triangular nose. The cartoon doesn't have what you'd call a handsome face, but it's definitely a friendly one. "According to my Mum, I'm named after a Chelsea midfielder," he says. "I'll try to make up a better story if it will help."

"You're from London?" I ask.

"Born and raised."

He holds out his gloved hand, and I'm about to shake it when he pulls it back. Avoiding shaking hands is on the long list of precautions we've been issued. I can't see that it would matter if both people are wearing gloves, but Deb says we should be cautious of everything until they work out what we really can and cannot do.

"Sorry," he says. "That was idiotic." But in the space where our hands almost touched, something happens, like an invisible sponge ball has come between us, pushing our hands apart. A strange sensation worms up my arm, heat traveling through my body the way a hot drink travels down your throat and warms your stomach on a cold day. That's exactly how it feels now, except the sensation doesn't stop at my stomach; it keeps heading south.

"Listen, I think I might have been a bit abrupt with you the other day," he says.

I shrug. "You're just doing your job."

"My job is supposed to be humanitarian," he says. "But it's not easy to be warm and fuzzy sealed inside one of these."

"I'm sure." I stand there forcing a patient smile and hoping he'll get the hint that I want him to leave.

"I just wanted to say that, well, I'm here to help. If you need anything. I'll do what I can. Just ask."

I am so unbelievably tempted to tell him that a one-way ticket to somewhere a long, long way from here would be really useful, but I can tell he's just trying to make the best of a bad situation. I might be stuck here, but he came of his own accord—why, I can't imagine—and the least I can do is appreciate that he's trying to help.

"Thanks," I say, and I mean it.

He smiles again, this time holding my gaze for an uncomfortable moment too long, as if he has more to say, but can't. My face burns, and I'm surprised when my heart thuds a little faster. *What is wrong with me? My life is on the line, and I'm getting my knickers in a twist over a man in a plastic suit?* And yet my senses slow down, as if I'm moving through water, and even though my brain tells me to walk away, my legs have no intention of moving.

He's finally called away by another alien, and the tension inside me dissolves, leaving room for the guilt to unfold. I'm on my way to meet Ro. My *boyfriend.* I'm acting like a silly kid around this guy, and I'm not even available, let alone interested in him. But it's like they say, you always want what you can't have. And human connection—making out, holding hands, or even getting close enough to whisper sweet nothings in someone's ear—is strictly forbidden. The lack of physical contact is starting to affect my brain. Honestly, I'd sell my little sister for an elbow bump right now.

As I resume my route to Cucklett Delf, I can tell I'm walking funny, as if the communication between my legs and my brain has been lost. And though I don't turn around to check, I know that Alien Boy—Aiden—is watching me go. It's not until I'm past the church and halfway up the hill that I realize what a prize idiot I am. If I'm hoping to push at the edges of the rules, the last thing I need to do is single myself out to one of *them*, especially one who might actually notice if I went missing.

At the top of the path, I take a last glance over my shoulder and slip between the rocks into Cucklett Delf. The grassy, tree-rimmed valley looks exactly as I remember it, as if I've slipped through a time warp, back to when everything was normal. I can almost pretend Ro will come across the fields from his family's farm to meet me, that we'll find a hidden spot among the trees to be together, that I'll get to feel the warmth and electricity of another human body against mine. At the bottom is the stream, looking just as it's always done. The quarantine map in my pocket might show a harsh red line, but in the real world, the stream is still the stream, just a band of running water that I could easily wade across.

I text Ro to see if he's close, and I jump when I hear the *ping* of a text alert in the trees on the opposite side. I press against the wall, like a spy in an old black and white thriller, praying there's no one else around to hear it.

There's movement in the trees, and a moment later, Ro slips into view. His head flits from side to side, like a rabbit on the lookout for hunters, and then he steps out into full view. I remind myself we're not breaking any rules, that we're too far apart to even speak, and I step out so he can see me too.

He looks like a mirage, like a long, tall drink of water in a dry, dry wasteland, something ordinary and desirable, but utterly unattainable. And beaming out from the center of his being is the courage I've been looking for, the hint of my rebel that I need now. But the thing I want most is his freedom, and I have to focus on my mission. I need to find out what would happen if I ran, just put one foot in front of the other and bolted for freedom. What would I find on the other side?

I get my answer immediately.

Across the stream, a figure moves through the trees. He's dressed in green fatigues and combat boots, a dark beret pulled to one side of his head. Slung across one shoulder is a rifle. From his crisp body movements and cropped hair, I can tell he's a soldier on patrol. He follows the course of the little river, his eyes scanning back and forth across the quarantine border. I press myself back against the rocks until I'm sure he's moved out of sight.

Ro has gone. I stare at the spot in the trees where I last saw him, and I will him to come back. Nothing moves except a flicker of leaves in the breeze, a gentle rustle that sounds to me as if the trees are laughing at my stupidity. I want to text him, to tell him it's safe to come back, but I don't know for sure that it is, and I can't risk getting either of us in trouble.

Pulling the quarantine map from my pocket, I follow the soldier's route with my finger. A little further along, the red line and the river diverge, and the artificial border dives down a ravine and continues on the other side. In the opposite direction, the border crosses a small lane into the village. My guess is his patrol ends at those two points, and sure enough, a few minutes later, he's back. I watch for a while longer, timing his passes back and forth, like the very slow swing of a pendulum. After the second pass, Ro emerges from the trees. He pushes his long hair from his face and levels a defiant gaze at me. That look tells me all I need to know, that if I'm looking for a partner in crime, I'll find one in Ro. I stuff the map back into my pocket and send him a text.

You look good, is all I can think to say.

As soon as this is over, I'm coming for you, he replies.

It's all I can do to not drop everything and sprint across the boundary into his arms. But, of all the things I might be, an idiot isn't one of them.

Soon, I text back, but what I'm thinking is, *sooner than you realize.*

Before the soldier returns, we say our goodbyes, and I slip back down into the village, stopping along the way to pick up some interesting stones to show to Dad if he asks about my mosaic haul.

When I pop through the gate by the churchyard, Aiden is waiting. I swear under my breath. I am a prize idiot after all.

"Hiya," he says. "Y'alright?" His friendly tone is forced, and his greeting lands at my feet like a javelin. A little bit closer and it would have pierced right through me. His eyes narrow, as if he's trying to focus on my innermost secrets. His gaze is so sharp, I can't hide anything from it, and my guilt bubbles like a mouthy traitor inside me.

His eyes examine mine, and he looks as if he's trying to decide what to say next. Will he dare to ask me what I'm doing? Or will he accuse me outright and march me into custody? Does he even have the right to do that? I root my feet to the ground, ready for a fight. I have rights, and I'm ready to defend them.

"Listen," he says. "It's not my job to lay down the law or

anything." He taps an official Red Cross sticker on his chest, in the spot where the two pieces of tape used to be. "I'm just here to help. But I am supposed to report anything..." He shifts in his suit, like he's searching for the right thing to say. "Suspicious," he says.

"I'm not doing anything wrong." It comes out way more defensive than intended. I fumble in my jeans pocket and pull out the grubby cloth bag of stones as proof. He frowns. "I make mosaics," I say.

"Look, I'm not suggesting you're up to anything, but I'd be careful if I were you. People are a bit jumpy at the moment. Nobody's really sure what this is yet, and they're not taking any chances. If they thought someone was breaking protocol..." He glances over my shoulder at the path to Cucklett Delf. My instinct is to keep lying, but I know he's onto me, so I keep my mouth shut.

"Just be careful, that's all. I'd hate for you to find yourself in trouble."

I don't know what he means by "trouble," but I can't get my voice to ask him.

"Like I say, we don't know much about this yet. We don't even know where it's coming from or how it's spreading. Better safe than sorry is all I'm saying. One Emmott Syddall in the churchyard is enough, don't you think?"

I manage a quick nod to let him know I understand. I'm sure he intended to be helpful and reassuring, but a cold, hard fact stares me in the face: If I don't go soon, I may not get out of here alive.

The trickiest part of the plan I'm forming will be navigating our local train station at Grindleford. It's well over a mile from the quarantine zone, surrounded by woods, and you can see the train coming from a couple of miles down the track, so hiding out and slipping onto the train shouldn't be a problem. I know the station well because I used to help out in the café there for a bit of extra money. The problem is that everyone around here knows everyone else, and the café staff definitely know me. I can't assume they won't turn me in if they recognize me. The second problem is that the place is popular with hikers and day-trippers, and it's often full of people. The fewer people who see me, the better. What I could really use is a lookout to scope it out while I hide. I just need one brave person I can trust.

When Ro pops up on my screen, I can barely contain my relief. He's sprawled on his bed, his long, dark hair fanning out behind him. He's wearing the t-shirt from the concert we went to last month, the night Deb had an asthma attack and almost blew my cover because my parents thought I was at her house. Ro wanted to take me home, to march in and tell my dad we'd been out together and dare him to forbid it. I talked him out of it, fabricating an elaborate lie about why I hadn't come straight home when the ambulance came for Deb. But it's that rebel streak in Ro that I need now because, outside the quarantine, he's the best hope I have for escape.

"Sorry I didn't stay long," he says. "That soldier looked serious, and I didn't feel like getting shot."

I smile as if everything about this conversation is normal. "Completely understand."

"I have to say, you were a sight for sore eyes. You don't look ill, and you definitely don't look contagious, unless drop-dead gorgeous is catching."

I force a laugh I don't feel. Over the years I've tried various tactics for getting my way with people. Sometimes they've worked, sometimes not so much. Tears are a no-no in this situation; there's no way Ro's going to help a weepy female. Given what I know about Ro, flirtation and a dare are good bets.

"Maybe I should just leave," I say, testing the water.

"I would," he says. "I mean really. What's to stop you just leaving right now?"

You, I think, *if you don't help me.* But I don't say it. "Don't think I haven't thought about it. All I need is someone to keep watch, and I could do it. I could get on a train in Grindleford and be gone."

"Where would you go?"

I'm about to say, "Auntie Margie's," but something stops me. I know that trust has to be a two-way thing, but the less Ro knows about my plan, the more watertight it will be.

"Maybe somewhere hot, where I can lay on the beach all day," I say, keeping things light.

"How about Greece," he says.

"Or Spain."

"Or Tahiti."

"Australia."

I turn on my full-power flirting. I hate to resort to cheap tricks, but desperate times call for desperate measures.

"Maybe we could find an uninhabited island and start our own colony," I say.

He laughs. "If only."

But I'm not laughing. I have to take my chance now, while his guard is down. "We could do it," I say. "If we're careful."

He looks at me, and his eyes narrow. "You're not serious, are you?"

"About Tahiti? No. But what's to keep me from leaving, really?"

He pulls the edge of his lip between his teeth and considers me. "The quarantine?"

"But the quarantine's just an idea. You saw. I could cross that stream in Cucklett Delf and be outside the zone in minutes. There's nothing physical to stop me."

"Except an armed guard."

"Who passes every six minutes in one direction and eleven in the other. I timed it."

Ro looks afraid, and I think he's going to bolt.

"Ro," I say, "I don't want to die here. I can't do this by myself, and I need you to help me."

His eyes scan my face, like he's looking for any sign that I'm kidding. He won't find one. He swallows and gives the slightest nod of his head. It's enough to let me know that I'm no longer alone.

Chapter Ten

Saturday, July 30

THE PEBBLE RICOCHETS OFF THE stonework so far from Deb's window, it almost hits the neighbor's house. It clatters against the drainpipe and drops into the shrubbery below. I curse under my breath, wishing I'd been endowed with a cricketer's arm or at least some semblance of athletic ability. I search around for another pebble and try again. This time I get lucky and the pebble strikes the center of one of the small glass panes. I'm so busy watching for Deb's face at the window, I don't notice the front door open.

"Emmott?" Helena pokes her head out. Her light hair is scraped into a ponytail and her face, what I can see of it, is free of makeup. I'm not sure I've ever seen her like that before, and I'm shocked how pale and featureless her face seems without the shades and lines she draws on each day. "What are you doing?"

"Is Deb in?" I ask, feeling like an idiot for flinging pebbles instead of knocking at the door like a normal person.

"She's not allowed out."

"Please, Mrs. Elliot," I say, going for the most formal way of addressing her, a tactic almost guaranteed to win over parents.

Helena frowns and I think she's going to dismiss me, but instead she disappears inside, and moments later my friend replaces her.

"There's this thing," Deb says, her voice muffled behind her mask. "It's called a phone. Absolutely miraculous means of communication. Pebble flinging is so last century."

"I was trying not to alert the parents." I gesture toward the house where Helena is presumably describing my odd behavior to Deb's dad.

"Fail," Deb says.

"And with that phone registry, who knows what they're tracking or who's listening. I just need to talk to you."

Deb's face gets serious. She gestures for me to follow her to the side garden, where she settles in the tree swing, nodding for me to sit on the bench beneath an arbor of pink roses, a safe distance apart. "Tell," she says.

I adjust my mask and lean forward to share the details of my escape plan. I tell her that if I'm careful, I think I can make a dash for it between patrols at Cucklett Delf. Crossing the boundary isn't the problem, though. It's what to do on the other side. There are three main roads into Eyam, and I know they're all closed off because I've seen the barricades. I've wandered by several times, so there's no way I'm getting past those armored vehicles. According to what I've found from surfing the internet and watching people's posts on social media, it looks like the smaller lanes in the area are also being guarded. There'll be no hopping on my bike and pedaling out of here, or taking Dad's car and bursting through the barricades like they do in the movies. If I'm going to get out of here, I'll need to do it on foot.

If I leave tonight, I can go through Cucklett Delf and make my way down the crags. It's a scramble in the daylight, and will be treacherous even in the eternal twilight of midsummer, but there are no houses or farms in that area, no neighbors to spot me and raise the alarm. From there, it's less than two miles over Eyam Moor and through Stokes Wood to Grindleford Station. If I can get that far, I can hop an early train on Sunday, when there won't be many people around, and be in Manchester or Sheffield in less than half an hour. From there, I should be able to travel freely, blending in with the other travelers. Ideally, I'd go straight to London, pick up my new life as if nothing has changed, but given all my correspondence about the flat and job, I'd be too easy to track down.

I have one big niggling doubt. What if I carry this thing, whatever it is, out of the village? What if I get all the way to London only to discover I've brought something infectious with me?

I recount my plan, then look Deb straight in the eye. "I know this is a very bad idea, and I know you're going to try to talk me out of it, but I can't just stay here and wait to die."

"It *is* a bad idea, one of your worst, which is saying something. But I think you should try."

I almost lose my nerve, right there. I want to hug Deb, but I can't. And I want to cry on her shoulder and tell her she's the best friend I could ever have hoped for, but I can't do that either.

"But don't go to London," she adds. "Go to your auntie's. It's less populated and they can take precautions until you know you're safe."

I want to argue that I can't risk harming my family, but I know Deb is right. I'll do everything I can to avoid contact with other people and, once I'm at Auntie Margie's, Mum will know what to do to keep us all safe.

"Come with me," I blurt.

Deb pushes off and leans back in the swing. The ropes around the tree branch creak as she glides back and forth. Even though I can only see her eyes, I can tell she's considering my proposal, maybe weighing her odds between making a run for it with me and taking her chances here in the village. To me it's a no-brainer, but Deb's hesitation causes me to second-guess my decision.

"I can't," she says at last.

I start to object, but she stops me. "They'd hear my wheezing before we even got to the top of the hill. And two miles across the moor? I can barely make it to the end of the village without having to sit down. I wouldn't make it, which means you wouldn't make it either. I'm not going to hold you back. It wouldn't be fair."

"Well, I'm not going to leave without you. That's what wouldn't be fair."

Deb shakes her head, no.

"I'm not leaving you here to die." The words catch in my throat as the reality of my decision hits me.

But Deb just laughs. "Salty, do you know how many different pills and potions I already take each day just to stay alive? Whatever this thing turns out to be, I promise you, I'm already taking something to prevent it getting me. So just go. And send me a postcard when you get to your aunt's."

Deb reaches out to rest her hand on my back. Just in time, we both pull back, measuring the distance between us and shuffling around until we're far enough apart. I can see the anguish in her eyes at what we have to do, and I feel the same anguish in my gut. What kind of life is this that you can't even hug a friend? The skin across my back starts to ache where her hands should have landed. I roll my shoulders, trying to erase the tension, trying to remember what it feels like to be touched by someone. But all we can do is look.

"Remember when we were young," Deb says, "and we'd pretend to smooch?"

"Johnny Depp," I say, turning my back on her and wrapping my arms tight around my torso, running my hands up and down my back and making smoochie moans.

"Brian Cox," says Deb, doing the same. "Oh, Brian," she sighs over her shoulder, "I love it when you talk particle physics to me. Show me your Higgs boson."

I giggle. "You're sick in the head." But I hug myself tighter, and for a long minute we sit there holding ourselves and imagining the day we can hug one another again. It's a poor substitute for the real thing, but for the first time in days, I don't feel so alone.

I keep myself busy, trying to keep my head full of tasks so I don't have room to worry about what lies ahead. I honestly don't know if anyone will look for me if I leave. I don't know what the consequences will be if I'm caught. All I know is that I can't take any chances that could land me back inside the quarantine. If I don't make it to the station, I'm going to have to stay underground until I can make another plan.

I borrow Dad's backpack, something that's not conspicuous but will hold enough to keep me going for a few days: water, food, a change of clothes, basic first aid, nothing more than I can carry. I can't use anything that can be traced, like bank cards. And thanks to the registry, that includes my phone. I have nine pounds in a money belt, plus sixty pounds from my sock drawer that I've been saving toward a jacket. I send a telepathic request for forgiveness to Alice and shake out the contents of her piggy bank. She has almost fifty quid, and judging by the fact that it's all in coins and small notes, it looks like the little miser has been squirreling away her pocket money for months. I make a silent pledge to pay her back with interest and stuff the notes and a handful of coins into my jeans.

I find my hiking boots still packed for my move to London. Even as the days have ticked by, I've clung to a childish hope that the quarantine will be lifted, and we'll all go back to normal. My job, my flat, my future are all sitting there awaiting my arrival. I never dreamed that, instead of starting my new life this weekend, I'd be fighting to save my old one.

My passport is with the others in Mum's dressing table drawer. I don't have plans to use it, but I don't want to rule out any possibilities. If I need to keep moving and leave the country, I will. On the top of the dressing table is a photo of the four of us. The absence of Mum and Alice yanks at my heart, but I can't imagine what it would be like if they hadn't left for Auntie Margie's when they did. It would kill me to see my little sister go through this, and I know with certainty that, if she were still here, there would be no way I could leave without her. If my plan works, I'll see her soon. If it doesn't, I don't know what will happen to me. I can't think about that now.

In the back of the drawer is a flowered box that I've often caught Mum browsing through. When I lift the lid, I'm confronted by so many memories, all of Mum's favorite photos of Alice and me. Our entire lives have been documented and squeezed into four-by-six frames of nostalgia—family get-togethers with the other Syddalls, visits to Auntie Margie, school events, afternoons in the back garden, and walks in the hills. All the minutiae of life are gathered in these images. So many good memories contained in one small space, while the real-life people are scattered all over—Mum and Alice on the south coast, and Dad and me trapped here. Another twenty-four hours and I won't be here anymore either. Then it will just be Dad. The thought of leaving him alone here grips at my stomach and twists hard, but he'd never leave, and it's unfair of him to make me stay.

I'm about to put the box back when something catches my eye. Tucked underneath the liner in the bottom is a blue airmail envelope—nothing unusual except for the array of brightly colored stamps and the unfamiliar lettering of the postmark. I pull it out and see that the stamps are from Greece, and the envelope is addressed in bold, curly handwriting to Mum's work. The postmark shows it was sent more than a decade ago, long before Alice came along. I peek inside, expecting to find a handwritten letter, as this is clearly a personal correspondence, but all I find is more photos. There's one of Mum sitting on a restaurant terrace in the port town near Auntie Margie's house. The next is of Mum at some sort of party, chatting to people I don't recognize, a glass of champagne in her hand and her curls blowing in the breeze. She looks like the Mum I know, but I recognize in her a glimmer of the youthful Mum I've seen in old photographs, a relaxed, daring Mum. If ever there was a poster child for the restorative properties of holidays, Mum is it.

I flip to the next photo. Mum is sunbathing, but judging by her glow, it couldn't possibly have been during an English summer. She's leaning back on her hands, her chin held high, one leg tucked up and the other straight. And it's pretty obvious that she's posing for—and flirting with—her photographer.

This is a side of my parents I definitely haven't seen. *Go, Dad,* I think, as I try to place the setting where he took this picture.

But then I know. I recognize the varnished deck; the sunny, yellow cushions; and the pristine, white cockpit of Mark's boat—a boat I am sure my father has never set foot on. I stare at my mother's face, piecing together crumbs of information that have been gathering in my mind for years. But I can't reconcile this picture of a woman in love with the knowledge that this woman is my mother. Until I turn to the bottom picture in my hands. Because there she is, her head leaned against Mark's bare chest, his tanned arm around her shoulder, and they are beaming at the camera in a way I've never seen her smile with my dad.

There are so many thoughts vying for my attention, I can't keep them in any order. And yet one thought keeps scrabbling its way to the top. *My mother has abandoned me in a village of death so that she can sneak some time with her...*

And suddenly, all the missing pieces—the hushed arguments between my parents that I assumed were normal spats, Mum's insistence on visiting her sister every year, the sudden important meeting requiring a trip to London without Alice, Mark's offer of "help"—drop into place in a puzzle I hadn't realized I was trying to solve.

As I stuff the envelope back in the bottom of the box and stash my mother's secret back where it belongs, a sense of betrayal sinks deep inside me. I have known my mother for almost eighteen years, but now I am no longer sure I know her at all. The person I was counting on to shelter me is no longer a person I can trust, and suddenly my solid plan for escape is riddled with tiny fissures.

It's still mid-afternoon when I hear Dad come in. I curse under my breath. I can only hope that he'll be too preoccupied to wonder why I'm brewing strong coffee at this time of day. I can't exactly tell him I'm using it to dye my blond hair with its conspicuous purple streak back to brown so I can escape incognito tonight. With Andy's village shop closed, this natural option (courtesy of the internet) is the best I can do.

Dad drops his mask and gloves into a bucket he's set up by the door, then shuffles into the living room and plunks down on the couch. He looks tired.

"Are you all right?" I ask.

He sighs. "I will be. I've been all afternoon trying to explain to the powers that be that Mrs. Glover has special dietary needs that are not going to be met with this dehydrated slop they keep feeding us. It's like talking to the wall sometimes."

"Why is that your job?" I ask.

Dad looks at me like I've asked the stupidest question ever. "Well, who else does she have?"

Dad taking it upon himself to answer every call for help in the village is nothing new, but since the quarantine, he's run himself ragged. His support of the affected families has ranged from handing out reassurances and words of comfort to coordinating any number of special arrangements like these for Mrs. Glover. It's just Dad being Dad, but now that I've found the skeletons rattling around in the back of Mum's cupboard, I want to shake him by the shoulders and yell at him to pay more attention to his own family instead of fussing around everyone else's. But when I scan through my images of him, I see a slow progression, a gradual change from the Dad of The Early Years to the Dad of now, and I have to wonder: Does he already know about the skeletons? Does throwing his energy into everyone else's lives keep him from having to face his own?

For all the criticisms I could make of my dad, he doesn't deserve this. And suddenly I feel very protective of my fragile father.

I make him a big mug of tea (thankfully tea bags are included in our government rations) and tell him to put his feet up. He starts to fuss about dinner, but I tell him I have it under control, even though I don't. I feel like making one of his favorites, one of Grandma Syddall's old recipes like "cheese and egg" or toad-in-the-hole, but despite the recent lift of the food restrictions, fresh ingredients like milk, eggs, cheese, and sausages aren't yet included in our supplies. What I really want to do is run down to the Jolly Fryer for haddock and chips or ring up the Indian Summer for a chicken tikka and some onion bhajis, but everything that is normal and good about my life has been taken away.

I should tell Dad I'm leaving. I should give him the chance to get away too. But he wouldn't take it. I know he wouldn't break the rules, and I know he wouldn't allow me to break them either. I have to do this alone.

As I pull open the fridge door to see if there's anything remotely edible in there, a wave crashes over me, and before I know why, I am staring into the empty depths of the refrigerator and balling my eyes out. And once I start, I can't stop. I just stand there sobbing, my shoulders heaving up and down like I'm trying to shrug off the weight of the world. And I feel as if I am. I'm crying for choices that have been stripped away from me, the fact that I can't make my dad a simple dish of milk, cheese, and eggs. I cry for the fractures running through my family, the secrets stashed in cupboards, the denial that anything is wrong. I cry that my sister is so far away, that my mother is suddenly a stranger to me, and that I'm about to leave my poor dad alone. I cry that I'm going to break the law and break my dad's heart along with it. I cry that my best friend's body can't be trusted to save her life. That the future I had planned is gone, and the future I have is unknown at best and nonexistent at worst.

But most of all I cry for my loss of freedom. That I no longer have options in any part of my life. That I am now just a piece in a game I cannot control. That I am, one way or another, a statistic.

"What's the matter?" Dad's voice behind me is full of concern, but the way his question flips up at the end lets me know there's only one answer he could stand to hear.

I wipe my snotty nose across my arm like a toddler and press the heels of my hands under my eyes so my runny mascara won't make me look like a panda. "Nothing," I say. "I'm fine." I turn around and flash my dad a smile, blinking away the last stray tears.

"Come on," he says. "It'll be okay. I promise it'll be okay."

"I know it will," I say. "I'm just being silly."

All my life my parents have promised me things will be okay, and they always have been. But in this moment I realize something. All these years, they've just been lucky, and this is a promise my dad has no hope of keeping. For the first time in my life, my so-called rebellion could earn me a lot more than parental disapproval, and suddenly I am truly afraid for my future.

Chapter Eleven

A S SOON AS THE SUMMER twilight dims to gray, I go out through my bedroom window and make my way to Cucklett Delf. Near the top of the hill, I take a last look back at the only place I've ever called home. I don't know when, or if, I'll see it again. For a moment, the fear of what lies ahead roots me to the spot. I search the faint outline of houses until I find Deb's. I wish she could have come with me. Salt and Pepper: We're supposed to always be together. But we both understand that she wouldn't have made it. She gave up her own chance of freedom to help me secure mine. I have to keep moving, not only for myself, but to make sure her decision wasn't for nothing.

I tuck in against the rock and wait for the guard to make his pass toward the crags. According to my reconnaissance, he'll pass back this way in about six minutes, then I'll have eleven minutes while he makes his pass down toward the lane and back. Eleven minutes to get myself over the stream through the short open stretch at the bottom of Cucklett Delf, and over the crags to freedom. I have the feeling it's going to be the shortest eleven minutes of my life.

I reach for my phone, then remember I don't have it. All I can do is trust that Ro will be there waiting for me. I take a minute to gather myself together. I can't let my emotions get in the way like this. If I look back at all I'm leaving, I'll never have the guts to go. I have to keep looking forward, to my immediate future and no further. There'll be plenty of time for looking back and having regrets, and for building a new life, but not if I don't do what I need to do right now.

The guard makes his return pass and, once he's out of sight, I make my way down the embankment toward the river. I keep glancing over my shoulder, waiting for someone to see me. I half expect Aiden to have followed me, trying to be helpful. If he does, my whole plan is shot.

At the edge of the stream, I take one last look over my shoulder to check that the coast is clear, and then I wade in. It's not until the water runs over the tops of my boots that I realize I've made a stupid mistake. I'll have to walk in wet boots, which will undoubtedly bring me a slew of problems from blisters to boot rot, but I don't have time to take them off, and I certainly don't have the luxury of sitting on the opposite bank to put them back on. If anyone sees me outside the cordon, I am toast.

About halfway across the river, the most amazing feeling comes over me. I don't know where it comes from, but I'm grateful for it. A sense of determination fills me, along with the absolute knowledge that I can do this. I have a plan and resources, and I have my wits. Most of all, for the first time in my life, I have real courage. Yes, I am going out into the unknown, but suddenly I am not afraid. I wish Deb could see me now, because I'm sure she'd be proud of me.

My newfound courage suffers a momentary waver when I climb out of the river and onto the opposite bank. Another first for me: I am breaking the law. I am a fugitive. And as such, I need to run. Right now.

I hoist the straps of Dad's backpack onto my shoulders and secure the belt around my waist. Steeling myself, I take a deep breath, pick a direction, and go.

There's the silhouette of a clump of trees ahead of me. I dash toward it, hoping to be hidden as soon as possible. Even though it's almost August, the summer nights still don't get fully dark, and tonight the moon is bright. I'll have to stay hidden as much as possible, but at least it will help me pick my way through the undergrowth until I can get a clear shot of the terrain and, hopefully, Ro.

I'm not even a handful of steps from the river when a dark figure steps out from the trees. My heart flutters because I know that Ro is here. I can't keep the relief from spilling over my face in a goofy smile, but when I turn to run toward him, I see it isn't Ro. It's Will.

Ro's older brother is a thicker, darker version of Ro—*swarthy* is what my grandma would have called him, but not in a good way. He has a shotgun slung casually over one shoulder, and a thick rope swings from the other. A red bandana covers his nose and mouth, making him look like a Wild West outlaw. I square my shoulders and push my hair casually back.

"Hey, Will," I say, trying to keep my voice level even though my heart is thudding against my voice box. My brain scrambles to piece together why Will is here. Has Ro recruited help? Is this Will's way of sticking it to the establishment, or whatever statement he needs to make? But as I get close enough to see Will's eyes, it becomes very apparent that he is not here to help. His face is set in a tight, emotionless expression, and beneath his dark brows, his stare is cold and hard. That look stops me in my tracks.

"Going somewhere?" he asks. His voice reminds me of Ro's, but it's deeper and harder. I have no ally here.

"Where's Ro?" I ask.

"Stood you up." Will's tone is mocking. "Bet you didn't tell your old man about this either, eh?"

"Ro told you I'd be here?" My stomach lurches with the thought that Ro hasn't simply had a change of heart, he's deliberately recruited help to stop me.

"Got cold feet and asked for some brotherly advice. I gave him some."

I can't believe Ro would really be so stupid as to go to Will for advice on something as important as this, but I refuse to be held back now I've come this far. Even though my legs weaken beneath me, I hold my gaze firmly on Will. "I don't want any trouble," I tell him. "Just let me pass."

Will takes a step forward, seeming to expand in front of me like a brick wall. He hefts his shotgun almost casually, but I've seen him carry a brace of dead rabbits in the same way Alice might swing a basket of flowers, as if life is something that can be picked or discarded at will. The threat that his gun could also fell me is enough to hold me at bay. "Sorry, Syddall," he says. "Can't do that."

"I'm not going to hurt anyone, Will. I'm not sick, and I'm not dangerous. Look at me. I'm healthy. But I'm not going to be if I stay here. So just let me go."

Will shakes his head. "Can't take that chance, I'm afraid."

Fury builds inside me, but I have to keep it in check. If I lose it now, I'm never going to win this lug over. And if I'm going to win him over, I need to do it soon, before that guard comes back into sight. "If you were in my situation, Will, you'd do the same. Think about it."

He hesitates for a moment, and I think maybe I've struck a nerve, but then he raises his gun and points it straight at me. I've never looked into the barrel of a gun before. In a kind of slow-motion, artistic visual, I picture the twitch of Will's finger and a tiny brass bullet spinning down the barrel. It bursts out into the daylight and takes a clear, straight path toward my head. I even have a second to wonder what it would feel like to be here and then gone. Would I feel anything? Would I know it was over? Or would the lights simply go out as I close for business forever, like Andy Hawksworth's shop? If I wasn't completely convinced that Will was capable of pulling that trigger, I'd find this intriguing. As it is, I'm too terrified to breathe. I stare Will in the eye until all I'm aware of is his eyes and mine. The rest of me—my body, my thoughts, Cucklett Delf—melts into a beige blur around me.

A movement on the periphery breaks the powerful spell of Will's gun. *Is it Ro?* I dare to look away for an instant, hoping this is all some really sick joke, but three more men step into the clearing. Ro's two other brothers both hold guns pointed at me, although they are somehow less menacing. Into the front of the scene steps Mr. Torre. His face is stern, but I catch a softness in his eye that gives me hope. He pushes his arm down over Will's gun and steps in between his son and me. The power in that gentle movement is formidable.

"Go home, Emmott," he says. "For all our sakes, go home."

I stare at Mr. Torre for a moment, trying to find something to say that might touch that soft spot I see in him. But I've seen this man birth a calf, coaxing the cow with gentle words and easing the newborn out onto the floor of the barn. And I know he's taken his gun to that same cow when she's become too sick to produce. This is not a sentimental man. This is a gentle man who will do what needs to be done. And what needs to be done right now is to get this risky quarantine-breaker back where she belongs. He will do it with kindness if he can, but at the end of the day, it will be done.

I can't look at him any longer. I can't look at his family, and I can't look over the three Torre brothers without seeing the fourth one who is missing. In that moment, my situation becomes clear. I have no allies beyond the quarantine. There may be people who care what happens to me, but they care what happens to me within the village. Out here, I will not find any friends.

I turn and splash back through the river before the guard returns. I do not look back at the Torres. I do not give them the pleasure of knowing I am beaten.

Chapter Twelve

F ROM THE ROCK AT THE top of Cucklett Delf, the
Eyam skyline is silhouetted against the floodlights from
basecamp. I pick out my house and am once again faced with
creeping back into a place I've just escaped. Last time the
biggest threat was the wrath of Dad; this time I'm going back
to my indescribable hell.

I slump down into the grass and let Ro's betrayal engulf me,
my anger ballooning up inside me. I thought I could count on
him. I thought that if anyone would rebel against my forced
imprisonment, against unreasonable rules laid down by the
institution, it would be Ro. He was always the one daring me to
break free, to be my own person, to not let myself be confined.
What happened to my daredevil?

As soon as I get home, I will demand an answer. But as I
replay the confrontation with Will, snippets of understanding
cluster together, pointing the finger of blame at me. I am as
guilty as my father for prejudice against the Torres. Only I
relished Ro's bad-boy image, gravitated to the partner least
likely to please my dad. But Ro has never been a daredevil. Even
before I told him of my plans to move to London, I worried he
might back out. Even as I packed boxes and resigned from my
job, a little piece of me knew he might lose his nerve. To trust

him to risk his life to save mine was the logic of an idiot. I have no one to blame but myself.

But that still doesn't stop me from despising Ro.

From this vantage point I can see the whole village, nestled peacefully in its hollow. Beyond is the dark shape of two bands of hills stretching into the distance. Behind the first is the village of Grindleford with its cozy train station, and over the second is the city of Sheffield, at least twenty miles from here in the neighboring county. Beyond, far beyond, lies London, the place that once held my dreams. In the daylight I'd be able to see a network of roads and paths and borders of dry stone walls separating fields and farms. There are physical boundaries between here and there, but none that I couldn't cross or go around. And yet I cannot get there. I am trapped in this village by powerful forces—by an illness that has baffled the so-called experts, by government bureaucracy that considers me a threat, and by people too afraid to remember their friends. I have never felt so alone in my life.

I should have been in London tonight, unpacking boxes, starting my new life. Of all the obstacles I'd predicted might stand in my way, I had never imagined this. It seems I have no choice now but to go home and wait—wait to see what happens next, and wait to find out if I will die here. But that feels a lot like giving up, and giving up is unacceptable. Will may have got the better of me this time, but he can't guard every inch of the quarantine perimeter every hour of every day. There has to be some way out of here, and I am determined to find it.

I push up from the rock, taking one last look at the view beyond my prison walls, and march back down to the village, my wet feet squelching inside my boots. My mind churns with possibility, testing the fence like a caged animal, looking for a weakness the authorities might have overlooked. Vans full of supplies come and go all day long. Maybe I could hitch a ride out. What if I could get my hands on a hazmat suit and just walk out? That could work too. I'm just thinking about sewers and wondering if I'd have the guts to venture out that way when Aiden appears, startling me. It's like a magic trick or some kind of sixth sense that lets him know I'm here. I hold my ground, almost daring him to ask where I've been. *Do your worst; turn me in*, I think.

"You're out late," he says.

"So are you."

"I'm on the night shift."

Of course you are, I think without meeting his gaze. "I needed a walk."

He glances at my boots. Can he tell they're wet? "With the amount of stuff you've got with you, you look like you'd be gone for days. I was worried you were going to make a run for it."

I force a laugh, even though I know that, now Aiden has seen me, I will not escape from here. The trickiest barrier between me and my freedom is standing right in front of me.

"Your hair suits you that color," he says, holding his gaze on me just long enough to confirm he's on to me. "Come with me." He turns down the street and gestures for me to follow.

I know I'm in trouble. He wasn't joking about me making a run for it and, despite all his talk about his role here, now he's going to turn me in. What is it with these men who get their thrills from landing me in hot water? "Where are we going?" I ask.

"I want to show you something."

"Show me what?"

He turns around and peers through his visor at me. "Are you always this stubborn?" he asks.

"Yes," I say. "Only I prefer to call it *determined*."

His eyes smile, and I'm sure I glimpse a look of admiration. The cartoon face on the front of his suit smiles up at me too, friendly and trustworthy. Even though my gut instincts have been unreliable lately, I sense that this isn't a man on a vindictive mission. Trusting my gut, I walk with him through the village.

When we reach one of the trailers near the village green, he opens the door and calls out a quick hello. When no one answers, he reaches inside the door, hands me a clean mask, gloves, and a long paper coat, and tells me to put them on.

"What's going on?" I ask as he ushers me inside and locks the door behind us. I try to sound more sure of myself than I feel. Even though he's not giving off any creepy vibes, I keep my distance from him. Thanks to Ro, I'm no longer willing to trust anyone, and I can't assume that anything I do outside of my house will be safe or private.

"You can't do a runner, Emmott," Aiden says at last.

I start to object, but he stops me.

"I know you were thinking about it. I can see it in your face," he says. "And your hair."

I pull the edge of my bottom lip between my teeth, pressing the soft flesh and trying to decide on a tactic. The weight of my backpack roots me to the floor like a ball and chain. It's pointless to deny it because it's clear he knows. But I'm not about to confess my guilt either.

"I can't blame you," he says. "I know what it must be like for you here, but I'm urging you not to try it."

"Honestly," I say, looking him dead in the eye now, "you have absolutely no idea what it's like. You have your nice protective suit and you get to leave anytime you want. You don't have the first clue what it's like to be trapped here not knowing if you're going to live or die."

"Actually, I sort of do," he says, inching his words out. "I've been on the other side, where you are."

As this is the first I've heard of an entire village being quarantined, I find that extremely unlikely. "Where?" I ask.

"Rwanda." His eyes seem to darken, as if the sun has gone in. "I worked with a relief team there. We had a protocol breach, and almost half the team was compromised. They put us in isolation for three weeks—a giant tent away from the main camp. Twelve of us watching one another to see who would start showing symptoms first."

"And did you?"

"No, but I had to watch the others who did."

For a moment his eyes lose their focus, and I can tell he's thinking about his friends. The cheeky glint is replaced by a deep sadness. I avert my gaze, not wanting to pry into his most intimate memories, or to let him see the unexpected kinship I suddenly feel.

"There was nothing I could do to help them," he says at last. "It's the most helpless and frustrating feeling I've ever had."

Yeah, I think. *That just about sums it up.* I'm uncomfortable with this personal admission. Aiden is supposed to be the enemy, and I prefer my enemies cold and unfeeling, more like Will. But Aiden gets it. He understands what it's like to be here. For a moment, my anger at Ro and his cowardice is softened by this tiny nugget of compassion. A friendly smile flickers into Aiden's eyes again, and I find myself smiling back, grateful for his kindness.

But there's something else causing my discomfort, some awful, niggling feeling wriggling in the pit of my stomach.

"The people you worked with... what did they have?" I ask. Images of news reports flash into my mind, hundreds of people dying of a terrible disease. Ebola. I can barely think the name, and I can't bring myself to say it out loud now. "Is that what we have?"

Aiden shakes his head, but not with sufficient conviction to assure me. He leans over one of the computer consoles set up in the trailer. It has a modified mouse and oversized keyboard so that he can operate it without removing his gloves. He taps a few keys and pulls up a map of the British Isles. "There's been a development," he says.

"A *development*?" I drop my backpack to the floor, shoving it under the desk with my foot.

"The official word will go out tonight, but don't tell anyone I told you first. Turns out this flu is a bit more unusual than that."

"That's not going to come as news to anyone around here," I say.

"I'm sure, but up until now they've had absolutely no clue what it is, and you can't treat what you can't diagnose. But now it's starting to look like a familiar virus."

"What kind of virus?" I ask, although I'm not sure I want to hear his answer.

"That's what they still don't know. Viruses come in families. Ebola and Marburg are filoviruses, nasty things they are. Measles and mumps are in another family, and your common or garden variety flu is in a different family again."

"So what family is our virus in?"

"That's the question. The symptoms we're seeing are typical

of a lot of viruses—fever, headache, body pain, nausea—the kind of thing you'd expect from the flu. But they're saying the pathology looks a lot like something they've seen in Siberia. There've been a couple of small outbreaks in nomadic tribes there. They've managed to contain them, and that's the only place it's been seen, so it's never become a major epidemic."

"How did it get here?"

Aiden shrugs. "That's part of what they'll be trying to find out."

I wrack my brains, sifting through the health classes I daydreamed through, trying to ferret out any information I have about viruses. All I can come up with is that they're really, really small, and very infectious. I also know that, as with a cold, someone can become infected and pass their virus along to others before they even know they're sick. Dr. Spencer could have been harboring our Siberian visitor long before he felt ill. He could have already had it when he peered into my ears and down my throat. The only indication that this is nothing more than a fear-fueled hypothesis is that—so far—I'm still here to worry about it.

"Now they know what it is, can they cure it?"

"Let's just say that research funds have been a little thin. But now it's here, things will move a bit faster, I'm guessing."

I wonder how many people had to die before we became a priority, but I keep my mouth shut in the hope Aiden will keep talking and divulge information I can use, such as how to stay alive.

"So here's what I want to show you," he says, turning back to the map. "The thing is, this isn't public knowledge, and I could probably get in a lot of bother for this, but I wanted you to see it."

"Okay." I feel a spark of excitement at his trust. "But why me?"

He glances over his shoulder and appraises me, as if he's thinking about this question for the first time. "Because, one way or another, I'd like it if you stuck around."

Before I can ask what he means and if he's actually flirting with me, he clicks on the map, causing big splotches of green to appear. They're patchy in some places and dense and dark in others. I can identify the dark patches as major population centers—London, Birmingham, Sheffield, Leeds, and Glasgow over the border. He clicks on a spot in the middle of the country, probably pretty close to Eyam, and a single red dot appears. "This is all hypothetical, a computer model based on the limited data they've managed to collect. But let's say this red dot is one person, could be anyone. Let's say he—or *she*—is carrying the virus but doesn't know it, doesn't have any symptoms or anything, in fact, he or she may never show symptoms. And let's say he or she finds himself—or *herself*—outside the quarantine zone."

"Okay, I get it, it's me you're talking about."

"Purely hypothetical, like I say. But, let's say this person comes into contact with another person and gives them the virus, but neither of them knows it, so they go about their business as usual." He clicks the mouse again. "Now watch what happens."

At first nothing seems to happen, except in a box at the side of the map labeled "Days," where the number changes from one to two to three, and so on. At about ten days, the red "me" dot changes and starts to grow. I have to really stare at it because the change is so gradual I'm not even sure it's happening. Then, just as the growing dot morphs into a splotch, another red dot springs up close by and then another around the London patch of green. In between the "me" dot and the London dot, other dots appear along an invisible line, each following the same pattern as the original. Each grows slowly, then suddenly blossoms as new dots appear.

Something else catches my eye on the panel near the numbers. A graph starts to form, a red line rising up from the axis like a charmed snake. As it lifts, the London dot bursts open like a rose bush blooming. Then other flowers spring to life around the map until the original green patches have all but been replaced by red.

I don't need to ask Aiden what it means. I know how quickly a cold could spread around school. One person gets it, then another, and before you know it, everyone's sniffling and hacking. But even that first-hand knowledge can't compare to the visual image in front of me. I only have to think about how many people I come into contact with on a normal day to see how this would spread. My one dot could easily become ten or more in a single day, and each of those ten dots could become a hundred, then a thousand, and so on. And in the space of the week, two thirds of our country's population would be infected. Put even a handful of those people on trains or planes, and the consequences are unimaginable.

As the red line on the graph climbs higher, the weight of the country bears down on me. This isn't just data. These are real people with lives and dreams, like me. I imagine if the four people who'd prevented my escape had helped me instead. Four potential new red dots. And Ro, another, then the people on the trains and buses I planned to take, and anyone else who gave me a hand along the way. In return I might have given them a death sentence. I might have taken our virus all the way to Auntie Margie's, all the way to Mum and Alice. My escape and infection of the whole population would have made me infamous. Typhoid Mary, meet Siberian Emmott.

Aiden watches me watch the map, but he doesn't say anything. He doesn't need to. We both know what might have been and what now is instead. Will may have prevented me from unknowingly spreading the virus, but he's also kept me here, in the heart of the first red bloom.

I turn back to the map to see what happens next. As the Days counter hits twenty-eight, something unexpected happens. The red graph plateaus and within a couple more days turns downward again. The map changes too. The red dots begin to disappear, and patches of green spring up again, smaller than before but definitely there. By sixty days, the red dots have all gone. What's left is a similar pattern of green as before, just lighter and patchier. When I look back at the graph, the line is a perfect hill, rising up, cresting, and disappearing again. Deb would love to see this.

"What's this line?" I ask, pointing to the symmetrical curve of the graph.

"That's new cases," he says.

"It's stopped. What happened?"

He gives me a half-smile, like this is going to be good-bad news. "The virus burns itself out."

"So it's gone?"

He kind of shrugs. "That's what we think, based on data from the Siberian outbreaks, although we can't be absolutely sure. We *think* this is the kind of virus you can't usually get twice, like measles or chicken pox. Once you have it, you're immune. After a while, there's no one else for it to infect."

"That isn't either immune or dead," I add.

He nods. "Sixty-two days is what they've modeled, based on the virus having access to the mainland population."

"And if it only has access to four hundred people?"

"Same," he says. "Sixty-two days and, in theory, it will be over."

"In theory," I repeat.

"In theory."

It's been a little over two weeks, that's all, since Dr. Spencer came down with his "flu," our first red dot. But if the two earlier deaths were related, as some people are now speculating . . . What's that? Twenty-one days? Maybe twenty-eight? Within the week it should reach its peak. All I have to do is hold on for another month after that. It may as well be a lifetime.

"According to the news, there are four hundred and twenty-three people inside the quarantine," I say, more to myself than to Aiden. "So, according to the numbers, a hundred and . . ." I try to use my fingers, but my brain is so muddled and foggy, I can't work it out.

"One third is one hundred and forty-one," says Aiden.

One hundred forty-one of us will not make it out alive. One hundred and forty-one people I know, some of whom I've known my whole life, will cease to exist in the course of sixty-two days. Every day, at least two people I know will die.

"The last I heard, there've been thirty-six deaths so far," I say.

"Thirty-seven, I believe. As of an hour ago."

I don't dare ask who the latest victim is. I just know it's not me, probably not my dad, and hopefully not Deb. All I can think is, *104 to go*. According to the graph, we're a week away from the downward side of the slope. After that, my odds of becoming one of the 141 will lessen every day. "All I have to do is wait it out," I say.

Inside his suit, Aiden nods. It's just a slight nod, and I can barely see it. I know what he's thinking, because I'm having the same thought: *All I have to do is wait it out and hope that 104 people catch this before I do.*

The idea of this makes me want to throw up.

"Aiden?" When he turns, I'm not sure what I want to say next. That he's provided a twisted ray of hope in this gloomy place? That in another time and place we might have been friends? That his kindness has touched a part of me that I can't identify? It all sounds stupid, so all I say is, "I'm glad you showed me."

He holds my gaze for a second and gives me a nod of understanding. "Be careful, Emmott," he says. "Don't do anything dangerous, okay?"

"Okay."

"You promise?"

I nod because it's what he wants to see, but, thanks to this virus, my entire existence is dangerous, and I'm not sure how to avoid that.

As we step out of the trailer, I realize I've left Dad's backpack under the desk. I'm just about to turn back when something down the street catches my eye, something familiar—the yellow flash of a suit. Three suits, to be exact… and my dad.

"Oh, bugger," I mutter as the group strides toward us. "Everyone's on the bloody nightshift tonight." From their decisive movements, it's clear this isn't a friendly visit. I know I've made a big mistake. "I think I've got you into that bother after all," I say to Aiden.

"I was about to say the same to you," he says. "It's Reynolds, my boss."

Before I can respond, one of the suits takes the lead. "Is anything the matter here?" she asks.

I wait for Aiden to rat me out, because there's no good reason for either of us to be here otherwise.

"Just answering a few questions, Dr. Reynolds." To my relief, his voice is matter-of-fact.

Reynolds peers at me. "And what are you doing out at this hour?"

"Just asking a few questions." I try to sound innocent.

"I'll handle this." My dad steps to the front, asserting his rights as my father. "What the hell are you doing out at this time of night? I've been looking all over for you."

Aiden flinches as if he's about to move forward, but I step ahead of him. I got us both into this pickle, so the least I can do is speak for myself.

"This is my fault," I tell Dr. Reynolds.

"It usually is," my dad says, just loud enough for me to hear.

"I couldn't sleep. I got up for a walk. I ran into Aiden and we got talking, that's all."

Dad gives me no more than a tiny nod of his head, enough to let me know the best thing I could do for myself would be to keep my mouth shut and follow him home.

It takes only an instant to decide I'd be safer abandoning my backpack than exposing my plan to escape. I step toward Dad, turning back only once to catch Aiden's eye in the hopes of sending a telepathic message to make sure it isn't found. I can't read his look, but he seems to be telling me everything will be okay. He's either lying or delusional, but I appreciate his reassurance.

Chapter Thirteen

Monday, August 1

IN THE BOTTOM OF ALICE'S toy box, I find my old Super Ball wedged under a doll that long since fell out of favor. A couple of bounces on the hardwood floor lets me know it still has enough life left in it to serve its new purpose. I take up position on my bedroom floor, back pressed against my bed, and take aim. The ball arches from my hand, hits the bare wood floor just beyond the rug, bounces against the closed door, ricochets back with a final *thud* off the floor, and right back into my hand. I haven't lost my knack. Off it goes again. *Thud-thud-thud*-catch. *Thud-thud-thud*-catch.

It takes about three minutes for my plan to take effect.

"Emmott!" Dad yells up the stairs. "Cut that out!"

Two more rounds and I stop. I've succeeded in expressing my annoyance to Dad. Now I have to come up with a way to spend the rest of my day.

I try to work on a new mosaic, but my heart is no longer in creating when everything around me is dying. I was supposed to start my new job today. I should have been stocking the fridge with drinks and collecting empty glasses, unpacking my boxes at home, going to bed tonight with Ro. But no, that dream is all in my past now. Big thanks to Ro and Will and yes, my dearest father.

Dad and I have skirted one another for the past twenty-four hours. My father isn't usually what people refer to as "a man of few words," but he's managed to make an exception for me. He's been kind enough to let me know that he doesn't approve of my "fraternizing" (his words) with Aiden, although it's not clear whether it's because Aiden is "one of them" or because he just can't stand the idea of his daughter in the company of any other male. He's reminded me that "this isn't a game" ("this" being the quarantine), as if I haven't already worked that out for myself. I'm not exactly sure what he thinks Aiden and I were up to in that trailer, but I decide that his punishment for "fraternizing" has got to be less than for attempted escape, so I don't bother to defend myself. Dad has quarantined me within the quarantine and committed me to his version of house arrest. "I'm not trying to be an ogre, Emmott," he told me. "I'm trying to keep you alive." Still, I'm convinced he finds some pleasure in keeping me prisoner, and the only revenge I can come up with is my Super Ball annoyance and making him field Mum's calls. Honestly, though, both are already losing their sweetness.

According to what Aiden showed me on the model, I have a week before this thing sees a turn, and then another month before I'll know I've survived. Now that we know for sure this thing is a virus, and that it's contagious, staying away from other people seems like a good idea. But, looking around at the four walls of my room, I am almost as worried about going insane.

I send a text to Deb, filling her in on the events of the previous twenty-four hours, and giving her an update on my relationship status. Whether Ro was a chicken or an idiot, the end result is the same. *It's over*, I tell Deb.

Never liked him, she writes when I tell her about Ro's part in my failed attempt. I know she's just being a faithful friend, but I still can't believe what he did. I had fooled myself into thinking Ro was different, that his swaggering rebelliousness made him more like me. But in the end, he turned out to be just like everyone else. I can't help but wonder if he would have had the courage to go to London. Now I'll never know.

Changing the subject, I tell Deb about Aiden and the virus model.

No word on transmission? she asks.

You mean how we can catch it? No. Not yet.

If it's airborne, we're done for, she says. *Keep your mask tight. Wear gloves. Watch for nicks and tears. If you get a cut, keep it clean and protected. Viruses love bodily fluids. Have you got vinegar?*

Probably. Sarson's for fish and chips.

Use it.

For?

Sterilization. Make a solution and dip your hands. Use it as a mouthwash too. You should try rinsing your nose out with a saline solution as well. Just keep yourself clean. Same for the house. Bleach is your friend.

Deb is scaring me more than anything else I've heard so far. My friend is not prone to drama, so her warnings hit like spikes, each one stinging with danger. Suddenly, I feel sick. I scan my body, imagining the virus swirling around me, looking for a way in. I can picture it mixing with my blood to create beautiful patterns, a Jackson Pollock swimming through my veins. I grab a mask and press it against my face, willing my breathing to still to shallow sniffs. All that does is make me dizzy. I'm scared. I want to pretend I'm being brave, but I can't. I wish I were more scientific, like Deb. I wish my brain would organize the facts and come up with practical measures it could take. Instead, my brain creates nightmare images. But I can't let it take over. I have to stay alive and, scared or not, I need to take every bit of Deb's advice, anything I can do to stay alive.

One more thing, Deb adds, and I brace myself for more bad news. *Go back to blond. You look weird as a brunette. Plus, how can I call you "Salty" when you're not?*

I promise her I'll do it as soon as I can.

When Dad leaves that afternoon, I scour the house, gathering everything Deb suggested. My own internet search turns up information on the right way to wash my hands, plus old wives' tales for staving off infections, so I add those to my arsenal. Out of curiosity, I google "deadly Siberian virus" and am shocked to find I have to scroll through several pages of news about our village before I get to anything about Siberia. But when I do, I wish I hadn't.

Alongside maps of the region and the images of the virus that Aiden showed me are photographs of frightened-looking people surrounded by teams of protected aid workers and close-ups of victims' symptoms. I gaze into the terrified eyes of people a continent away. And I see myself.

I scrub my skin under a hot shower until the water runs cold. I rinse my nose with a salt solution, gargle with vinegar, and scrub my hands with salt and lemon juice until they're almost raw. If this thing is going to take up residence inside me, it's going to have to fight for squatter's rights. I put clean sheets on my bed and slip into fresh pajamas. With no better plan in mind to stay healthy, I climb into bed. It's barely three o'clock.

I must have dozed off, because the next thing I know

my phone is buzzing beside my bed. *This is Aiden*, I read, an unexpected thrill jolting through me. *You OK?*

I flop back on the bed, trying to come up with a witty response, something more than "yes" to keep the conversation going.

Good, is all I can say. *Did I get you in trouble?*

Within seconds, three little dots appear on my screen to let me know he's typing. I wait, dreading that he'll tell me he's been fired or transferred. *Told her I was offering humanitarian aid. Which is true.* :-)

Did she ask what I was doing there?

Don't worry. Your secret's safe with me.

Where are you? I type.

Mess tent. Dinner. You?

I don't tell him I'm lying on my bed, even though I sort of want to. *Just chilling out*, I type instead.

We banter back and forth, snippets of chitchat, until we fall into a rhythm, like two old friends catching up. Everything feels wrong about this, about flirting with Aiden while people around me are fighting for their lives. But I long for something that feels normal and, outside of Deb, Aiden is one of the few people I can really talk to.

But when he mentions London, I feel a pang of sadness, a reminder that this isn't a normal conversation, that my whole life has changed in the past couple of weeks.

I was supposed to be there now, I write. *Got a job.*

I'm sure they'll hold it for you, he types back. I'm sure they won't.

Only place I ever wanted to live.

What's wrong with here?

Apart from the obvious?

Apart from that.

I try to frame my response. What specifically *was* wrong with here? Everything, but nothing, really. I am descended from ten generations of village-dwellers, but somewhere in my blood courses the DNA of a city girl.

Just never belonged here, I typed. *Does that make sense?*

One hundred percent, he replied. *My mum always says that some people are just itchy, and they have to keep moving until the itching stops.*

Is that why you wanted to leave London?

Sort of.

I wait, hoping he'll explain, but when the next text comes through, all it says is, *Just wanted to be somewhere I could be useful.*

And they sent you here?

Actually, I requested it. Got itchy again.

Lying on my bed, I smile to myself. I've never been able to put into words what drew me so powerfully to London, but Aiden has worded it perfectly. London scratches my itch.

As the sun makes its slow descent to the horizon, I lie in the fading light for hours, my mind tossing around thoughts about the virus, how it got here, and if it will really go away. I bat around a jumble of images—of Ro, of Will, of Aiden's concern and the feelings of attraction it has roused in me. Which brings me back to the village and the people who are no longer here. None of it seems real. As mad as I am with Mum, I keep waiting for her and Alice to come bursting through the door, laughing themselves silly at the great prank they've pulled on Dad and me. I'd do anything to have that be the case.

I squeeze my eyes closed and tell myself to sleep. Deb keeps sending me ideas to build my immunity, but they won't make an ounce of difference if I don't get some rest. It's almost impossible to sleep with the noise in my head and the absolute silence in the village.

It's always been quiet here at night, but there was a sense of life happening. I'd hear cars pulling up and doors closing. The rumble of wheelie bins trundled to the curb, washing machines lurching into their spin cycles, and the village cats spatting over territory. Now I don't hear anything but the distant, dull thrum of generators and the occasional relief worker passing by. Everyone's on lockdown, nowhere to go and no reason to leave the house. It's so quiet I wouldn't be surprised to open the curtains one morning and find the village gone, our house perched on an island of rock with nothing but darkness as far as the eye can see. I roll onto my side and pull the blankets up. I hate when my thoughts turn dark like this. They seem to do it so often these days.

I sleep fitfully for a few hours, waking around dawn feeling restless and fidgety. I pull Alice's Pandicorn into bed with me and wrap my arms around it, resting my cheek on my own hand. I need to feel something warm and alive, even if the something is only me. I miss Alice. I miss her soft hair and her strawberry smell. I think of all the times she'd want to get in bed with me, and I'd be irritated by her wriggling and the heat she gave off. I'd give all the Pandicorns in the world to have her cuddling with me now, innocent, unencumbered love.

Except I wouldn't. I would not want her to see us like this, for her to be in danger. Better that she's away. I don't know what she'd do if anything were to happen to Dad and me... but I can't let myself think about that now. I'm not sure I can let myself think about that ever.

I push Pandicorn to his own side of the bed and pull my

hands inside my pajamas, wrapping my arms around myself like Deb and I did. The sensation of touch on my skin is shocking, even though the touch is my own. When was the last time anyone touched me? I run my hand across my belly, and my thoughts jump to Ro. Ro's was the last human touch I felt, and the thought makes me sick. Underneath the hatred and resentment that cloud my thoughts of him is a flicker of a memory of something good. His touch. I wish I could float out of bed and away across the hills to a time before it all went to hell. If Ro touched me now, it wouldn't feel the same, but his is the only touch I know, so I push aside all that I know now and go back to what I need.

I wriggle out of my PJs and let the cool air spark against my skin. I keep my eyes closed and conjure an image of Ro's face from a time when things were good. I see his long hair and his mischievous smile as he looks down at me. I arch my back against the cool sheets and feel the prickle of desire between my legs. I imagine him standing at the foot of my bed and opening his shirt. I stretch my toes toward him, willing him to come to me.

But when I open my eyes in the dim, early morning light, it's Aiden's image I see. The details of his features aren't clear, but I know those eyes. They light up, and I know underneath his respirator, he's giving me one of his cheeky grins. He holds my gaze for a moment, and the grin drops into a gentle smile, but his eyes don't leave mine. I like his eyes, his tiger eyes, and I'm struck by how much of a person you can get to know through these two small windows, and how much you can get to know through actions. He covered for me with my dad, and even hid my backpack. That shows kindness and trust. He's seen a world way beyond my little village, and you can almost see his experience crackle in him.

And he's funny too. His last text said, *Please don't run away. It would be no fun here without you.* Underneath was a repeat of his cartoon face, but instead of circles for eyes, he'd drawn two little hearts. The drawing made me laugh. *Yay, me. I got a boy's phone number with zero chance of a date.*

A date. If it wasn't for the suits and the rules and the protocol, would that really be a possibility? Or have those things forced our simple attraction to bloom into something more, a natural pursuit of the forbidden? If Aiden and I had met under other circumstances, would the attraction have been the same? Would we have even noticed one another? If I saw him now, in the street, without his suit, just an ordinary guy going about his business, would the attraction be there? I know the answer. I saw it in his eyes, and I felt it in me.

I wish I could see you without that suit, I think, and immediately my face burns. I meant I want to see him in normal clothes in a normal situation, but now that the thought of a suitless Aiden has popped into my mind, I can't seem to erase it.

I close my eyes again, sweeping his image aside with reason after reason for why he doesn't belong in my head. The thoughts collect in little piles of jumbled memories and ideas. For a second, I admire my handiwork in cleaning up my mind, until I sense an unfamiliar gnawing in my bones, urging me to see what's really there. I push myself back into my pillow and crack open my eyes.

The image of Aiden is still there in the early dawn light. And he's still smiling. His is a gentle smile, a kind smile. There is no mischief or lust in his eyes. I know what the look *feels* like, but it's a ludicrous idea. You can't fall for someone you've never even seen. Can you?

I don't even have any idea what Aiden looks like underneath his suit. All I have is my imagination, and *it* has decided he's hot. I pull back the covers, giving Aiden a flash of thigh, and invite him in.

I'm sure those suits take ages to get into and out of, but my imagination has gone for the quick release version, and in a matter of seconds, Aiden is moving toward me and climbing into bed. His body is perfect, of course—tight chest, taut abs, sculpted arms that fold easily around me. He has freckles across his shoulders, my imagination has decided, so I kiss them, one by one. He runs his hands over my body—the thing I've so longed for—and in a moment we're pressed together, and he is kissing me like I've never been kissed in my life. His kisses start at the lips, like any other kiss, but they shoot tendrils of sparks down my body until, I swear, they make my toes ache. I melt back into my pillow and wrap my legs around his, feeling the scratchiness of his rough hairs against my smooth calves. *This*, I think, *is what it's supposed to feel like.* This isn't lust or rebellion or even an escape. This is something different, something new to me.

He buries his face into my neck, and I hear him murmur, "Emmott."

"Aiden," I whisper back. I love the way the sound of his name barely touches the backs of my teeth. It's a sensual name, so I say it again. "Aiden."

In the silence, I listen to his breath against my ear, his skin against mine, and I wait for what I know—and want—to come next.

"Emmott," he says again, and I hear a change in his voice. "Emmott?"

The sound is not coming from my room. It's coming from downstairs, but getting closer. My eyes fly open, and Aiden vanishes.

"Emmott!"

It's Dad.

I dive out of bed, grabbing my pajamas and tripping into them as I run to the door. What was I thinking, fantasizing about strangers when my neighbors are dying? There's no time to grab my robe, but I don't need it. I'm already wrapped head to toe in a blanket of guilt and shame.

Chapter Fourteen

Tuesday, August 2

B OLTING DOWN THE STAIRS, I find Dad hanging out of the front door. He pulls me next to him, and I follow his shocked gaze out into the early morning street. A convoy of ambulances moves through the village, all heading toward the cricket pitch. Scattered in between and heading in the same direction are groups of our neighbors and friends.

"Where are they going?" I ask. "Are they leaving?" For a delusional moment, I think that perhaps the quarantine has been lifted and we'll all be free to go back to our lives, but even as I allow the idea to dance a jig in my mind, I sense that I'm about as far from the truth as is humanly possible. There is fear in the air, a tight, sharp cut of dread and uncertainty. I don't know where everyone is going, and I pick up the feeling that neither do they.

Dad and I step into the street to find out what's happening, holding back so as not to get too close, as if the stream of people contains some unseen force that could pull us along if we don't keep a safe distance. Across the street, two suited paramedics wheel a sealed bubble gurney toward a waiting ambulance. From the spill of dark curls protruding from the white blanket, it's clear that Mrs. Wainwright is being taken away. Her face has the now-familiar yellow pallor; her red-rimmed eyes stare skyward. She's followed closely by her husband, who walks from the house unassisted. He moves as if he's off to the rugby club for a practice game, his broad shoulders square to his loping gait. In other words, he does not look in the least bit sick. My fear has come true. They are rounding up the sick and rounding up the healthy too. Does this mean they'll be coming for us?

As they leave, a suited crew moves in. One alien sprays a few feet inside the door of the Wainwrights' cottage from a large, white canister he carries on his back. When he's done, another crew member seals the edges of the door and sprays a large, red X across the middle. Mr. Wainwright follows his wife's ambulance into the parade. Around the village, several cottage doors have been sealed and sprayed with red Xs. Others bear white Xs. It's not clear to me yet what the difference is, but I know the red one is something I never want to see on my door.

"What are they doing?" I ask Dad. "Where are they taking everyone?"

"To a new isolation unit," he says. "Too many sick people for the village hall."

"Mr. Wainwright doesn't look sick."

"No." Dad offers nothing more reassuring.

Unconcerned by the fact that I'm dressed only in pajamas, I go with Dad as he follows the caravan down to the cricket pitch, where the tents I'd seen being built are now complete. Across the pitch, three enormous, rectangular marquees stand side by side, each fenced off from the other by a double row of orange plastic webbing. At the front entrance of each is a green shed that looks like a double-wide porta-loo, along with a plastic trough, also green, that I'm guessing is for washing off boots. At opposite corners of the fenced-in area are two additional tents. The line of people files into one, suggesting it's the entrance. By process of elimination, the other must be the exit, but I doubt it's intended that anyone will walk out that way. Beyond that tent, a high screen has been hammered into the ground, making whatever lies behind it invisible to us. Whatever is back there, it's the final destination for the dead. The entire camp is fenced in by more plastic webbing, with an additional orange boundary about ten feet outside that. It's like its own mini city, a busy hive of suited workers buzzing around with an air of competence and efficiency. But unlike an ordinary city, there is something cold and sinister about this.

Dad and I watch as Mrs. Wainwright's bubble gurney is wheeled through a back entrance to the furthest tent. Mr. Wainwright is escorted through the camp's main entrance, reappearing moments later inside the compound and headed toward the first tent. Some of the others who walk in are directed into the middle tent. It appears that each tent houses patients at different levels of sickness, the third tent clearly being where the sickest and the dying are kept. A family of four from higher up the village are divided between Tents One and Two, the children crying as their parents are pulled apart. An altercation erupts, and suited workers swarm to help. They hesitate, the parents conferring for a moment, before agreeing to go their separate ways.

The second I get home, I text Deb to ask if she's seen what's going on. She doesn't answer. I'm overcome with a terrible fear that Deb and her family have been taken away. I pull on clothes and run back out into the village, ignoring my dad's warnings to stay inside. I'm shocked to see how many of the houses are painted with white or red Xs. Still running, I scan the lines of ambulances and walkers, looking for Deb's familiar black hair. I'm relieved to see she isn't there.

I hit my phone's call icon and listen as it rings. Four rings later, I hear Deb's voice. "This is not the Deb you're looking for. Move on. Or leave a message." And then a beep.

"Deb," I say, "all hell has broken loose. If you're okay, send up a flare. Just let me know, okay? Ciao for now."

As I sprint past my house and round the corner to Briar Lane, I see two people outside of Deb's cottage. I can't tell from this distance, but they appear to be Deb's dad, Mr. Elliot, and Tommy, her brother. As I get closer, I can see they're hauling boxes. For a brief moment of panic, I think they're moving out, but of course that's not possible. From the way Tommy struggles with his box, I can tell it's heavy. I trot up to see if I can help.

Tommy sees me first, but before I can offer my assistance, Mr. Elliot turns and glares. I give a friendly wave and peer over my mask. He looks like he doesn't recognize me. "It's me, Mr. Elliot. Emmott." Without waiting for his response, I walk over to Tommy. "Which way are we going?" I ask, bracing a corner of the box. But when I look up, Tommy and Mr. Elliot have both pulled back.

"We don't need your help, thanks." Mr. Elliot doesn't make eye contact with me.

My first thought is that he's worried about contagion. I let go of the box, and my hand unconsciously moves to my mask, pressing it closer to my face. Then it dawns on me that the boxes have official stickers on them, like the supply boxes we receive each week. Dad and I are rationed to two a week, but these boxes hold enough supplies for a month. Enough to get through the rest of the quarantine.

"Wait," I squeak. "What are you doing?"

"Go home, Emmott," Mr. Elliot says.

"Where did these come from?"

"Emmott. You really should just go home."

The sharp tone of his voice makes me pull away. I've never heard him speak this way to anyone, let alone me. Deb's dad is Funny Dad, Laughing Dad, "Who Wants Ice Cream?" Dad. This man is none of those. This man is "Nothing Comes Between Me and my Family" Dad. My stomach gives a sickening lurch at the realization that I have just helped imprison my best friend.

"I want to see Deb," I say, squaring against him.

Mr. Elliot scans my face, as if I'm some kind of raving lunatic that he can't comprehend. "Where's your dad, Emmott?" he says.

"At home."

Mr. Elliot's face softens. "You need to go home too, Emmott," he says, as if he's talking a child into letting go of something she's not supposed to have. "Someone's been going around ratting out people with symptoms. Well, I'm not standing for it. My wife isn't infected, and I'm not letting anyone take her away."

So Helena is sick. I want to remind him that if she doesn't have the virus, she doesn't have to go anywhere, assure him that it's probably something else. That whatever Helena has will pass, and she'll be okay, and so will he, and so will Deb. But Mr. Elliot's face is a picture of such sadness and resignation that I'm overcome with an urge to throw my arms around him. I'm not a hugger at the best of times, less so now it's become dangerous, but I suddenly feel a fierce solidarity with him and his determination to preserve some semblance of dignity for his family. I grab him by the arm and squeeze.

"Tell Deb I say 'hi.'" It's such a pointless thing to say when I have so much I want to tell my oldest and best friend. But Mr. Elliot only nods, and I watch as he and his box disappear from view.

Before I turn to leave, I glance up at Deb's bedroom window just in time to catch a glimpse of her face in the shadows. I hold up my hand to wave, but she pulls back behind the curtain. Staring at the empty space where she stood, I'm struck with the thought that this glimpse could be the last time I see her. It's totally morbid, but not impossible. What if Helena *does* have the virus? What if Mr. Elliot is sealing his whole family inside with this thing? I wait, willing her to come back so we can share some kind of farewell, just in case. When she doesn't come, I whisper "goodbye" into the air between us.

Suddenly, hiding in my room until this is over doesn't seem like such a bad idea. Better there than out in this. I trudge home to wait, although for what, I'm not sure.

Chapter Fifteen

Friday, August 5

THERE IS NOTHING TO DO but wait. Wait to see how long this lasts. Wait to see who is next. Wait to see who will get out and who will not. Deb and I text to pass the time, but as the days pass and nothing changes, and as neither of us does anything worthy of sharing, our conversations dwindle. She isn't sick, and Helena isn't any worse. Good news all around, but her dad won't let any of them leave the house, and that is very bad news for me.

A reprieve comes when I get a summons to the village school to complete a "Contact Tracing Survey."

"What kind of survey?" I ask when Dad gives me the news.

"They're just trying to gather information to see who we've been around over the past several weeks."

"That could be hundreds of people."

He nods. "They seem to think it's a good idea, so we'll do as we're asked."

I don't argue with him this time about acting like sheep. The chance to get out of the house, even for a while, is enough to make me obey. Plus, there's a chance I might see Aiden. That would be an excellent perk.

"Straight there and straight back," Dad says as if he's reading my mind.

It's been years since I've been inside the school where Deb and I first became friends, and I'm surprised by how small everything is. I walk through the hallway, looking at the paintings posted in galleries on the walls, remembering my creative teachers who understood how to make learning colorful and fun. As I pass the cloakroom, I try to remember which of the rows of hooks and cubbies was mine. I spot one with a picture of a lamb posted on one end, the corners turning up. I can't believe it's the same picture, stuck there for more than a decade. I'm shocked to see how low the hooks are. I can remember stretching up to hang my coat on a hook that would poke me in the chest now. The whole place makes me think about Alice. I miss her more than I could have imagined, and at the same time, I'm more relieved than ever that she isn't here.

She texts periodically, always silly pictures of her having a good time, oblivious to what's happening at home. Yesterday, we got the news that a girl in her class had died. She was eight, barely tall enough to hang her coat, and now she's gone. Dad is trying to organize a memorial service for all the victims. He says it will help the rest of us get through it. It's a nice idea, but I don't know how any of us will ever get through this. Alice has all this to come back to. How will she ever make sense of it?

Outside a classroom door, a being in a suit stands guard, his presence silencing my thoughts. As I approach and present my papers, I peer up into the face mask in hopes of finding a friendly face, or more specifically, of finding Aiden's friendly face. It's been days now since the one time we texted, and I hoped it would happen again, but I haven't heard from him. The sight of his familiar smiling eyes would be reassuring. I want to know he's still here and hasn't been reassigned due to our "fraternization." Instead, the unfamiliar suit hands me back my papers and, without a word, ushers me into a classroom.

The room immediately looks familiar, and the view across the playground jolts a memory. How many hours did I spend staring out of that window instead of paying attention to Miss Carmichael's lessons? A lot, as I recall.

All the tables and plastic chairs have been stacked against one wall. Was I really ever able to fit in those tiny chairs? Seeing them makes me feel detached from my body. I've always been me inside this body, and I've always felt like me, so it feels odd to think of myself in a body I can no longer recall, as if the physical me and the spiritual me are on different journeys, always tethered, but by a long piece of elastic that stretches and contracts. Right now, it sags as the two parts of me reconnect in this odd memory from my childhood.

"Miss Syddall?" A voice pulls me back into the present.

In the middle of the classroom, booths have been set up like stalls at the Summer Fair, but instead of the Hook-a-Duck and Coconut Shy, each houses a desk, computer, two chairs, and a suited being. My being is female, and when I peer beyond the edges of her respirator, I recognize her as Aiden's boss, the woman who caught us together. She must recognize me too, but she doesn't mention it, and for obvious reasons, neither do I.

"My name's Jo. I'll be doing your interview today."

The official-looking name tag taped to her suit reminds me she's Dr. Joanne Reynolds. Unlike Aiden, she has not drawn a cheery cartoon interpretation of herself on her suit. Although she's friendly enough, it's clear she's the business end of things.

"Can I get you something to drink?" she asks in a tone that

suggests this is a formal offer, part of the routine, and not an invitation to get comfortable.

I shake my head. Now that I'm here, my stomach is churning with nerves. My anxiety must show on my face, because the skin around Dr. Reynolds's eyes crinkles into a reassuring smile. "There's nothing to worry about. This isn't an interrogation. Our purpose is to collect contact data. We wish to monitor everyone who could have been in contact with the virus, so that we can stop the spread." Her voice has the same tenor the school vaccination nurse used, right before she stuck me with a giant needle. "It's a monumental task, but we have a very powerful computer that uses modeling software to show us where we're most likely to see the virus pop up next. That way we can take preventative measures."

"Is this going to help stop it spreading in the village?" I ask.

The smile drops from Dr. Reynolds's eyes, which gives me my answer, but she responds anyway. "I wish I could tell you we knew how to stop it, Emmott. Is it okay if I call you Emmott?" I nod. "We're looking at every facet imaginable. Local containment is first, of course, hence the quarantine, but we're also looking at preventing further spread, which might mean expanding the zone or creating other small, local zones."

"Okay." I feel bad for Dr. Reynolds. It's an impossible job to come up with good news in a place where everyone knows there's none.

"So," she says, getting back to business. "You can really help us by giving us as much information as you can, even if you think it's trivial and won't be any help. We've nicknamed our computer Sherlock because it notices even the most elementary details that we humans would think insignificant."

If Dr. Reynolds is attempting to put me at ease, it's not

working. Ever since I got my first phone, Mum's gone on about how I have to be sensible about what I post online, so the idea of old Sherlock gathering every scrap of data on me and making some brilliant deduction about my behavior is frightening.

"All right," I say, deciding to play along. "What juicy gossip can I give Mr. Sherlock?"

We start with the basics: name, address, date of birth, doctor, parents, *blah-di-blah*. As I churn it all out, I can't help but think my brain could be put to better use than storing all this data. I've got almost eighteen years' worth of useless information in there, all accessible for me to offer to Sherlock.

Next, Dr. Reynolds hands me a list of people from the village. Dr. Spencer is at the top of the list, followed by Karen Cooper and the other people who have died. Below them is another set of names. Given that neither Dad nor I are on the list, I'm guessing this is a list of everyone who's been infected so far. It's already several pages long, and it makes my stomach contract to think it's only going to get longer.

"Okay," Dr. Reynolds says. "What I'd like you to do is mark the level of contact you've had with each person on this list in the past twenty-eight days. This will help us to ascertain how the virus is transmitted. We have four levels we're interested in: Airborne, Physical, Biological, and Sexual."

My stomach gives a sharp clench. Even though the list is only for our village, it makes me think of my interactions with Ro and the fun times we had together, which ultimately reminds me of what a weasel he turned out to be and what an idiot I was to trust him.

"I think the levels largely speak for themselves," she continues, "but just to clarify, Level I is Airborne, that means coming close enough to hold a normal conversation with someone, even if you didn't actually speak. If you got as close as we are now, even passing in the street, that's Level I."

"Okay." I nod in understanding.

"Level II is Physical, and that can mean any kind of physical interaction—shaking hands, a pat on the back, a hug. It also includes unintentionally brushing against someone, even if your skin didn't touch. That's a bit trickier, because you might not realize you touched someone, so I want you to really think about it."

I don't have to think hard to recall Dr. Spencer pressing his stethoscope to my chest and back, or shaking my hand as I left and wishing me luck for the future. Ironic that my luck ran out around the same time as his future. I know I've hugged Deb since then, and Alice. If I'm one of those carriers that Aiden warned me about, there's a chance I could have passed it to them. I start to feel light-headed. If Dr. Reynolds thinks this survey is nothing to worry about, then she's living on another planet. I take the pencil she's given me and fill in the bubble for Level II next to Dr. Spencer's name.

"Level III is Biological, and that includes a number of things. If you've been caring for someone where you might have come in contact with bodily fluids of any kind—mucus, feces, vomit, blood, saliva—that's Level III. So, if someone sneezed on you or kissed you, even on the cheek. Or if you kissed *them*," she says, lifting an eyebrow and giving me a conspiratorial smile, "it's Level III.

"And Level IV speaks for itself, I think." She levels her gaze at me. "I know this can be a bit embarrassing, and there might be things you'd rather nobody knew, but it's absolutely crucial you fill this in accurately. It could quite literally be a matter of life or death."

"I have nothing to hide," I say, even as the heat rushes to my cheeks. Dr. Reynolds is just doing her job, and I'm sure she's the bastion of privacy, but I'm glad the list only includes people from the village so I don't have to confess the details of my personal life to Sherlock.

"Right then," she says, pushing up from the table. "I'll leave you to it. I'm going to get myself a cuppa. Sure I can't tempt you?"

I think I could do with something a bit stronger than tea for the task at hand, but I'll take any comfort I can. "I actually think I will," I say, and she disappears through the back curtain of the booth.

I turn my attention to the card and scan the list of dead. It's numbing to think that all these people are no longer with us, but I can't allow myself to dwell on that now. The only way I'm going to get through this awful task is to treat it like a shopping list. If I think about the people attached to the list of names, I'll never be able to do it. I need to try to remember as much as I can, but so much has happened in the past weeks, it's started to blur together. I've already marked Dr. Spencer, so I start back at the top, working my way name by name, trying to think of when I last came into contact with each person. Some I saw at Dr. Spencer's funeral, others in the post office or in the street. It's hard to remember which people I talked to and who I might have touched. But as I go down the list, I'm shocked to realize how many of the sick and dead I've been near, to realize how much we interact with others every day of our lives. I keep thinking too about Mum and Alice, and how I kissed them both before they left, and how much time I've spent with Dad, how many times we've bumped into one another in the kitchen.

Dr. Reynolds slips back into the booth and slides a paper cup of tea and a paper plate of biscuits across the table to me. That's something else that's changed. Everything's become disposable, and there's no offering someone a proper cup of tea on your best china anymore. You can't trust that anything reusable has been properly cleaned. We had to turn in all our money because coins touch hand after hand. We've been told we'll get the same sum back in new money once the quarantine is lifted, but there are some in the village who think it's a swindle. I choose a biscuit and nibble one edge while I go through the horrible task of remembering every interaction with all my sick or dead neighbors.

Dr. Reynolds keeps busy as I fill out my form, turning to the computer and keeping her eyes off my answers. When I'm done, she slips my paper into a folder without looking at it. I appreciate her discretion.

"This next part's a bit trickier," she says. "Are you holding up okay?"

"Fine." The tea and bickies have revived me, at least for the moment.

Dr. Reynolds slides another form across the table. This one has four sections with blank lines underneath. The sections are labeled with the same four levels of contact. She pushes a small notepad and a pen across the table.

"Now I want you to think of all the places *outside* the village that you went in the week or so before the quarantine. Did you go into school, into town, to a friend's house, on the bus, to the gym? Try to think of absolutely everywhere you've been." She slides a calendar toward me, open to this month's picture of four puppies sitting in a hay wagon. "This might help jog your memory. You can use the notepad if you like. Then for each level, I'd like you to list everyone you can remember being in contact with, whether that's people you met outside or people from outside who came into the village."

I pull a face. I can barely remember what I had for breakfast this morning, let alone where I was three weeks ago. And to mark all the people I've been around, every tour I've taken, every interaction I've had. *Ugh*. I could be sitting here for the rest of the week.

"I know it's a lot, but do the best you can. I'm going on my break in a few minutes, so I'll see if I can rustle up a sandwich for you. I don't want you fainting."

I thank her. Even though what she's asking is a total pain, at least she knows it is, which counts for something.

I set to work trying to remember everywhere I've been and all the people I've seen. I try not to focus on what it might mean if our virus has traveled elsewhere. At first, I'm glad I haven't been far, and that my list isn't too long. My classes ended not long before the quarantine, so I've been catching up on sleep and milling about the village mainly. And working. My heart sinks as I think about all the tours I've taken in the past few weeks. Most of those contacts would be Level I, but how often did I grab an arm to steady someone or squeeze someone's hand as I accepted a tip? I don't even have their names, just a number of how many to expect in each party. If any of those people were infected, the implications don't bear thinking about.

There's one more problem niggling in my mind. And that's Ro. I'm not ashamed to have a Level IV contact on my list. I'm seventeen. It's normal to have a boyfriend. In fact, I'd be more embarrassed if I didn't have someone to write down. I don't even care that the secret I've managed to keep could be out. But his name will stick out like a sore thumb and, given his recent turn of loyalty, I'd sooner forget we ever had those particular interactions.

I go on with my list, until I've exhausted my memory. My hand hovers over the Level III box, tempting me to relegate Ro to a more chaste level. But I don't know who will see my answers. Will a faceless administrator feed the information into Sherlock, or will they check with Ro and know I've lied? It doesn't matter anymore anyway. That's all in the past, so I may as well tell the truth.

I'm just about to scribble in Ro's name when the curtain swings back and a yellow suit appears, accompanied by a heavy whiff of bacon that jangles my taste buds to life. I look up, expecting Dr. Reynolds, but it's not her. It's Aiden. He steps toward me, and I'm reminded that the last time I saw him was in my imagination. My face colors.

"Room service," he says, his eyes sparkling as he ambles over with a fantastic-looking bacon sandwich and a steaming cup of tea. I start salivating at the unfamiliar smell of real food, and when he sets the plate in front of me, it's all I can do not to cry. I'm about to dive in and devour it when I remember the list. I slide an elbow over it so Aiden can't see what I have—or haven't—written.

"What are you doing here?" I'm unable to keep the mixture of glee and worry from my voice.

He pushes the plate across the table. "I heard you were under the microscope today."

I lift the sandwich to my mouth and bite. My teeth cut through the grittiness of the bread to find the warm, greasy center and the sharp tang of brown sauce. If there's a heaven, this is what it would be like.

"Did she say anything about the other night?" I ask, lowering my voice. "She acted like she didn't recognize me."

"Hard to imagine." He grins. "Luckily, she didn't see you with *this*, or it might have been a bit trickier to explain." Aiden pushes a large plastic bag around to my side of the desk. Inside is my backpack. I thank whatever lucky stars shone on me that night and made me leave the backpack behind. And I thank the same lucky stars that Aiden was the one who found me. I don't know why he's so willing to stick his neck out for me, but right at this moment I am very grateful.

"Thank you," I tell him. I want to ask why he's protecting me, why he's singled me out over everyone in the village, but a warm feeling snakes its way through me, giving me my answer. My face flushes as I realize that something has happened between us, something that we might never get the chance to do anything about. "And you're sure I didn't get you into trouble?"

He shakes his head. "But you will if you don't finish your survey. It's important."

He turns away with the same level of discretion as Dr. Reynolds, but I don't turn back to my paper. Instead I watch him moving papers around the desk and try to guess what he really looks like without that suit. He's average height, average build, average everything, as far as I can tell. Except for his eyes. And his heart. It's both of those things that make him exceptional.

When I turn back to my form, I know I have to write in Ro's name somewhere. Ro, who was always above average in so many ways, until I needed him to be exceptional. Ro, who would have turned me in to save his own skin. Ro, who didn't keep my secret safe. It would be easy to get my revenge now.

But that kind of pettiness was for the old world. There is no room for it now. People's lives are at stake here—lots of people's lives—and every day I see what this virus can do if it isn't stopped. I could lie about my interaction with Ro to save face, but even after all he's done, I still care enough about him to try to save his life.

I scribble Ro's name in the Level IV box and flip the list facedown.

"All done." I return my attention to the sandwich and avoid eye contact with Aiden, not wanting him to see my humiliation.

"Looks like you have quite the appetite," he says.

Color rushes to my face. "What?" I ask without looking up. I can't believe he's reading my "confidential" survey. I've a good mind to report him for this.

"Looks like you were hungry." I glance up to see him nod toward my bacon sandwich.

"Oh!" I glance down at what's left in my hands. Two small pieces of bread stuck together with congealed grease, all evidence of the bacon devoured. I laugh, embarrassed. "Apparently so."

Aiden is gazing at me. He's not laughing; he's not even exactly smiling. But I know that look; it's become entirely too familiar to me. It's the look of someone who wants something they know is unreachable. And the thing I'm sensing he wants… is me. If things were different—if *every*thing were different—I think I might reach back.

Chapter Sixteen

Monday, August 8

Dad is out in the village again today, and I'm tempted to go looking for him. I don't want to be alone in the house, but everything is changing so quickly that home now feels like the only safe place. For the first time in a very, very long time, I really wish my dad were here.

I get my wish a short time later, but it's not quite what I had in mind. Dad slams the front door behind him and pushes out a sharp breath like an athlete preparing to deadlift twice his body weight. His keys hit the table in the hallway before clattering to the floor. I don't have to be an ace sleuth to know he's in a foul mood, but I creep to the top of the stairs anyway.

A floorboard creaks beneath my foot, and Dad looks up. His face contorts, and he stomps toward me, an angry finger punctuating the air in front of him.

"You." The word hisses through his teeth. "You!" He slides to a halt, both hands raised in front of him, fingers splayed like he wants to grab something and crush it with his anger. "You," he says again, his voice rising.

"What have I done?" I ask, backing away. I've been the model of good behavior for days now, and I have no clue what

I could have done to stir up this anger. Still, my mind flits immediately to Aiden. Guilt by imagination. Even though Dad has never laid a finger on me in my life, at this moment his track record isn't enough to convince me he won't hurt me. His face is red with fury, his eyes slashed to narrow, steely slits. His brow seems to have folded over his eyes and cast his face into a dark shadow. I've only ever seen one on TV, but everything about him makes me think about tornadoes, and this dark, swirling, entity looks as if it's about to knock me off my foundation. He's so mad he can't even speak, and he shakes as if every ounce of his strength is being used to stop him from hurling himself up the stairs and pounding me into pulp.

"Roland Torre!" he yells. "Roland *fucking* Torre."

My eyes sting with tears. Dad has never ever sworn at me. Never. This is an unfamiliar animal tearing toward me, and I'm scared of what he might do.

"When did you see him?" Dad yells. "When?"

"I haven't seen him," I squeak, backing away from him. I try to wrap his question around what I think he knows, but nothing fits. "I haven't done anything wrong," I cry, but even as I say it, I know that's not true. I've done everything wrong. Everything. I shouldn't have tried to escape. And I shouldn't have trusted Ro.

"That's a lie," he spits.

"How could I see him when I'm stuck in this stupid prison?" I scream. I'm beyond defending myself to Dad. I'm defending myself to myself. I try to grasp onto a single emotion, a single regret, but there are too many. I'm angry at Dad, at myself, at Ro, and especially at Mum. I wish she were here, though. She'd step between us and calm him down and make us talk to one another like civilized human beings. But Mum isn't even in the village, let alone in the house.

"Then why did you put on your survey that you... ?" He sucks in a breath, as if choking down the words, but he can't hold them in. "You had *sex* with him?"

"What?" The heat of humiliation gushes up inside me so fast that for a moment I think I might black out. That survey was supposed to be confidential. How did my most intimate secrets make it to my father? And who else knows? My thoughts flit again to Aiden. Could I have misjudged him so badly? Or is it just the village grapevine, still hard at work? Mrs. Glover. It has to be Mrs. Glover and her interfering nose. "How could you know that?"

"So you're not denying it!"

"Who told you?"

"Everybody told me, Emmott," he screams. "Roland Torre's been quarantined because of Level IV interaction with someone in this village."

"And you're jumping to the conclusion that it was me?"

"No," he says, his shoulders sagging. "I jumped to the conclusion that it couldn't be you. I foolishly believed that my daughter had more sense than to waste her time on anyone in that thieving bloody family. But no. Turns out not to be the case."

My insides twist as if they're trying to wring the shame out of me. Everything about this situation is upside down. Sex is something dads aren't supposed to ever know about, or if they do, they're supposed to pretend they don't. But now my dad is confronting me about something I wish had never happened. He looks up at me, and my heart shatters into a million pieces. How can I tell my father something I can no longer explain to myself? That I loved Ro and he let me down, that there was nothing wrong with what I did, that yeah, it might have been a poor choice, but it shouldn't have been a life-altering error, not for Ro, and not for me.

"Yeah, well, that was before all this. I didn't break the quarantine, and I'm not seeing him anymore."

"No. Now you're hanging around with that Red Cross fellow. I don't understand you, Emmott. I don't know where this constant urge to do the wrong thing comes from."

This man below me used to be my dad, but I no longer know him, and it's evident he doesn't know me. No wonder Mum was so anxious to get away.

"Well, maybe if you didn't have so many rules, I'd do better at not breaking them. No wonder Mum always wants to get away," I spit.

My regret is instant. Dad seems to freeze in space, but not in time. In a matter of a blink, I see history spooling backward across his face, sticking barbs into wounds that have scabbed but not healed, taking him all the way back to the point he was first betrayed.

I can't watch any longer. I twist away and run to my room, slamming the door behind me. I hurl myself onto my bed, flinging Pandicorn across the room and out of my sight. And I cry—great sobs of humiliation and indignation—because there is nothing else left for me to do.

I lie in the indentation in the middle of my bed and stare at the ceiling. When my text alert pings, I grab my phone, anxious for some relief and hoping it's Deb. Or Aiden. But it's neither; it's Mum. No doubt Dad has alerted her, making sure to share his side of the story before she can hear mine. *The more things change, the more they stay the same.*

I push the phone aside. She is the last person I want to talk to. Well, second-to-last, after Dad. Mum should have been here. She should be the one asking me about Ro, not Dad, not the person voted least likely to understand.

I glance at my phone. *Em, are you OK?*

No, Mum, I want to write, *I am very, very far from OK.*

I'm fine, I type, so that she knows I'm still alive. I owe her that, I suppose.

My phone rings, and I see it's her, but I don't want to talk yet. I send the call to voicemail with a text that I can't talk now.

I'm worried about you, she texts back.

Don't be, I write. *I'm fine.*

But I am not fine, and my mother has a hand in my not fine-ness. If I talk to her now, I might not stop talking ever. Better to say nothing until I'm sure I can say the right thing . . . whatever the right thing might be.

I don't know what to do. I feel like one of those tigers you hear about in the zoo, pacing its cage around and around in the same pattern, day after day after day. If I don't get out of here soon, I swear I am going to eat my keeper. But there is no "out of here," and the "here" just keeps getting worse.

I reach for my phone and scroll through to Ro. I need to know where he is, if he's been brought inside our quarantine or placed on lockdown at home. It doesn't change anything. He's still been quarantined, and it's still because of me. I keep telling myself his quarantine is precautionary and that Ro has nothing to worry about because I haven't contracted the virus, so it's unlikely he will. Unless I'm an unwitting carrier. I should warn him. But what good would it do? I can't undo what's done, and there's no chance we'll be in physical contact again as long as I'm on this side of the quarantine, or ever for that matter.

Finally, my guilt gets the better of me. No matter what has happened between us, I did love Ro, and I don't want anything bad to happen to him. I text him to see if he's okay, but he doesn't answer. Maybe they've taken away his phone in the quarantine, I think, but more likely he doesn't want to talk to me. I try to imagine the series of events between my survey confession and Dad's tirade. Did Dr. Reynolds read my answers, march over to Ro's, and drag him from his bed? That sounds a bit dramatic. And what about his family? Are they quarantined too? And do they blame me for this? It's not my fault, but… For a brief instant, I'm glad I'm on the opposite side of the cordon from Will and his shotgun.

And how did word make its way to Dad? I don't need to ask. It travels the way news always travels around here—person by person, whisper by whisper, until everyone knows some version of the truth. I used to say that around here, gossip spreads faster than the plague, but that analogy is no longer funny. I sink back into my bed and close my eyes. So, now everyone knows the most intimate details of my life. I'm branded. Instead of going about my day carrying a personal secret, something shared between two people, I'm now the girl who spread the virus because she couldn't keep her knees together. I may as well pin a scarlet letter to my chest—*I*, for *Infectious*—and stick my head in the stocks.

Downstairs, Dad is talking to someone. It's a one-sided conversation, a phone call. No doubt he's on the phone with Mum again, discussing what to do with their mess of a daughter. I can't help but think they ought to be talking about their mess of a marriage instead.

It feels like hours later when I hear a rap on my door. It's a gentle tap, but I can't be sure it's friendly, and I'm not ready to face another bout of The Wrath of Dad. Still, I say, "C'min," just loud enough for him to hear.

He pushes open the door with one elbow. He has a mug of tea in each hand with a plate of bread and jam balanced on top. He sets a mug down on my bedside table and keeps the other for himself. If he were Mum, he would perch on the edge of my bed to talk, but instead he pulls up a chair and sits in the middle of my room looking awkward.

"You must be hungry," he says.

I'm starving, but I shrug, not yet ready to accept *his* peace offering.

"I'm sorry I swore at you," he mumbles. "I shouldn't have done that."

"S'okay," I whisper. "I'm sorry I said what I said too."

He nods. "Your mum and I, we've had some problems in the past, but she'd never leave you, Emmott, not intentionally."

"But she did," I say, taking my tea and curling my legs under one another.

"No," Dad says. "She just picked the wrong time to go on holiday, or rather we picked the wrong time *not* to go."

His face twitches into an attempted smile, and the anger I've been lugging around with me deflates. He's right, of course, but I needed to be angry about the photos I found, and Mum was the ideal target.

"So you and Mum are okay?" I ask.

"Yes, but…" Dad seems to be searching for a way to break

bad news, and I find myself bracing for the impact. "Em, your mum and Alice have been quarantined as well."

"What? Why?" They can't do this to Alice. My little sister is nowhere near the village. She's completely *out* of danger. Am I responsible for sending the danger with her too? "Because of me?"

"No," he says. "Because they were here, in the village, in direct contact with us right before the outbreak. They've been taken to a special facility for observation. Now the surveys are out, lots of people have been taken in. Mum says it's just precautionary, and they're fine. She doesn't want us to worry."

"Right." I struggle and fail to keep the sarcasm out of my voice. "I'll just get right on with that not worrying business." I twist "precautionary" around in my mind until it no longer feels like a government buzzword for "trouble" and instead feels like an overzealous concern. Aiden's map flashes across my mind, the blotches blooming and spreading. An imaginary vine of danger sprouts from our village all the way to Auntie Margie's and the two red blossoms of my mum and sister. I shake the image away. I can't let myself imagine Alice in danger, and if I'm really honest with myself, I don't want to imagine that for Mum either.

Dad inches up from his chair, as if he's about to come toward me, but he sits back down. He twitches again, as if battling with himself over what to do next. Finally, he sighs. "If your mum were here, she'd handle all this better than I am."

"I don't think anybody knows how to handle this, Dad."

"No, but she'd do a better job with you."

I don't say anything, because it would be a giant fib to tell Dad he's doing a good job, but Mum will hardly be up for Mother of the Year, either.

"The thing is," he says, concentrating hard on his tea, "you're not my little girl anymore. You haven't been for a long time, and I'm not sure what to do."

"I don't think there's anything you can do, Dad. It's sort of the way things go."

"You know what I mean. When you were little, my job was to keep an eye on you, point you in the right direction, keep you safe. I knew how to do that. But now they tell me I'm supposed to let you go and trust I did a good job, trust you'll do the right thing, and I don't know how to do that bit. And just when I think I'm ready, this happens. And I can't protect you anymore."

"That's not your job. I have to look after myself."

He shakes his head. "I never wanted you to go to London. I was terrified in case something happened to you and I wouldn't be there to do anything about it."

"That's silly."

"Maybe, but when you were born, I promised your grandma I wouldn't let you go off alone."

"Like Auntie Sandra."

He nods. "But, as you got older, I could see San in you. You're so much like her, that streak. She couldn't wait to get away, to be anywhere else but here."

I smile. "She was itchy."

"Yes. That's what she used to say. Itchy. But the irony is that keeping you here has put you in more danger than I could have ever imagined."

"I don't think anyone could have imagined this, Dad."

"No. So, now we just have to look after each other. We all have to look after one another."

I think about the graph Aiden showed me. "About the

others, Dad. I know you want to help everyone, but the more people you come into contact with, the greater your chances of being infected."

He narrows his eyes at me. "Has that Red Cross chap been telling you that?"

"Yes," I say. "And he's right."

"They come in here and start ordering us around."

"Because they actually know what they're talking about, Dad. They're the ones who've done this before."

"But they don't know our village."

"Dad. You can't go out helping everyone like you used to. What if you catch it?"

"I'm not going to catch it."

"What if you do?"

"Emmott," he says. "These people are our friends. I've known some of them my whole life."

"I know that," I say. "But it's not your job to take care of them."

"No. That's beyond my capabilities now. But it is my job to care *about* them. We're all in this together, and if we don't have each other, what have we got?" His voice cracks. "This is killing our village."

I can't stand it. I push up from my bed and go to put my arms around him, but he pushes me away. "Don't, Em," he says. "The protocol."

"Bugger the protocol," I say.

"Emmott!"

"Bugger the virus too. And twice on Sundays." I wrap my arms around my dad and rest my head on the top of his. He smells clean and antiseptic, like manly shampoo, and the curls of his hair tickle the end of my nose. I feel the muscles in his shoulders from all that digging and planting, and a faint aroma of blackberry jam. He reaches up and rests his hand on mine. The sensation of his touch jolts through me like a warm electric buzz. I need my daddy's hug, and I sense that he needs mine too.

"If anything happened to you… ," he says.

"It's not going to."

"But if it did…"

"We have to stick together."

He nods, his curls tickling my ear where my head still rests against his.

Neither of us says another word as we hold each other. I don't know what he's thinking, but I know what's in my head. I don't want to lose him either, and I don't want him to lose me. But I can't tear my mind away from one thing: the image of the virus and how quickly it can spread.

"Dad," I ask, "can I ask you a favor?"

He pulls away, giving me a look as if I'm about to sucker him into adopting a puppy. "What sort of favor?"

"Just for now, what if you stopped going out to check on people? What if you just phoned or texted or put notes under their doors instead?"

"I can't," he says, looking away from me. "They need me."

His words twist in my stomach, and I wonder if he can even hear what he's saying. "*I* need you, Dad," I tell him, and the truth stings me. I do need him, because he's more or less all I have now.

Dad turns and looks at me as if all this time he hadn't realized I was there. "You *don't* need me," he says. "That's the trouble. You haven't needed me for a long time."

I almost smile. He was paying attention after all. "Maybe not, but I do sort of want to keep you around."

"Thank you," he says. "But some of our neighbors are not as strong as you. They need me now, and I can't let them down."

"I know." I'm all too familiar with the concept of being let down.

"And the truth is," Dad continues, "I need them too. I know you don't think that's big or important, but I'm completely helpless, and it's the only thing I know how to do."

Something inside me bends and snaps, the frayed ends reaching out and touching something unfamiliar. It's the part of me that understands my dad. I've always seen him as a big fish in a small pond, someone wasting his life on the trivial and mundane. But I know what it feels like to long for something you can't explain to others, and I know now that all these years, that's what Dad's been doing. Not taking care of others' needs, but taking care of his own.

"Then I need you to be careful," I say.

Dad rolls his eyes, and I see why Mum hates it so much.

"You promise?" I ask.

Dad holds out his little finger like he used to when I was a girl. My lips twitch into a smile, and I curl my little finger around his.

"Promise," we say together.

Chapter Seventeen

Tuesday, August 9

I F I'M GOING TO BE really honest with myself, Dad wouldn't be my first choice of person to get trapped with in a crisis. If I had my pick, I might choose someone a bit more practical, like Deb. But Deb has been incommunicado all day, and what I have in terms of real and available is Dad. So it's with Dad that I make a plan for survival.

Or, more accurately, I make a plan, and Dad sort of listens.

I show Dad the right way to wash up, and we practice holding our hands under hot running water, soaping up, and doing an elaborate set of moves to make sure every nook and cranny is clean, all the while singing two rounds of "Happy Birthday" as suggested online.

"It's a bit like the hand jive," Dad says as he rubs the splayed fingers of one hand over the other, twisting them around to repeat on both sides. Per my instructions, he curls his fingers under the others, rubs his palms in circles, and massages between his thumbs.

"The what?" I ask.

Dad grins and starts to dance, waving one hand over the other and tapping his fists together. He throws a hand up, spraying the kitchen counter and walls with potentially virus-inundated soapsuds.

"Dad!" I yell, fighting to keep from laughing.

"Sorry," he says, but I hear him humming some ancient rock and roll tune as he goes through the rinsing procedure.

I bump my hip against his and he pretends to lose his balance. We both understand that now should not be a time for levity, but these few moments of laughter with my dad do me more good than any medicine.

Dad and I come to an agreement that imposing a further quarantine on ourselves and sealing ourselves in the house (an option that we actually consider) would end in a one-way ticket to insanity. Even the short periods of time I've spent indoors have left me agitated and grumpy, so I can't imagine what would happen if Dad and I locked ourselves away together. Instead we agree to limit our excursions and devise a strategy to reduce our risk of exposure. Despite the warm weather, we will always dress in long trousers and long-sleeved shirts, and we'll keep our heads covered with the woolen caps Grandma knitted us one Christmas. We practice taping the wrists of our latex gloves to the ends of our sleeves and making sure our masks are firmly in place. I make Dad promise to stay the prescribed distance from everyone, no matter what. He agrees, albeit reluctantly. I set up a bath of bleach solution by the back door that we'll step through before we come in, and I place bowls of Deb's magic vinegar water by the door and at other spots around the house. At this, Dad nods his approval.

When we stop for a tea break, I ask Dad something that's been bothering me for a while.

"Why do you think some people are getting this and others aren't, even if they've obviously been exposed?"

Dad shrugs. "Luck?"

Deb would say there's no such thing as luck. She'd probably propose a scientific investigation to examine which factors make people immune. She'd want to know how Dr. Spencer's wife, Louise, is still healthy, despite not even knowing her husband had a deadly virus, let alone taking precautions to prevent catching it. And Mrs. Glover. She's old and has so many ailments you could spend an entire afternoon listening to her list them. She's always got her nose in everyone else's business, so I have no doubt that she's been in contact with every sick person. And yet she's as fit as a fiddle. What Deb would want to know, and what I want to know, is why? But I can't exactly march up to her front door and say, "Oh, hello, Mrs. G. How come you're not dead yet?"

"All we can do is try our best to keep ourselves healthy," I tell Dad.

"There's always your mother's exercise DVDs."

I give him a look that says, "Really, Dad?" and we settle on doing five sets of stairs.

"I found loads of information about how to build immunity," I tell Dad as we march up and down the stairs. I tell him about everything I've discovered, from eating sauerkraut to popping vitamin C. As we have neither in the house, it doesn't help us at all. "I really miss your homegrown veggies."

Dad stops and seems to consider me for a moment. He sniffs, as if sucking in resolve for a decision he's made. "There's something I want to show you," he says. "It's our secret weapon."

For a minute I wonder if Dad has been building nuclear warheads out in the shed, but that's not what he means. I follow him out to the hall, where he flicks on the light to the cellar.

"Are we going to tunnel out of here?" I ask.

He laughs. "I've always fancied myself as a bit of a Steve McQueen, but given we're built on bedrock, I don't think I have the stamina to dig my way out with a couple of teaspoons. Come on." He heads down the narrow stone steps.

I half expect him to have built us a bunker, like the old Anderson shelters they had during the war, complete with Army-issue camp beds, gas masks, and piles of sandbags—air raid sirens whirring above ground every time someone with the virus approaches the house. But of course, that's not what Dad has up his sleeve.

He stops at a wooden box against one cellar wall. It's the kind Andy used to have in his shop, filled with cauliflowers or apples. He pulls back a piece of sacking that lies across the top to show me what's inside.

"It's a box of sand," I say.

He grins like he's about to show me the best ever magic trick and brushes away the top layer of sand. Underneath, a long, brown cylinder emerges, but as Dad brushes away more sand, I see it's not brown, it's orange—and it's not a cylinder either.

"Carrots," I say.

"Proper ones. All the vitamins you could ask for."

"What are they doing down here?"

"They're from my garden. I'm storing them."

I look around and see other likely-looking containers. There are sacks of potatoes and boxes of turnips against the walls, bunches of onions and garlic hanging from a rack, and on a set of makeshift shelves sit jars of beetroot, tomato sauce, and jam, and bags of dried beans. With a flourish, Dad presents his final surprise: Inside an old chest freezer are bags of frozen green beans, squash, cauliflower, and Brussels sprouts.

"Weren't you supposed to turn these in?" I ask.

"Well, yes," he says, averting his eyes. "But now that we know they won't make us ill, I thought a bit of roughage might do us some good."

"But why didn't you tell me sooner? We could have been eating these instead of that powdered slop."

Dad looks chagrined. "I broke the rules. I was afraid I'd get caught."

I suppress a small giggle. "Good to know I'm not the only one with a rebellious streak."

"I could learn a lot from you." He grins at me like I'm six again, sharing a moment of mischief with Dad before *I* grew up and *he* got so serious. "Can I tempt you with bit of *proper* shepherd's pie? Or perhaps some minestrone soup?"

I'm stunned, both by his deceit and his excitement. We've been condemned to an unknown fate, and Dad's big act of rebellion is contraband vegetables.

But it's still an act of rebellion. I glance at my dad in the dim light of the cellar and see a small ray of hope. The faint glimmer of an idea has started to sparkle inside me. Could Dad's vegetable stash be the key that opens the door to Mrs. Glover's secret?

For that alone, Dad is King today.

I get dressed, per our agreed protocol, and leave Dad happily chopping vegetables for our shepherd's pie. There aren't many people out in the streets anymore. Why would there be? There's nowhere to go and nothing to do. I pass a couple of neighbors walking toward the cricket pitch and give them a small nod in greeting. I'm still aware that I am the subject of recent village gossip—Ro's quarantine—and I'm not in the mood to stand and explain myself. Nor do I wish to see those awkward, tight looks people get when they're trying not to be judgmental, but judge you anyway. Besides, I'm on a mission.

Mrs. Glover's doorbell poses the first complication in my plan. Thanks to my research, I now see every surface as a potential colony of virus cells, just waiting to find a new host in which to set up camp. This new paranoia can't be good for a person, but I can't stop myself imagining some infected person's virus lingering on Mrs. G.'s doorbell, just waiting to hitch a ride on the end of my finger to every other thing I touch. You don't realize how many surfaces you touch on a daily basis, and how many times you unconsciously scratch an itch or rub your eye, until you're faced with every contact having the potential to kill you.

I find a stick under one of Mrs. Glover's rose bushes and poke it at the doorbell. I hear the chimes on the other side of the door and wait. Out of the corner of my eye, a movement catches my attention, a slight twitch of the curtain. I'm not quick enough to see who it is, but I've no doubt it's Mrs. Glover. I poke the doorbell again, twice this time, to let her know I know she's in there. *Come on out, you nosey old bat*, I think, then remind myself to be nice. Although I have come bearing gifts for her, ultimately it's she who has what I need.

It's a few more seconds before a stooped shape ambling up to the frosted glass door. I hear a jangling noise, and the door creaks open, the security chain hanging in a low arc and one lens of Mrs. Glover's metal-rimmed glasses pressed into the gap.

"What is it?" she asks, her voice wary. I sense an undertone of curiosity and hope it will find its way to the surface.

"Hi, Mrs. Glover." I turn on the smile Mum always begs

me to save for the school photographer. "It's me, Emmott. How are you?"

"What do you want?" She sounds justifiably suspicious.

"My dad sent me over to make sure you're okay. And he asked me to bring you these." I hold out the basket in my hand and show her the contents, a clear plastic bag containing half a dozen carrots. They are like gold, homegrown and packed with nutrients. More important, thanks to the earlier food panic, they're as rare as hen's teeth, as my grandma would say.

Mrs. Glover eyes them. The door creaks open a hair more, but she makes no move to take the offering.

"Are you keeping well?" I ask.

"Who wants to know?"

"My dad." I struggle to keep a friendly tone in my voice in the presence of such a cantankerous old biddy. I can't understand why Dad would care more than half a whisker about people if this is how they're going to treat him. "He just wants to make sure you're all right."

Behind her glasses, Mrs. Glover's eyes narrow. I can't believe she'd be suspicious of my dad checking up on her. Dad, for all his faults, doesn't have a malicious bone in his body. But I can't blame her. It's no longer clear who to trust and who might turn on you in an instant.

"I'm fine," she says finally. "No thanks to our government." I wait patiently as she rattles on about her rights and about the old days when you knew the country had the best interests of its people at heart. I make sympathetic noises as she explains what it was like during the war, and how neighbors looked after one another, and there wasn't this feeling of mistrust. "Now we have no one to count on but ourselves. If I get out of this alive, it will be of my own doing."

I press the basket forward, tilting it to show her the carrots. At last, it's too much for her to resist, and she pokes a liver-spotted hand through the door and curls it around the bag. She isn't even wearing gloves.

"What's your secret, Mrs. Glover?" I ask.

She yanks the carrots into the house and squints at me. "I don't have a secret. What do you mean, 'secret'?"

"What are you doing to stay so healthy?" I want to come straight out and ask, "How come you haven't caught this yet?" but that would be rude, and Mrs. Glover won't stand for that. But it doesn't stop me wanting to ask.

"Good genes," she says, "and a resilience your generation couldn't hope to understand."

And with that she closes the door, with me on one side and our carrots on the other.

I swing a foot back, ready to kick her stubborn old front door, but I catch myself just in time. It's just the kind of thing that would prompt a phone call to my dad, and I don't need *that* right now. Instead I settle for slamming her gate behind me, relishing the clanging echo that rings long after I'm gone.

My dad has got this whole thing wrong. There is no community here anymore. It's every man for himself, and every miserable old woman for herself. After all he's done for the village, the old bat treats me like this. I don't know how she has the nerve.

I need to talk to Deb. I need a Bitch Fest, a sympathetic ear to listen to me vent and do nothing more than nod in agreement, like any good friend would. But Deb's still subject to her dad's quarantine, and she hasn't answered any of my texts all day. I turn and head in the direction of her street. Maybe if I walk by, she'll see me. Maybe we can talk through the window, or maybe she'll at least send a message somehow.

The house looks quiet, but not empty. I stand under Deb's window and hurl pebble after pebble until, finally, her curtain twitches. Deb's face pops into view for a second, then vanishes again. I'm not leaving until I talk to her. I fire off a series of well-aimed stones, one after another, until Deb comes back to the window. She holds up a piece of white paper. On it, she's written, *Phone's dead.*

For a second, I'm just relieved to know why she hasn't been in touch. I seriously thought she was ignoring me. Then it dawns on me what a lame excuse that is. I motion that she should perhaps consider plugging it in, but she doesn't respond.

"Are you okay?" I mouth.

She gives me a look that, even from this distance, burns with sarcasm. *What do you think?* it says.

"I need to talk to you. Open the window."

Deb shakes her head. She glances behind her, as if someone is there. I duck behind Helena's hydrangea. I don't know what's going on in their house, but for some reason Deb doesn't want to, or can't, talk to me.

I peer out, and Deb holds up her hand for me to wait for a minute, then disappears, returning a moment later and beckoning me toward the house. Her window pops open a crack, and a folded piece of paper drops to the ground by my feet. At Deb's urging, I scoop it up and run for the cover of the hydrangea again.

Unfolding the sheet, I see Deb's familiar handwriting, tiny rounded letters crushed into neat rows of purple ink. *Dad's banned phones and internet. Worried we're being watched. Totally lost his mind. Helena sick. I'm fine. Miss you like mad. Destroy this note.* It's signed with a very un-Deb-like purple heart.

When I look back at her, Deb has hung a single black sock from the window latch. She grins at me. I force my mouth into a smile, but my heart cramps. When we were young, before we had our own phones, the window sock was our secret signal. It meant that we were at home, bored, and looking for company. During the summer holidays, we'd hang our socks as soon as we were up, and whichever of us was out first would know it was okay to call on the other. It was stupid, really, because we could have just phoned or knocked on the door, but the window sock gave us a secret that no one else understood, and that made the bond between us all the more special.

Now, all Deb and I can do is stare at one another. I can't knock on her door. I can't ask her to come out with me. Deb is at home, scared more than bored, and looking for my company, but there is nothing I can do about it. Her black sock is now our secret signal that everything has changed for us. Overnight my friend and I have grown old together, but not in the way we'd once planned.

Chapter Eighteen

Thursday, August 11

DAD AND I PUT ON our protective gear to attend a memorial for "The Victims"—our friends and neighbors. Dad finally got approval from the authorities and has been organizing it for days. He has permission to hold it in an open outdoor venue, where we can all get together and still maintain a safe distance between us. He even managed to get special dispensation for the families of the sick and dead to attend, with precautions, of course. And with the cricket pitch taken over by Bubble City, he's chosen Cucklett Delf. As we open the front door to leave, an official-looking paper taped to the door flutters up. Dad gets to it first, tearing it from the door and scanning the information. At first I hold back, wary of new information and the changes it might bring.

It was two days after Bubble City was erected that we finally received an official explanation, long after the news feeds had speculated about its appearance. As most of us had already guessed, the compound is a staged isolation center. The first tent is for those who exhibit some symptoms, but whom medical personnel deem low probability. So, if someone has the sniffles they can be admitted, but if the doctor thinks it might not be the virus, they stay in Tent One for observation. The second tent is for anyone that the medical staff deem "high probability," someone whose symptoms look iffy or who's been exposed to the virus because of direct contact with an infected person. Admission to the center for any unusual symptoms is recommended but voluntary. But if someone is clearly infected, evacuation to the isolation unit is mandatory. Once someone is confirmed infected, all members of the household must remain isolated, even if they don't have symptoms. If they choose not to enter the isolation unit, they will be placed on in-home isolation and provided with a home aide. These houses will be considered high-risk. As such, their doors will be marked with a white X and may only be entered by official personnel. Any member of an isolated household who shows symptoms will immediately be removed to Tent Two. Fully evacuated homes will be decontaminated, sealed, marked off-limits by a red X, and monitored by armed guards.

It all sounded so clinical and cold. I was reminded of the old black and white films my granddad used to watch, ancient grainy war movies with rugged heroes outwitting the enemy. I pictured coils of barbed wire, fierce Alsatian dogs on thick chains, and shouts of "Halt!" quickly followed by the *rat-a-tat* of machine gun fire. I hated those films. Now I'm living in one.

According to the new paper, everyone admitted to Bubble City will be tested but will have to wait in the tent until their results come in. Results, it says, could take twenty-four to forty-eight hours.

"Anyone testing positive will be moved to the Care Ward," Dad reads from the sheet.

"For treatment?" I ask, wondering if Deb knows this.

But Dad shakes his head. "Palliative care."

I know what that means. They'll do whatever they can to increase the odds of survival, but there is no treatment. Half the Care Ward patients will be carried out in bags and, as no one has yet been infected and recovered, it's not clear what will happen to the survivors. As much as I hate that Deb's dad is keeping his family locked away, I can't blame him for not wanting to send Helena to a place from which she's unlikely to return.

"What happens if your test comes back negative?" I ask.

He scans the information and reads on. "They'll be moved to an observation unit for seven days, and if no symptoms develop, they'll be free to leave the village."

"Why aren't they testing everyone?" I ask.

"It's a new test, so they're doing a trial. They're starting with those at highest risk first." He looks up from the paper. "This is good," he says. "The more high-risk people they move out, the safer it will be for the rest of us."

I wonder if Deb will be considered high-risk? If she tests negative, does that mean she'll be able to leave soon? I'll be glad for her if she gets out of here—of course—but I can't help feeling like the wallflower on the edge of the dance floor, everyone else waltzing into the sunset while I'm left behind.

"Does it say where they'll go?"

Dad flips the page, and his face flickers into a twisted half smile, as if what he's read would be good news, if it wasn't such bad news. He makes one of those little *humph* noises that means, "well fancy that," and hands me the paper.

"Elmington?"

I close my eyes for a moment and picture the famous, stately home a couple of miles from our village. I know from about a million school trips that Elmington Hall is the ancestral home of the duke of some county that's nowhere near here, and it's one of the few grand estates still running, mainly because the duchess decided to let throngs of school kids and tourists traipse over their ancestral carpets on tours. Dad has been trying for years to form a partnership with the tour office to try to funnel some of their visitors down the road to us. Looks like the history of Elmington and our village will now be inextricably linked.

I picture the old house clearly, perched on a hill overlooking the river, the grounds speckled with herds of deer and flocks of sheep. I can see the wide terrace with its stone balustrade overlooking the manicured gardens, the long reflecting pool, high fountain, and cascading waterfall that flows down through the trees. I picture Deb and me sitting in wicker chairs, tartan blankets draped over our knees like a couple of old ladies, breathing in fresh country air and knowing we are no longer in danger from this terrible disease.

Now I have something to aspire to. Goal number one is to avoid getting infected, of course. Then all I need to do is get myself a place in line to be tested and pack a bag for Elmington. For the first time since my failed escape attempt, hope flickers inside me.

As Dad and I make our way through the village, I glance toward Deb's street, hoping her dad will decide to let her come today. We pass by the church, where our village last congregated to say goodbye to Dr. Spencer. It feels like a lifetime ago that we all gathered there, but the alien invaders have brought with them a means of distorting time, bending it around us so I no longer know where I stand in the world. I realize that Dr. Spencer's funeral wasn't an age ago. It's only been two weeks.

Behind the church is the old vicarage, where the Reverend Mompesson lived until he admitted himself to Bubble City for possible symptoms. The vicarage used to be such a gorgeous, ivy-covered building, with decades, maybe centuries of growth climbing up the stone walls and spreading like a protective blanket over the house. Then, one year, it got blight. The leaves curled and turned black. So the once-green curtain became a dark, sinister cloak. They took the ivy down, but it had put its roots into the stonework, and when they pulled it away, it took the structure of the building with it. Most of it had to be rebuilt, and what stands now is a modernized version of the former, solid home.

The gloominess of the old vicarage washes over me, and I steel myself for what lies ahead. There is still no word from Deb. She must be going crazy without her phone; I can't believe her dad is really that paranoid about being watched. Still, it's like rubbing salt in a wound. It's lonely enough being cut off from the outside world without losing my one source of sanity inside as well.

A low murmur of voices drifts toward us as Dad and I pass through the narrow rock passage and out into the open air of Cucklett Delf. My eyes dart immediately to the stream in the bottom, and a brief thought flashes across my mind about where I'd be now if it hadn't been for Ro. I push it aside; it won't do me any good to dwell on that now.

Below us, small clusters of people, all wearing face masks, stand at abnormal distances, as if each were standing alone and talking to himself. Some wear plastic ponchos; others have somehow acquired respirators; almost everyone wears the same weary, stunned expression, as if it's become a uniform. No one touches, no one leans in to listen, and no one laughs. I think back to Dr. Spencer's funeral, when our whole village gathered to pay their respects, everyone packed into the church, shoulder-to-shoulder, hugging and consoling one another. I wonder, had we known about the virus then, would we have taken that risk? And did our lack of knowledge help fuel the spread? But there's no point hashing over that again; it's in the past, and what's done is done.

As we step in, Dad greets a cluster of neighbors. "Thanks for coming," he says.

"Not much of a turnout," one says in a way that makes me think he's doubting his own decision to attend.

I scan the paltry group. Last year we held a Midsummer Festival here. There was barely a blade of grass visible as the entire village packed in to enjoy the festivities. Today there are barely fifty people.

Around the Delf, the small crowd forms into sparse rows, everyone jostling to maintain space, shuffling one way to avoid one neighbor, then back again to stay away from another. The Talbot family huddle together, their arms draped around one another in a show of solidarity. Around them is a clear circle of grass that no one else dares to enter. Everyone is assumed infected until proven clean, and an air of mistrust swirls around us.

Dad steps forward, his hand extended to shake Mr. Talbot's. I grab his arm and pull him back. He gives me an apologetic look, but in his eyes I see intense sadness. It's killing him not to be able to connect with his people, but it could actually kill him if he does.

Behind my mask, my breath heats my face, and a thin

layer of perspiration gathers across my nose. I sense the faint aroma of last night's dinner and this morning's toothpaste, as if everything I do from now on will linger with me inside this wretched mask. I pull at it, trying to get some fresh air, but as I do Millie Talbot takes a step backward. Like everyone else, I am now an unknown entity.

We step down into the Delf, and I search the crowd for Deb or her family. They're not here. Close by, I spot Katie, Alice's holiday friend. She comes every summer to stay with her grandparents but spends most of it at our house. Clutching her grandfather's hand, she looks so small and afraid, just like Alice would if she were here. I'm struck by how rash fate can be, plucking my sister out of danger and dropping Katie in the thick of it. Had the quarantine been imposed a week later, I might have been one of the lucky ones too.

"Friends," Dad calls out, taking up position at the bottom of the Delf and raising his arms until a reluctant hush falls over the gathering. "I'm standing here today where our good friend Reverend Mompesson ought to be. I'm sure you'll join me in sending our good wishes to him and his family." He raises his hand in our direction, and I turn to see Elizabeth, the vicar's wife, standing not far from me. A ripple of nods and murmurs wafts through the crowd, but from my position up the hill, I can see another ripple. As if someone has dropped a pebble in a pond, the crowd pulls away from Elizabeth, propelled by an instinct for self-protection. Then everyone falls back into place when good manners and guilt kick in. I give a polite nod toward her and try to stop my feet from inching away.

"The latest report shows a slowing in the spread of the virus," Dad says. "And although that sounds like good news, we're not out of the woods yet."

He shouldn't be talking about this, I think. This is supposed to be a memorial. I shoot him a look, warning him to stick to the plan, but if he sees it, he doesn't acknowledge me.

"For the foreseeable future," Dad says, "all quarantine limits and precautionary measures will remain in place, and we must continue to cooperate."

"For how long?" shouts a voice from the crowd, followed by a murmur of assent.

"Like I say, for the foreseeable future."

"It's out of order," the voice says again. I can see now that it is Martin Bamforth, always one for picking a fight. "Even criminals know how long their sentences are going to be. Are we supposed to just stay here forever and wait to die?"

"They're trying to contain this, and the only way to do that is to—" But Dad is drowned out.

"It's not right for those of us not infected!" Bamforth shouts. "It's a bloody death sentence."

"You wouldn't think that way if it were your family!" one of the Talbots shouts back.

"But it's not," Bamforth retorts. Then everyone jumps in, each shouting an opinion from their safe patch of ground.

"Everyone should stay at home!" someone cries.

"Then what are you doing out here?" comes a response.

"How do we know we can trust the tests? They don't seem to know anything about this!" someone else yells.

"If you're suggesting I'm a threat... ," Elizabeth starts to say, her voice straining to maintain control.

"Yeah, what are you saying?" another voice shouts.

Suddenly there are people yelling in favor of the quarantine and those demanding we form a united front to break out. There are shouts of "murder" and "selfish" clashing with chants for "unity" and "community." A scuffle erupts around Elizabeth, and Martin Bamforth's fist hurtles toward Mr. Talbot. Two people dive in to break up the fight, while the rest pull away. If blood is spilled, no one wants to be nearby.

In one corner, a group of people forms a circle, hand in gloved hand, their heads bowed as if trying to shut out the mayhem around them. A small band of families scrambles down the embankment, splashing through the stream to freedom, as I had done. Others slip quietly from the gathering, disassociating themselves from the rabble.

I want to yell for both sides, against those who'd condemn me to death and against the others who want to run free—and with whom I am compelled to run. Tension surges in the confines of the shallow valley. At the front of the crowd, Dad looks like he's about to go off. The pressure building inside him radiates out toward me.

Inside, my rage begins to grow too, as everything my dad has worked so hard for begins to crumble in front of our eyes. Instead of watching the kind, gentle people I've known for most of my life, I am standing in a Roman arena watching wild animals fight to the death. It is a bloodbath I don't want to witness.

Then Dad tears off his mask and yells "Stop!" above the crowd, but if anyone hears him, they pay no attention. He yells again and claps his hands, trying to make a noise that will stand out above the din, but it's impossible. Suddenly, he yanks off one of his gloves. I watch, stunned, as he holds it to his mouth and blows as hard as he can. The glove puffs up and deflates. He stretches it out, like he's about to attempt a balloon animal, and tries again. This time, the palm of the glove bulges into a ball, and the fingers swell. He blows again and again, until the glove is inflated as far as it will go, twisting the end closed. I still don't know what he's doing, but I don't like it. Suddenly he lurches for something on the ground and comes up with a small stick. Before I can run to stop him, he points it at the glove, like an arrow, and with a sharp movement, thrusts it at the glove balloon. It bounces off. He tries again. The stick hits the glove and the balloon disappears. In my split second of confusion, a resounding *pop* ricochets around the Delf like a gunshot, and all exchanges stop as everyone looks up.

Dad stands there, the stick still extended, his open mouth uncovered, and the deflated remnant of a rubber glove in his bare hand. It's probably just my imagination, but I'm almost sure I can see the invisible virus swirling around our neighbors and swimming toward my father's open mouth.

A second later another *pop* reverberates through the trees and then another. They do not come from my dad. Our heads all turn as one to the trees on the opposite side of the stream. Grouse hunting season doesn't officially start until tomorrow, but we all recognize the sound of real gunshots. Only this quarry is human—escapees. Our friends.

I grab Dad by the arm and all but drag him through the crowd. I'm angry at him for taking off his mask and gloves, and also for being so naïve about trying to bring our fractured community together. I'm afraid to open my mouth in case the high-pressure gush of words knocks us both off our feet, and anyway, there's no time for a lecture now. We have to get out of here; both of our lives depend on it.

Once home, Dad obediently starts his decontamination process. I make him go through everything twice, adding a vinegar gargle and a saltwater nose rinse to the routine. Finally, he plops down at the kitchen table, his face pink from scrubbing and his eyes red and watery from the salt and vinegar. He looks like a little boy who's just realized Christmas has come and gone, and he hasn't had any presents. I'm overcome with an urge to hug him, but that's the very last thing I should do.

"They shot them," he says.

"We don't know that. It could have been just a warning."

Dad shakes his head. He lets out a breath, trying to find the words he needs to say among the chaos of those he *wants* to say. "All our friends, fighting among themselves. It makes me sad. And there's nothing I can do."

"You can't risk getting infected," I tell him for about the thousandth time.

"I just don't know how to not be involved."

"There's nothing left to be involved with," I say. "You saw what happened back there. No one else matters anymore, Dad. It's every man for himself, dog eat dog, law of the jungle. It's just you and me now. We are all we have."

Dad's head drops. "If ever there was a time for this village to pull together, it's now. I can't give up on them."

"What about us, Dad? What about *me*?"

"I won't do anything to put us in danger, Em. I promise you that."

"Dad." My voice is cold as I push up from the table. "You already did."

I leave Dad at home and step out into the village, walking determinedly toward I-don't-know-where. I wish I could just take my bike and ride until everything in my head falls into place, but my saddle would barely be warm before I reached the boundary of the quarantine and had to turn back. So I push forward on foot, trying to make sense of my dad. Yet again, he feels like a stranger. *I've lost him*, I think, but now I'm not sure

I ever really had him. *Is this what it feels like to be an orphan?* I wonder. *Or is this just what it feels like to be an adult?*

I turn up the lane and make my way to Deb's. I know I won't be able to talk to her, but maybe she'll come to the window again so I can at least see her face. She is my voice of reason, and her silence is killing me. I march on, determined to see her one way or another.

But when I reach the house, all the curtains are drawn, and there's no sign of movement or life from within. Across Deb's front door, someone has painted a big red X.

My friend isn't here anymore. My friend is in Bubble City.

Chapter Nineteen

M Y BREATH TEARS AT MY chest, scrabbling its way to my lungs, but not quick enough. My mask is wet from the exertion of sprinting with all my might to Bubble City. I run to the front entrance, grinding to a halt when I realize I have no idea what I'm hoping to accomplish. To fight my way in to see Deb? To put myself among the sick and the dying? Even I'm not foolish enough to take that risk. But I need to see my friend. I know she's not okay, but I need to see for myself how "not okay" she is.

I peer through the entrance, straining to catch a glimpse of her. I know it's futile, but it doesn't stop me from trying. I move down the line of tents, half desperate to see Deb, half hoping she won't be there. I skirt the perimeter, keeping my distance from the medical personnel scurrying around. I need to know if she's in there, but I know no one will tell me. I scan the suits, looking for Aiden. Just when I really need him, he isn't there.

A new tent has been set up just outside the main compound. It's more a canopy than a tent, the kind used to provide shade at a fair. It looks out of place. Underneath, something flaps in the breeze, like a bigger version of Himalayan prayer flags, only made of white paper. Everyone is too busy to notice me, so I hurry over to see what it's all about.

Once inside, I can see they aren't flags; they are in fact sheets of paper. The top of one reads "Status Update" along with today's date. The top of another sheet reads "Admitted" followed by a list of names. The next few pages look the same, except these are printed with "Confirmed Cases." Below is another list of names. There are four pages of people I know; more than 150 people have now been infected.

My stomach turns as I move to the last set of pages, labeled "Deceased." I scan the list, taking in all the familiar names of people I have known, people who are now gone. The names are grouped by week, each with a date of death. Weeks One and Two show the names of my two elderly neighbors, and Week Three contains Dr. Spencer's name. After that, each week has a longer list until this week shows twenty-five familiar names, almost fifty people in total who have not survived. Unless something changes soon, half the confirmed cases will eventually make that list.

I'm struck by the coldness of the lists, all these people I've known reduced to nothing more than a few words. There are no photographs, no celebrations of the lives once lived, no record of accomplishments. We are all reduced now to statistics.

I scan the list of dead, knowing Deb won't be there, but needing that crumb of good news. I can barely move the breath in my throat as I check the list once, twice. Deb's name isn't there. I move backward to the Confirmed Cases list, scanning this week's names, my eyes finding what I'm looking for this time: Elliot.

But it's not Deb; it's her stepmum. Mr. Elliot's barricade wasn't enough to halt the protocol. Helena has been found out. I scoot backward to the Admitted list, knowing what I'll find. All three Elliots are listed: Deb's dad, her brother, and Deb.

Next to each name is the same location, "Low Prob." They are all in Bubble City.

"What are you up to?"

I turn at the sound of the familiar voice behind me. Aiden stands on the threshold of the tent, his friendly eyes smiling back at me. I'm transfixed, momentarily unable to reconcile this welcome feeling of comfort with the information newly buzzing around my brain.

"I'm sorry about your boyfriend," he says. "It's just precautionary."

"He's not my boyfriend." The words shoot from me so fast, I don't have time to stop them. "Not anymore," I add, willing myself to stop answering questions I am not being asked.

"You find out who your friends are in times like this," he says.

I nod. "Turns out I don't have many."

"Are you looking for someone in particular?" He indicates the papers behind me.

I manage a small nod.

"Family?" I shake my head, and his gaze softens. "Are you looking for a friend?"

I tell him about Deb. "She's here on this list, but I don't know what that means. I don't know where she is. I don't even know if she's okay." My throat tightens, and I hear my words squeeze into a higher and higher pitch as my eyes fill with tears.

"It's all right," Aiden says. "Show me your friend's name." He follows my finger as I point to "Elliot, Deborah." Reading her full name like that makes her sound old. I'm struck by what a curious name "Deborah" is, longer and more exotic written than spoken. It reads like an ancient name, perhaps a goddess or an early African queen. No longer just "Deb," my oldest friend is suddenly more complicated, her importance on display for the world to see.

"She's Low Prob. That's good news; it means she's not sick. Let's go and find her."

"Where?" I ask.

He points me toward Bubble City. "Go around to the visiting area, and I'll see if I can find her."

"Am I supposed to be there?"

He smiles. "For once, yes." He prods me off around the back of the perimeter and heads toward the entrance.

At first I don't move, uncertain of the idea of a "visiting area." Everything we know so far has warned us to keep a distance, to avoid getting too close to anyone else in case they're carrying the virus. The thought of venturing into an area where I *know* people are infectious is alarming. But I need to see Deb; it's the whole reason I'm here.

Behind the tents are two sets of fencing with a wide gap in between. I move tentatively toward the outermost fence, taking in everything around me, as if waiting for something to happen. The air is heavy with a damp, unidentifiable smell. Even through my mask, the scent of harsh disinfectant burns the back of my throat, triggering memories of the locked room where the school caretaker kept his supply of mops and buckets. I glance up, and my eyes find an opening at the back of the Care Ward. The inside of the tent looks like frog spawn, a mass of plastic sheeting forming individual bubbles, the dark shapes of yellow suits moving around still, dark figures within. The antiseptic smell suddenly seems to clear, and underneath is a raw, human smell—the smell of sickness, of death. And something else, something burning.

Beyond the farthest corner of the compound, almost to

the woods, an area has been shielded from view by high, solid barriers, like a giant white windbreak. From behind the wall, a steady plume of pale gray smoke rises into the clear afternoon sky, and I know immediately what it is—a crematorium to dispose of our dead.

I push my mask against my face and hurry toward the visitor area, blinking away the images of the sick and dead now seared on my mind. The thought of what I might find when Deb appears fills me with terror. I know she isn't sick. She isn't like the people in the Care Ward. But even though I know she's in Low Prob, probably not infected, merely under observation and awaiting the results of her test, geographically speaking, she's only two tents away from the sick.

Then my thoughts begin to spiral. What if she's been admitted? Is she showing symptoms? Will she be wheeled out to see me in her own plastic bubble? From this distance, will I even be able to tell if it's her? What if Aiden comes out to tell me Deb isn't even here anymore? What if… ? But a few minutes later, Aiden pokes his head out of the tent and Deb walks out toward me.

At first she looks exactly the same as she always does, dressed in black, her dark hair flopping over one eye. She grins at me and rolls her eyes, as if to say, "Honestly, can you even believe they've dumped me in this place?" But as she reaches her side of the barrier, I can see she is not the same. Something in her face, the way her smile is forced into action, tells me that something profound has changed.

"Are you okay?" I gasp.

Deb screws up her face as if confronting the biggest idiot ever. "Um, no?" she says. "I'm camping. In a field. With a load of other people I don't really want to spend time with. And we don't even get to sing 'Kumbaya' by the fire at night." It's the same Deb humor I've always known, but the edge in her voice tells me it's all a front. My friend is terrified.

Through the opening in the tent behind her, I can see the rows of camp beds, each not much more than an arm's length from its neighbor and separated, for all intents and purposes, by a shower curtain. Considering they've been set up for a group of people at risk of exposure to the virus, they don't look all that safe.

"How's Helena?" I ask.

Deb twitches one shoulder and looks away. "She's in the Care Ward. They tell us she's doing well, that she's still strong, but we're not allowed to see her. Dad's about to lose it, I think."

"But what about you? Are you, you know... ? Are you okay?"

"I'm tired, that's all. But they don't think we have it. They'll probably let us go once the tests come back."

"I wish there was something I could do," I say.

Deb's face crumples. The stoic lines of my brilliant friend's face fold into one another, hiding the wisdom of her years until she looks no older than Alice. In the center of my chest, a dull ache opens up, reaching tentacles of love toward Deb, but in an instant, her face changes again and I see her suck in her fear, fighting to regain her composure.

"Your friend seems nice," she says with a fake, cheery grin.

"Aiden?" I blush and look away. "Yeah, he's been really helpful."

"I don't think much of his sense of style, but my radar's picking up that he might have a thing for our Emmott."

I start to object, but Deb holds her hand up to stop me.

"Don't be a twit, Em. He's your best ally right now. Maybe your *only* ally, so don't start playing Miss Innocent with me."

"Are you suggesting I use him?"

"No," says Deb. "I'm suggesting you don't let Ro be the standard by which you measure all men. You have to do *everything* you can to stay out of this hell hole, and if you've got someone like Aiden on your side, you shouldn't throw that away."

I nod to let her know I understand, even though I'm not sure I do.

"Use your strengths, Salty. That's all I'm saying." Deb wraps her arms around herself, the way we used to as girls, pretending to smooch. "Love you loads."

I'd do anything to be able to hug her for real, absolutely anything.

All the way home I think about what Deb said about using my strengths, and I worry that her estimations of me are all wrong. I don't even know what my strengths are. I thought I was good at sneaking out at night until I realized Dad knew all along. I have terrible judgment when it comes to trusting people, as evidenced by Ro. And Mrs. Glover's refusal to share valuable knowledge has shown that I have no allies in the village. I used to think of myself as determined and independent, both positive traits, I thought. But they're only a whisker away from stubborn and alone, which is more or less how I feel.

I'm still noodling the whole thing as I splash through the disinfectant bath by the back door and let myself into the house. I can hear noises in the kitchen and assume Dad is scrabbling around in there. He's not making cooking noises though. It sounds like he's mending something or wrapping a present. *My birthday.* It's less than a week away, and although it's been nowhere near the forefront of my mind lately, I haven't forgotten. You don't forget your eighteenth birthday, do you? I'm not expecting any kind of celebration, not in the middle of this mess, but is it possible that Dad has found something to stand in for a gift? I push open the door slowly, giving him plenty of warning that I'm coming, but when I look in, he's not wrapping presents. Instead, I'm confronted by the most ridiculous sight I've ever seen, and I can't make head or tail of it.

Dad is dressed in an old, navy blue boiler suit, fastened up the front with rubber buttons. He has yellow plastic shopping bags over his feet, and his legs are wrapped in bright blue plastic and taped in place with wide bands of duct tape. There's more of the blue plastic strewn around the kitchen floor, and once I can make out the words "Gro-Mor" written up Dad's right leg, I realize they are the empty fertilizer bags that he uses to protect his veggies in the garden. On the table are a pair of plastic goggles, a mask, some washing-up gloves, and a lot more plastic.

"Dad?" I ask. "What are you doing?"

Dad's face lights up with what I assume he thinks is joy, but to me he has the look of a mad scientist. "If you can't beat 'em, join 'em," he says.

"Join who?"

"The plastic bubble brigade. I've been trying to get them to fork over a hazmat suit so I can get out to check on people. I heard about this thing called a Community Liaison, someone local assigned to help in a crisis so that people get to see a familiar face. I've tried to convince the authorities, but no luck. Apparently they say it will increase the risk of spread because they can't monitor if people are using correct protocol. Most people won't."

"That still doesn't explain why you're standing in the kitchen wrapped in fertilizer bags."

"I am not *most* people. I've been paying attention, and we already have a protocol of our own to follow. I don't know why I didn't think of this before."

"Of what, Dad? What are you doing?"

He looks up and studies me as if trying to decide if I've really asked such a stupid question. "I'm making a hazmat suit."

It takes me a moment to fully grasp this. I hear what he's saying and even understand the implications of what he's telling me, but my mind can't quite grasp the idea that my own father is doing this.

"No," I say. "Oh no, you're not." It sounds exactly like something my mother would say to me.

"Em, I know I promised you I wouldn't take risks, but I have to be able to get out and see people. This way I can do it safely."

"I think you've finally lost it." I head for the sink to scrub up, trying to think how I'm going to talk my dad out of this ridiculous idea on which he's so clearly set. "I've just been to see Deb, Dad. She's in Bubble City. Helena's in the Care Ward. Nobody's really sure exactly how this thing gets passed around, but given that the workers are still wearing fully sealed suits, I'd say this thing is fairly aggressive. We have to do whatever we can to protect ourselves, and I'm really sorry, but this is not it."

Dad seems to deflate and plunks himself down on one of the kitchen chairs.

"There," I say, pointing to the seat with my elbow. "Right there is why this is a bad idea. What if you go into someone's house being all neighborly, and you sit down to offer your words of comfort, but they have the virus in their house. So what happens? You take your infected posterior to the next neighbor and leave the virus on their kitchen chair. Or you bring it home to us. See? This is a very, very bad idea, Dad."

"I've thought of that already. I'll hose myself off after I leave. We'll create a new protocol."

I shake my head in disbelief. "A new protocol. Great idea. Because you are *so* qualified to do that."

He doesn't say anything.

"I just think this is one of those things that seems like a good idea all the way until it suddenly becomes a bad idea. And I know you don't want to be the person responsible when it does."

He sighs. I hate that he looks defeated, but I can't let him win this one. "I have to do something," he says.

"No, you don't. Not anymore. You've done as much as you can, and now it's time to stop."

Dad narrows his eyes at me. "It's not like you to give up so easily. You're usually so much more... determined."

It's the closest thing to a compliment I can expect from my dad, and it pings around inside me like a moth around a light. I'm not ready to give up either, but when it comes to other options, I'm flat out of ideas.

"I know, Dad," I say. "But for once, it's all we can do."

All evening, I think about Deb, wondering what she's doing, if she's sleeping, or if she's lying awake waiting to find out her fate. I wish I could be there with her. I imagine myself strolling into the tent in Dad's homemade suit. It would be a death sentence. I can't believe Dad would think for one minute it could be a good idea. And yet, would I take that chance to be with Deb?

Does my dad really care so much about our neighbors that he'd risk his own health for them?

Dad's idea isn't completely idiotic. In a way, it's sort of noble. And suddenly I realize that it's brilliant. Just not in the way Dad had planned it. If we are to survive this, what better way than to isolate ourselves fully from risk?

I pull out my phone and scroll to Aiden's name. Deb's right about him being an ally, but where is the line between asking a friend for a favor and asking too much?

I suppose there's only one way to find out.

I tap a brief, *How are you?* And then I wait to see if I really do have an ally, to find out where that tricky line is drawn.

It feels like a lifetime later that his response comes back. *Better now*, it says, and I am filled with hope.

Chapter Twenty

Saturday, August 13

There's a buzz in the air today. Something big is happening, and those of us still able or willing to venture out gather around Bubble City. Word goes around, hopping the gaps we leave between one another: Almost a month after the start of the quarantine, the first survivor is being released.

It's not long before a bustle of activity flares up around the exit to the Care Ward and an orderly wheels someone out to a waiting ambulance. I barely recognize him at first. He's dressed in pale blue scrubs that look as if they're hung on one of those hangers designed for baby clothes. They fall around his meager frame, catching on the bumps of pointed shoulders and sticking-out knees. His face looks as if it has been sucked in from behind and, even though the waxy yellow pallor has gone, I'd be hard pressed to say he looks better. But he must be, because Dad's friend, Andy, is leaving.

A pair of medics helps him to a decontamination shower, and he emerges several minutes later looking like a drowned rat. As the waiting ambulance pulls around to the exit, a group of medical personnel comes to the fence to wave him off. I find myself waving too. Andy's departure has burst open a bud of hope I hadn't dared feel before.

"Are they taking him to Elmington?" I ask around, wondering if anyone knows for sure.

The response comes from a man a few feet in front of me. "Yep, Elmington. Jammie devil. They've opened up another wing for survivors. He'll be free to leave from there… assuming he can find anyone willing to take him in."

I'm not sure "jammie" is how I'd describe Andy's fortunes. If anyone is lucky, it's those of us gathered to watch his departure, those of us "jammie" enough to have avoided infection. Who would risk taking him in, knowing he'd been here? And what about when the quarantine is lifted? Will he ever want to come back? So much of what made this village "home" is gone. Andy's shop has been boarded up, and even if it wasn't, he'd have nothing to sell and a rapidly dwindling group of customers to sell it to. Many of our friends and neighbors are sick or dying or dead. Before all this began, I swore that once I left, I'd never come back, but now I wonder: when all this is over, will *any* of us want to return?

"I wouldn't come back here," I say. "Put myself at risk of catching it again?"

"Can't catch it twice," says the man. "That's what they're saying."

So Aiden was right. This thing is actually going to burn itself out. It's the first bit of good news we've had in ages.

As I turn to head home, I notice a group of people gathered inside the compound, watching Andy's departure. A hand shoots up and waves in my direction, and Deb steps away from the group. She smiles at me, and even from this distance I can sense a shift in her, in everyone in the group. Andy has given them hope, given us all hope, that maybe we'll make it out of here after all.

Back at the house, I find Dad staring out the kitchen window. He barely acknowledges my presence. I tell him about Andy and what I heard about him being immune now. I think this is good news, but Dad only nods. He's gazing out into the village, but it's clear he's far, far from here.

"Earth to Father," I say.

It takes him a second to react, then all he does is shake his head. "That's good news," he says. "Good for Andy."

I get the sense there's more to this thought, but before I can pry further and offer an ear if he wants to talk, the doorbell rings.

"I'll get it." I'm grateful to step out of the circle of melancholy that seems to have descended around Dad.

Through the glass in the front door, I spot the edge of a yellow suit. I open the door with my guard up, always on alert that a moment's good news could turn bad in an instant, especially when suits are involved. But I'm relieved to find Aiden on my doorstep, peering at me over the top of a large cardboard box.

"Delivery," he says, but he doesn't offer the box to me. I reach to take it from him, but he pulls it back. "*Special* delivery," he says. "Meet me around the back."

My heart flickers. *Did he get it?* I close the door and hurry into the backyard to meet him, calling to Dad to come with me.

"Mornin', Mr. Syddall," Aiden says, striding into the garden and setting the box on the patio table. "Brought a few extra supplies in case you need them."

"Good of you." Dad's tone is polite, but skeptical.

Aiden opens the flaps and lifts out packets and boxes, which he then sets on the table. "Face masks; gloves; vitamins; unidentifiable, government-issued dehydrated slop. Indian takeaway. Chicken Tikka masala, lamb Rogan josh, biryani, poppadoms, and onion bhajis." He turns and grins at me.

"Really?" I ask as he hands me a large, lumpy bag, the distant memories of soothing aromatic spices already tantalizing my taste buds.

"Sadly not," he says. "But it's almost as good, I think."

I can barely hide my disappointment as I peer into the bag. It's not Indian food. It's not even edible. It's something even better. I reach in and pull out a pile of yellow fabric. I don't need to unfold it to know what it is. A hazmat suit. "You got one," I say. Mixed with my awe and appreciation that Aiden granted my request, a pang of guilt flares in me that I've once again risked getting him into trouble. But this time it's for a good cause... my dad.

"Technically there are six," Aiden says, setting the bag on the table. "You can't use them more than once, but they should last a few days."

"Thank you," I tell him, doing an internal dance that he brought extra suits, perhaps one that I could borrow. "A lot. Thank you," which causes Aiden to smile. It's a smile that goes all the way to his eyes, which is fortunate as that's all I can see of him.

"What is all this?" Dad asks, nosing at the suit.

"Special dispensation," Aiden says. "You've been officially designated Community Liaison, which means as long as you follow protocol, you'll have a little bit more freedom around the village."

Dad looks from Aiden to me, and back again, and I can see

he's worked out the approximate sequence of events that led to this. He beams at me as if he's been given the best gift ever. "Thank you," he says, to both of us.

I shuttle the supplies into the house while Dad gets instructions on how to properly put on, seal, and then take off the hazmat suit. I'm pleased to realize that our makeshift protocol isn't too far off from Aiden's training. We've been putting layers on in order and checking one another for leaks and tears, just like they do in Bubble City. Aiden explains the "decon" procedure they use, with the footbaths and timed shower, and when I show him our setup, he looks impressed. Even so, when he shows Dad how to safely remove and destroy a used suit, I start to worry. There are so many things to remember and so many mistakes that could be made.

Finally, he's all suited up and ready to go. As he turns so Aiden can check his hood one last time, he catches my eye. His shoulders slump, and I've no doubt he's thinking about all the rules he's breaking, but he's so excited about being able to visit his people in safety that he says nothing. He may be having second thoughts, and he's not the only one, but when I study his face, I can see how much he wants to go, how much he needs to be helpful. I glance at the official Red Cross badge clipped to his chest. *J. Syddall, Community Liaison.* I give him an encouraging smile and a little nod. It's my way of telling him it's okay for him to go, even if I'm not sure I'm right.

"Be careful out there, Mr. Syddall," Aiden says.

Dad's eyes crinkle into a smile through the narrow slit left for them. "I will," he says, and then he's gone, leaving Aiden and me alone.

I can't help but wonder what I'd have to do to get Special Dispensation so I could get into Bubble City and spend some time with Deb, but I've already asked enough of Aiden. "Do you want a cup of tea?" I ask instead, before realizing how stupid that is. Of course he can't sit here and drink tea with me. But he surprises me.

"If you're making one, I will. Cheers."

I duck into the kitchen and don't point out his mistake. It doesn't matter that he can't drink it. It feels so good to be able to do something normal like offer a guest a cup of tea. My grandmother used to say that tea makes everything feel better, and when so much is wrong, I'm glad for this brief moment of normalcy. I like Aiden's company, strange though it is to contemplate drinking tea with a man covered in plastic, but I'd make all the tea in China and India combined if it meant he would stay a little bit longer.

"How did you manage to wrangle this?" I ask, returning to the garden to set out the teapot and mugs. "Community Liaison? Is that really a thing?"

"Believe it or not, it is. It's something we've learned from other…" He catches himself, and I can see him searching for the right word. "… from other situations. It helps bridge the gap between 'us and them.' You know? It makes people feel more comfortable to have someone they know on their side."

We sit across the table from one another, me sipping my tea and him watching through his visor as his goes cold. As I suspected, he has no intention of drinking it, but I think he appreciates the normalcy too.

"Is he going to be okay out there?" I ask.

"As long as he follows protocol," Aiden says.

"I wish he wouldn't do this. I wish he'd just stay here and worry, like a normal dad."

"I'm not sure he is a normal dad. It's fairly brave what he's doing."

A little bubble of pride swells and pops inside me. My dad, the hero? I've never thought about him like that. Perhaps all this village stuff hasn't been meaningless. Perhaps it's only me who's seen it that way.

"Thank you for making his day," I say.

Aiden shrugs off my thanks. "When I left to come up here, my dad told me that if all I did was make a difference in the life of one person, I'd have done my job."

"In that case, you should be getting double pay."

Aiden grins, and my face flushes. But honestly, he's the only thing making this whole mess bearable, and I don't know how to tell him how grateful I am for all the chances he's taken for me.

"There's something I want to show you," he says.

"More contraband?"

"Sort of." He reaches into his bag of tricks and tells me to put on fresh gloves and make sure my mask is secure. I put down my tea and do as I'm told. Then he takes out a tablet sealed in a double plastic bag. "I think this is going to be good news, but you have to promise me you'll keep it to yourself."

I make a small cross sign roughly over the spot where my heart is, and he prods the tablet to life and slides it across the table. The screen fills with a cluster of cells, an image I recognize immediately from biology class. "Each cell tells a story," my old teacher used to say, and my guess is that these cells have something to do with the mess in Eyam.

"This is our virus," Aiden says.

The images are beautiful, I have to admit, blooms of pinks

and yellows and greens. Like the most exotic flower I've ever seen.

"This is the host cell." Aiden leans across the table and points to the pink area. "The human cell. And this is the virus here." He points to the yellow clusters at the top of the screen. I'm shocked to see that the virus is the most beautiful part of all. There are clusters of yellow petals, with delicate fringes, the kind of thing you'd expect to find bees buzzing around. I half expect to see a spotted ladybird crawl across the screen. How can something so beautiful be so deadly? The drop-dead gorgeous assassin. The virus is pretty enough to put on display, like one of my mosaics, and yet it's the last thing you'd want to do.

I point toward the chain of green emeralds sprinkled between the virus and host. "What's that?"

Aiden smiles at me through his mask, his eyes lighting up with barely contained excitement. "With luck," he says, "that's our hero."

I stare at the row of green blobs. Is this what's going to save my life? It looks so fragile. "What is it?"

"It's descended from an ancient plant with a fancy Latin name I can't pronounce. It's found in hostile environments."

"Like Siberia?"

"You are quick. The nomads make tea from it, a health tea. They think there might be a link between the tea and those who show immunity to the virus."

"A vaccine?"

"Not yet," he says. "It has to be tested, but it's looking hopeful."

The thought that the vaccine won't come quickly enough for my neighbors—or my best friend—flits through my mind.

I allow it to run its course but keep my lips pressed together tight, as if speaking the words might make them real.

"A group of our doctors is pushing for a trial, but the government won't approve it without data."

"That's stupid. What harm could it do?"

"Unfortunately, that's the bit they don't know."

"But if it kills the virus, why not try it?" I ask, furious now that they could be so cautious when people are dying.

"That's the thing. It doesn't kill it, not exactly. If you think about two pieces of Lego and how they fit together—you know, how the nub of one fits perfectly inside the bottom of the other—that's how the virus attaches to the host." He presses his gloved thumb and forefinger together to demonstrate. "So the vaccine, it acts like a protective barrier to prevent the cells connecting." He glances at me from the corner of his eye. "A bit like this suit. Between you and me."

His directness makes me flinch, and for a second I'm reminded of Ro, egging me on and daring me to be his rebel. But when I glance at Aiden, I feel something I never felt from Ro, the thing that was always missing. He *has* touched me—not with his hands, not with his body, but with something even more powerful. A feeling. It's as if some part of him has reached through the layers of his suit and connected with something deep inside me. It's the most ridiculous notion ever, and yet, instead of being thrilled about the protective vaccine that will keep the virus from my cells, all I can think about are those two bricks of Lego. A smile tugs at the corners of my lips as I wonder if our two matching pieces could ever get together.

Aiden leans toward me, and I'm certain he's going to reach his arms out toward me. All I need is a twitch from him, a sign that it's okay and I would go to him. I wait, but the touch doesn't come. When I dare to look up, his eyes are pools of agony, and I can tell he feels the same way. I slide one foot toward him underneath the table, and he puts up his hands.

"No, Em." His voice is strained. "Don't."

"It's not fair." I try to keep the tears from coming. I don't want to show him my weakness, but I'm not sure I can contain it any more.

He twitches his arms, and for a moment I think he's going to hold them out to me, but he doesn't. Instead he clasps his hands behind his head, pressing his elbows together in front as if trying to hide his face. Then he shakes his head and turns away. My body feels like two entities, the real me trapped inside an exterior shell. I want to rip myself open so I can get to Aiden. The sensation is so overwhelming my nails start to ache with the desire to let myself out. I scratch them across my belly, over the spot where the feeling is trying to burst through, but it's no use. The ache won't go away.

So I gather up the cups, still filled with cold tea, and hurry inside the house. I dump them in the sink and run the water, covering the sounds of me trying to collect my breath. When I'm sufficiently pulled together, I return to the patio. Aiden has left, and I am more alone than ever.

Chapter Twenty-One

Monday, August 15

TODAY IS MY EIGHTEENTH BIRTHDAY. I'd envisioned Deb taking the train in, the two of us dressing to the nines and having afternoon tea at the Savoy. Then Ro and me hopping from club to club, coming home to our little flat on the first morning Tube. In my wildest fantasy, my parents, having fully accepted my decision to leave, would have come down to take us out for a meal in Covent Garden. I never pictured turning eighteen shut in the house with Dad.

There doesn't seem much point in getting out of bed. I stare up at the patterns in the textured ceiling of my room, watching the shadows shift as the morning sun makes its way across my bedroom window. *Happy Birthday to me*, I think, but I can't muster any enthusiasm to celebrate. By the window sits the stack of boxes, still packed for my move to London. All my plans and dreams for the future boxed up with nowhere to go. Deb should be getting ready to leave too, preparing for Freshers' Week at Oxford, making new friends, starting her life, *not* trapped in a virus-ridden village. Eventually, there's nothing good left to think about, and I have no option but to go downstairs. I'll make my pilgrimage to see Deb, which I've been doing daily since she was admitted to the Low Prob tent, and hope I don't run into Aiden. I can't stand the torture of being close to him but kept so far apart. Better I don't see him at all.

Dad stops me at the bottom of the stairs with a curt, "Morning." He tells me there's tea in the pot and offers me a cup. He doesn't mention my birthday, but I can't be upset. There are much more important things to worry about now. I go to take a seat at the kitchen table, but Dad ushers me into the living room instead. There's an air of seriousness about him that leads me to think he has bad news to break, although these days bad news is so commonplace it no longer warrants a living room talk.

As I wander into the living room clutching my tea, something seems out of place. It takes me a minute to register the burst of color around the table. Strung across the window are chains of colored paper, like we used to make in school, and a clutch of multicolored balloons hangs from the ceiling. On the table, glass jars are filled with every kind of flower imaginable, loose rose petals scattered around them like snow. There are a small stack of cards, some in regular envelopes, others in what appear to be folded magazine pages, and three brightly wrapped boxes. In the middle of the table sits a cake, the top smeared in pure white icing, bright jam oozing from its center. Someone has written "18" in tiny Alpine strawberries.

I gape at my dad, unable to find the right words.

He grins at me. "Happy Birthday, Emmie." He hasn't called me that in years, and the gentle sound of my pet name wraps itself around me.

I can't comprehend all this. I can't fathom how he put this together, or even that he *thought* to put it together. And he made a cake? "How did you... ?" I stammer.

"I had a lot of help," he says, pointing out each item and listing off the villagers who contributed ideas, materials, and time. The Ashton kids who made the paper chains, the neighbors who cut flowers from their gardens for Elizabeth Mompesson to arrange, and those who gave up their scarce rations of sugar, flour, and eggs. "And Mrs. Glover made the cake," he says.

"Mrs. Glover?" But she hates me. "Why would she do that?"

"People care about you, I suppose." He gives me a wry smile. "Imagine that!"

I do imagine it, and the notion brings with it an unfamiliar sense of peace and belonging.

Dad and I have strawberry cake for breakfast, and we agree that it's absolutely divine. I open the cards, a mix of generic greetings and homemade numbers, some drawn, some collaged with cutout pictures, and one painted in watercolors. Each has a note from someone in the village, wishing me a happy birthday, a long life, and good fortune. For a few minutes, I soak in the warm feelings and the belief that everything in my life is as it should be. Then I open the gifts: a box of scented soaps from our neighbors over the fence, a pair of socks from another neighbor. Dad hands me the last box, patchily wrapped in a piece of shiny paper that's not quite big enough, and tied with a creased ribbon.

"From me," he says.

I undo the bow and peel off the layers of tape to uncover a small, leather-bound box. I throw Dad a questioning look, but he encourages me to open it, so I ease off the lid. Inside is a pendant, a miniature statue of a woman in perfect gold and green detail, no bigger than the tip of my thumb. She's perched on a gold swing, hands clutching the chains, and a green dress swirling around her legs. Flaxen hair and a pair of green and gold wings flutter behind her. The overall effect is one of freedom and abandon.

"It was your great-great-grandma Syddall's," he says. "You know her name was also Emmott."

"I know," I say.

"This was passed down to my sister, your Auntie Sandra, but after... well, your grandma thought it should go to you someday."

"Thank you," I say. "That means a lot."

"I'm not sure if it's your style, and you don't have to wear it, but I wanted you to have it."

"I love it," I say. "She's beautiful." I unclasp the chain and hand it to Dad, turning my back so he can place it around my neck. I feel the pendant rest against my skin, the tiny woman arcing under my collarbone.

"What do you think?" I ask, turning back to show Dad.

He pinches his lips into a look that says he's at a loss for words. "I love you, Em," he says at last. "I might not always be good at showing it, but I want you to know."

"I love you too, Dad."

"I've been thinking... maybe I should cut back on my visits, just for a while. Until we're sure we're out of the woods."

I almost tell him I think it's a good idea, but then I catch sight of the gifts, the balloons, the flowers, and the cake, and I understand now what a difference a small gesture can make, what a big difference my neighbors' gestures have made to my day, and what a difference Dad's visits have made to theirs. "It's up to you," I say. "But maybe now is when they need you more than ever."

Dad considers me for a moment, then says, "First day of being eighteen and you really are an adult." He hovers for a moment, like there's more he needs to say, but he's already said more than he's ever said before. "So," he says finally, his tone changing to playful. "How are you going to spend your big day?"

I think about it for a moment, crossing off all the things I'd like to do and narrowing it down to not much. "I think I'll have a bath and binge-watch cartoons, then drop in on Deb," I say. "And maybe have more cake for lunch."

"Sounds like a plan." He starts gathering up our dishes. "Don't forget to give your mum a ring too," he adds on his way out.

I want to protest that it's *my* birthday, and I shouldn't have to do anything I don't want to do, but now I'm officially an adult, I need to act like one. Mum and I chat for a few minutes, but my side of the conversation is clipped. I ask her about her quarantine and how Alice is coping. She offers reassuring answers that they are both doing fine, and more importantly, they're both healthy.

"I wish I could be there for you today," she says.

I don't want to spoil my eighteenth with an argument, but I feel one coming on. "If your friend Mark was going to pull those strings, now would be a really great time."

"He can't," she says, her voice tinged with regret. "Not anymore."

"Can't or won't?"

"Can't, Em. Mark's been quarantined too."

It doesn't make sense, and I'm about to ask why they'd do that when Mark hasn't been anywhere near our village, but then I think about the pictures I found, and all my questions are answered. They've quarantined Mark like they quarantined Ro. Because Mark is Mum's Level IV. Suddenly I see my mother clearly. Like the blighted ivy on the old vicarage, she covered our family in a lush, protective shield. We looked good from the outside, but when they pulled her away, she took the structure of our family with her.

"Well." My voice quavers as I suck back all I want to say about my mother's behavior. This is *my* day, and I'm not going let her ruin it. "That's that then."

"I'm so sorry," Mum says. "Emmott, I..."

But I cut the conversation short. Whatever she feels she needs to say, today is not the day I want to hear it.

I raid Mum's expensive toiletries, despite a niggling suspicion that they were probably gifts from Mark, and take a long soak in the bath. As hard as I try to focus on the amazing birthday my dad has put together, my mind won't stop wandering to the scattered mess that is my family. I don't know what stings the most: the fact that Mum has been seeing Mark again or that Dad is under the illusion that everything is all right. Everything I once believed about the people who raised me is falling apart at the seams.

Years ago, when we were maybe ten, Deb asked me a hypothetical question as we were walking to school one day: "If one of your parents had to die and you had to choose which one, who would it be?"

I refused to make the choice, but when she goaded me into it, I picked Dad. I imagined life without each of my parents, and things always looked a little bit easier with Mum still around. I thought that if Mum were gone, there'd be no one to take care of me, no one I could confide in, no one I could trust.

But I had it all wrong. Because I never imagined Mum would leave me. I never thought she'd lie to me. I thought that if she had to, she'd do whatever it took to save me. I never would have believed I could be so wrong. And I never could have imagined that my dad would fill those needs.

Chapter Twenty-Two

L ATER THAT MORNING I HEAD down to Bubble City to see Deb. The village looks a little bit brighter today, as if the dark cloud of fear and tragedy that hangs over us has lifted just a hair. There are three ambulances outside Bubble City. Three more people are leaving for Elmington, free of the virus and free to resume their lives. Every day the number of survivors increases, while the number of new cases falls. We've turned a corner, passed the peak of Aiden's bell curve. None of us is out of danger yet, but every day, that danger diminishes a little bit more. Another week or so, and I can finally feel safe again.

The one fly in this otherwise sweet-smelling ointment is that, once the virus is done with us, Aiden will be too. We've had news of isolated outbreaks around the country and overseas, all quickly contained, they say, but at some point he'll be called to another community in need, and away he'll go. I only hope I'll get the chance to say goodbye.

Okay, so that's not my only hope, but I feel guilty about my other hopes when there are so many things I should be hoping for instead… like people's survival, like this ending quickly. But the recent turn has me thinking about the future again. And that has me thinking of Aiden, wondering what it would be like to feel him against me, like I almost did the other day, of maybe (*oh, please, maybe*) seeing him in real life, without that stupid suit. I don't even care what he looks like, although I'm curious, of course. I want to be able to touch his skin, to feel a real, warm person, not a plastic-covered being. I want to talk to him and see his facial expressions. I want to know everything about him. I've never known this intense kind of feeling before, not even with Ro. Ro was exciting, and loving him was daring, but the desire to connect with Aiden is different. Inside my gloves, my fingers burn with the need to touch him. I rub them together and try to shake away the thoughts, but two steps later they come flooding back in.

I float down to Bubble City on my cloud of fantasy and sign in at the visitor check-in tent, as I've done every day since last Thursday. Visiting Deb here is still strange, but it's becoming almost routine. At least here we can talk, unlike at her house, and now she has her phone back things feel a bit more normal. Wandering around to the back of the enclosure, I text her to let her know I'm here, then wait for her to come out of the Low Prob tent. Yesterday, we didn't talk about Aiden, but I don't think I can keep my feelings to myself much longer. Besides, she's bound to work it out for herself sooner or later. I wonder if she'll approve.

A few minutes later my phone pings, but when I look over to the Low Prob exit, Deb isn't there. I spin around until I see her: Deb is standing beside the door of Tent Two. Inside my mask, my face prickles. Deb has been upgraded.

What happened? I text, scurrying over to the fence that separates me from the next enclosure.

Even from this distance, I can see her face collapse into tears. *Tommy's in the Care Ward*, she replies.

He's sick?

She nods, reading my text. *Now Dad and me are high-risk. Why?*

She looks up, and I see her answer. She looks paler than usual. She looks more than tired. I try to console myself with the thought that, if she were sick, she'd be in the Care Ward too. But I can see in her expressions that she's watching her fate unfold, and I pray she can't see it in mine. I want to tear away the fences that stand between us and run to hug my best friend, to give her some crumb of reassurance and compassion. But I can't. This stupid virus has built walls around each of us, leaving us all to fend for ourselves. If I could have one wish for my birthday, one perfect gift, it would be to hug Deb, to let her know someone cares.

I have to go back in now, she texts. Then she looks up and gives me a weak wave.

"Oh, Peps," I whisper, because I don't know what else to do. I can't tell her what I want to say, and that's, "Please don't leave me. Please don't die."

Deb disappears back inside the tent, and a second later my phone pings again. *Happy Birthday,* is all it says.

Back at home, I try to distract myself with a *Pinky and the Brain* extravaganza, but all I can think about is Deb. When something at the window catches my attention, I turn to find Aiden waving at me. For a second I'm startled, as if I'd forgotten there were other people inhabiting my planet. He gestures toward the front door, and I take it he wants to come in. I grab my mask and gloves and all but race into the hallway, all at once thrilled to have company and terrified he's come bearing bad news about Deb.

When I throw open the door, he gives me a smile. If he has news, it's not going to be bad. He hurries inside, and I wait for him to ask if I'm all right. If I had a penny for every time someone has asked me that in the last few weeks, I could buy a fancy neon sign that blinks, "What do you think?" But Aiden doesn't say anything. Instead, he hands me a bag, and even though I can see right away what it contains, I can't believe it. It's a real, proper bar of chocolate in a purple, oblong wrapper.

"Where did you… ?" I start to ask, but Aiden holds a gloved finger up to his face mask and shakes his head. I hold the chocolate in my hands, feeling its weight, something solid and real, familiar. Then I take it out of the bag and run my hand over the smooth wrapper. It feels like satin to my touch, as if the nerve-endings in my fingers have never felt anything so exquisite before.

"Happy birthday," he says.

"Thank you," I squeak, although it comes out as nothing more than a whisper.

"Well, aren't you going to try it?"

I peel back the wrapper and expose the first row of chocolate. Taking care to touch only the foil, I lift my mask, placing my teeth around a single square, and bite.

"Go on," Aiden says, "eat it."

I pull the square of chocolate into my mouth, pressing it upward with my tongue, the sweet flavor tiptoeing across my taste buds and the milky goo oozing against the roof of my mouth. It's not the same as I remember… it's better. It's the taste of real life, of everything I've been missing and of everything I've lost. And as the chocolate dissolves on my tongue, the numbness of the last few weeks falls away too. Something explodes inside me, igniting every cell in my body.

Heat rises in my face, and my jaw trembles. All of a sudden, the kindness around me is overwhelming. I gasp in a breath, trying to hold it all together.

And then Aiden holds something else toward me. It's a square bag of folded yellow fabric that I recognize instantly.

"I'm a Community Liaison?"

He shakes his head. "This is sort of contraband. You can't let anyone see it."

"What's it for then?" I ask.

"Emergencies."

"Okay," I say, not grasping what he's telling me. "What kinds of emergencies?"

"Well," he says, handing me a folded suit. "Emergencies like me."

The ache of desire flares up as I understand what he's saying. I shake out the suit, climbing into it as quickly as I can. I secure the hood and sleeves, pulling up my mask around it and snapping the goggles on top. All the while, Aiden gives instructions. I laugh at the irony of hurrying to get dressed to touch someone, especially when I am sure I look like a giant, wrinkled lemon in this oversized suit. But finally I'm ready. Aiden looks nervous, and I feel it too. With this distance between us, we are safe. We both know that, and we both know that being here like this is strictly forbidden. Inside my suit, I feel protected. I have nothing to lose. But Aiden does. I wonder if I've asked too much of him. I wonder if I should let him go, while he still has the chance to go back.

But then Aiden steps forward and, without hesitation, wraps his arms around me. He pulls me against the cool, lifeless fabric of his suit, but underneath I'm aware of his body—living, vibrant, real—and that single moment of human touch unleashes everything that has built up inside me. A moan escapes from my chest, followed by a whimper and another until I can't stop. My whole body convulses as sob after sob disappears into the dampening fabric of my mask.

I'm aware of his hands against my back and his arms bearing my weight. The cool surface of his face shield rests against the top of my covered head. I wrap my arms around him and pull him toward me, desperate for the warmth of human contact, of someone who cares. But I can't feel it. He is there, I can feel the shape of him, even his strength, but I cannot feel the person, the human being. In that second I want to rip his suit away, just to prove he's really in there.

And then his gloved hands rest on my masked cheeks. He lifts up my face until I'm looking into the space where his mouth should be. Through our face shields, I can see his eyes—his tiger eyes—locked on mine. I can read in them the frustration and agony I feel. He wants to know too. He wants to know I am real; he wants to feel that I am a person, not a number, not a statistic, not part of an assignment. But we both know we can't do that. There are only a few thin layers of fabric between us, but it may as well be a continent. The quarantine that keeps me from the outside world may not be physical, but the barrier that keeps me from Aiden is. In time, both will be lifted, but only time and fortune will dictate whether I am here to witness it.

Aiden holds my face and rests his face shield against mine. I lift my hands and place them on the sides of his, then I stretch onto my tiptoes until our eyes are inches apart. All I'd have to do is lift our masks, and I could kiss him. The only thing stopping us now is some fabric and plastic. It would be so easy, but that would be Level III contact. Dangerous. Contagious or not, I can't risk his life, and I know that he will not risk mine.

And in that moment, even through the suits and masks, something in him touches me. It's barely a fingerprint of a feeling on my insides, but it's there, and maybe it will be enough to sustain me until this is over. And maybe then, this thing that has bloomed between us will have a chance. I start counting down the days until I can find out.

Chapter Twenty-Three

T HAT NIGHT, I CRAWL INTO bed and pull the covers over my head, trying to block out this awful world and think about the small light of hope that has flickered on inside me. But I can't erase from my memory the anguished face of my friend or the helplessness I feel. It's only once I'm alone in the dark and quiet that an idea begins to form. In my vast repertoire of very bad ideas, even I know this one ranks among the worst. I push it aside and try to go to sleep, but the idea won't leave me alone. By the time I hear Dad come up to bed, I have never been more clear on what I need to do.

When I'm sure Dad is asleep, I creep down the stairs to the kitchen. The weather report's been threatening a storm all day, and through the kitchen windows I can tell it looks darker than usual. I'm not sure if the darkness will help or hinder my plans to move through the village undetected. I grab a bucket and make a vinegar solution, dunking a clean cloth into the water and rubbing it over my face, neck, and any other exposed skin. Then I dunk my hands into the water and scrub under my nails, rubbing my palms in determined circles and trying to keep my thudding heart quiet. When I'm done, I creep to the back door where Dad has hung his suit.

What I'm doing goes strictly against both protocol and

common sense, and yet it feels strongly, urgently necessary. Deb said I should use my strengths, and all this time I've been sifting through my positive qualities, trying to find something valuable I could use. I've been looking in all the wrong places. If there's one thing I'm good at, it's sneaking out to places I'm not supposed to be. Now Deb has provided the impetus, and Aiden has supplied the means. All that's left is for me to execute the plan.

And not get caught.

I find the box where Dad keeps his suits and am dismayed to see there's only one left. I make a note to find Aiden in the morning to see if he can snag a couple more. I wouldn't put it past Dad to reuse suits if it was the only way he could do his visits. I slip off the Community Liaison badge, making a careful note of exactly how he's placed it so I can put it back the same way when I return. He's bound to notice if it's not exactly right, but by then, I'll have already got what I want, and it will be worth whatever consequences I have to face. I hope.

Then I slip into the suit Aiden brought for me, aware that I'm reusing it, but rationalizing that I haven't been outside in it or in contact with anyone infectious. I clip on Dad's name tag, rehearsing in my mind that the "J" in *J. Syddall* will stand for *Jemma* if anyone asks. I go through the procedure of covering my feet and head and taping my gloves to my sleeves—not an easy task to do single-handed. I double-check my work, pressing down any seams to test for gaps, then crack open the front door, pausing to check for any stirring from upstairs, and step out into the night.

The first drops of rain from the threatened storm have splashed the parched street, landing in heavy splotches like the spots on a Dalmatian. The main road is deserted; there are no villagers around at this hour and very few workers. Even the television crews by the barricade have long since packed up and moved on to newer news. The small amount of action will be concentrated around Bubble City. As I approach, there is no sign of Aiden, and for once, I'm glad. I don't want to run into the one person who might recognize me in this suit. I don't want to get him into any trouble, and I also don't want him to know that I've betrayed his trust.

As I get close to Bubble City, I take a deep breath, the air already stale inside my mask, and press back my shoulders, striding toward the entrance as if I have every right to be there. If I look like I don't know what I'm doing, I'm bound to give myself away. I head for the entrance tent, where I've watched the other workers go in, nodding to a passing medic, but not making eye contact.

Inside, two medical personnel are checking one another's suits for gaps and tears before going inside. My online research verified what I'd already observed: Medics work in pairs. I walk up ready with my alibi.

"Hi guys," I say, trying sound as if I'm just "one of the team." "Sorry to bother you, but my partner hasn't turned up, and I need to get in to see a patient. Would you mind giving me a quick once-over?"

I raise my arms and turn my back, partly to give them no option but to do as I ask, and partly so they can't see my face. I hear a grunt of agreement, and one of the medics circles around me. She pauses to read Dad's Community Liaison badge but doesn't ask any questions. When she says, "All clear, Syddall," and gives me a thumbs-up, I follow them through the decontamination basin. They continue on to the Care Ward, and I slip through the makeshift gate into Tent Two.

The tent is dimly lit, but I can make out three neat rows of low, narrow beds, each with a chair on one side and a small table on the other. Beneath each sleeping occupant is the lumpy silhouette of stored belongings. The whole place has the feel of accommodation for a cut-rate camping holiday: basic, but not as scary as I'd expected.

Just inside the door is what I take to be a nurse's station of sorts. One suited medic lolls in a chair. From the rhythmic movement of his suit, I can tell he's dozing. I consider waking him and taking advantage of his disorientation, brazenly flashing my badge before carrying on. I opt instead for the safer option: sidle past and hope he doesn't stir.

I walk the rows of beds, pausing at each with a concerned cock of my head. I recognize Millie Talbot curled in a ball, her thin hair splayed around her. In the dim light, I can see her lips moving. She's dreaming. A pang of sympathy stabs at my chest. I can only imagine the images that dance through her dreams at night, her future so uncertain. I rest my hand on her covered foot and give it a gentle squeeze. *There but for the grace of Lady Luck go I.*

I move from bed to bed, sealing my heart in a protective case so that each stab of guilt and sadness can't reach it. I know everyone here, and any one of them could be me. But I can't think about that now. I have to find Deb. I hurry up one row of beds, but she's not there. Halfway down the next row, I find Mr. Elliot. That's good, I think. It means she's probably close by. I'm about to move on when Mr. Elliot turns over in his sleep. As I glance back, I see his eyes are open and staring up at mine. In the pale, yellow light, it's not clear if he recognizes me. I hesitate, wondering if I should move on. It's enough time for him to register who I am. He pushes up onto one elbow, and the sound of him rustling against the sheets rushes through the tent like a gale-force wind. I put my gloved finger to my face mask and urge him not to say anything.

"What are you doing here?" he hisses.

I duck down beside his bed, heart thudding in my chest like it's trying to escape its protective case and bolt for freedom. I can't allow Mr. Elliot to give me away now I've made it this far. I point to the badge on my chest and tease the lie to the tip of my tongue, the one that tells him I'm supposed to be here, that this is all aboveboard and nothing for him to worry about. But that lie won't come.

"I want to see Deb," I say. "Please don't say anything. I just need…" But I can't tell him any of the reasons I need to do this because that would make them real. I just want to see the friend I've known so long I can't remember not knowing her. I just want to give her a hug, as if everything is normal. I just want to let her know that someone cares. "Please?"

Mr. Elliot considers me for a moment. He nods.

"Where is she?" I whisper, looking down the row of beds for her familiar silhouette. But when I look back at Mr. Elliot, I get my answer. A dark haze falls across his face, and in his eyes I see a swirl of hope, longing, resignation, and sadness. In the center of it all is a look of deep fear that makes goose pimples spring up on my arms, despite the heat trapped inside my suit.

He glances over my shoulder. Behind me is a gated exit with a fenced walkway beyond. It leads to the Care Ward.

Chapter Twenty-Four

I STAND IN THE FOOT BASIN outside the entrance to the Care Ward, the rain now pelting down so that it streams across the front of my visor, blurring my vision. Still I can't move, not yet. I swish my feet in the disinfectant pool, back and forth, back and forth, delaying the moment when I will have to step forward. My stomach starts to tighten, and I can hear the shallow rasps of my breath inside my mask. My heart begins to race, and suddenly my senses flicker to life, as if waking up from a long hibernation. I'm aware of every part of my surroundings: the foggy view through my face mask, the scent of my own breath inside my suit, the heat rising from my skin, the sound of my blood pulsing through my veins, and the pattering of rain on my hood. Suddenly, everything feels real, as if I've been living behind a gauze curtain, seeing everything around me but not being a part of it. It's as if I'm waking up from a long and disturbing dream, only to realize it was real. It *is* real. This is real. I am here, alive, and my best friend is in the tent. Her condition is unknown.

I step forward out of the basin and through the entrance of the Care Ward tent. There is no air of a camping trip here.

The well-lit interior is draped with see-through plastic sheeting, dividing the tent into individual bubbles. Inside the compartments, medical personnel move around like blue-gray shadow puppets, tending to the sick, their motions accompanied by the beep and whir of medical equipment. The air is heavy with illness, although I can only sense—rather than feel—the heat and smell through my suit. But I can hear, and I can see. I try to shut out the moans and cries of once-familiar voices, try to focus on finding Deb.

Some inner instinct draws me to the end of the ward where there is less activity. I'm not sure if it's logic that tells me the newly diagnosed need less care, or if my fear of being discovered drives me away from the action, but in the last bubble in the row, I find Deb.

She is sprawled across the narrow bed, dark hair plastered to her damp face. Dark circles bruise the flesh beneath her eyes, the only hint of color in her pale, waxy face. It seems to have happened so fast, but I register now how weak she appeared this morning, how quickly she hurried back into the tent. She knew that she was sick and chose not to let on.

In Deb's arm, an intravenous drip bubbles in medicine and fluids—not a cure, but a balm, something to help her rest, perhaps to give her more strength to fight this. The narrow tube provides a tenuous connection to hope. It's a hope I find hard to feel, and yet the alternative—letting go, giving up—is even harder to face.

I perch on the edge of Deb's bed, trying hard not to move her. I rest my gloved hand over hers and watch. I don't know what to do next. I came to offer comfort, to give her hope that things will be okay, but now I feel helpless.

Beneath my hand, Deb's twitches. She opens her eyes and looks at me from under heavy lids. It takes a moment before her eyes flash with a brief light of recognition and surprise, and the barest hint of a smile flickers in the corner of her pale, dry mouth.

"Hi," I whisper, not sure if she can hear me.

Her red-rimmed eyes flicker toward the metal bedside stand where a plastic cup of water sits. I'm suddenly nervous. I don't know how to lift her, how to hold her so she can sip. If anyone sees me, they'll know I'm not supposed to be here. But I don't care. My friend needs me, and I have to do the best I can, even if it's not perfect.

I prop Deb on an extra pillow and lift the cup to her lips. Even through my gloves and suit I can feel the heat radiating off her. She closes her eyes, and her pale tongue flickers over her teeth, barely forming the words, "Thanks," and, "Salty." I wait for her to smile again, but she doesn't. My chest tightens as reality closes in, the possibility that I could lose my friend.

I can't let the thoughts get to me. Not now. I came here for Deb, and losing it now won't help her one bit. I need Deb to fight. I need her to stay alive.

I slide off the bed and crouch down beside her, moving as close to her as I can.

"Hey, Peps," I whisper, and her eyes flicker open. They track across the ceiling of the tent, where the rain is now hammering down, until they find me. "I have an idea." It's a bit of a fib, but it might buy me some time to work out something to say, because the only idea I have is to grab Deb and sprint from here as fast as I can. But for once, running away won't get me what I want. It won't save Deb. "When you get to Elmington," I say at last, "I'll give you twenty quid if you can get a video of yourself bouncing on the duke's bed."

Deb gives a small laugh that turns immediately into a cough. She sucks in a breath and closes her eyes again. I know

I should go. I thought seeing her might help, but now I think I'm making it worse.

I clamber to my feet, taking care not to snag the suit on anything. I rest my hand on Deb's thin arm and squeeze. I'm overcome with the urge to take off my suit and just sit with Deb, like two normal people. I know I can't, but the thin layers of fabric create a chasm between us, and just for a moment I want to bridge it. I want to hold my friend's hand and tell her it will be okay, but I'm no longer able to do either of those things. I lean down and rest my head on Deb's chest. It's the closest thing to hugging her I can manage. When I pull back, Deb smiles at me, and I can tell she's trying to say something. I lean in to hear. Her breath rasps in her chest, fighting to make its way out. Deb struggles to gasp enough air to tell me what she needs to say. Finally, it comes. "I'm glad you came," she says.

No matter what happens now, so am I.

"I'll see you soon," I say.

Deb starts to smile, but her face contorts. She gasps for air, and her whole body spasms with a wracking cough. She reaches for another breath, but it won't come. Her eyes fly open and fix on me, like she's begging me to help her, but I don't know what to do. Beside her bed, a machine starts to beep, a red light flashing out a warning. I hold onto Deb's hand, urging her to breathe, trying to soothe her with useful words. The next second, we're surrounded by a flurry of yellow, pushing past me to reach for Deb. As the medics yell instructions back and forth, maneuvering Deb and giving her a shot, her hand slips from mine. In the space between our fingers, Deb's fear pulses. I see it in her twisted face and body, and I know: I have to get out of here, and I have to make sure I never come back. I have to stop being a rebel if I'm going to survive.

I take a last look at Deb. Her eyes are closed now, and her body rests peacefully in the bed once again. Her chest rises and falls in a smooth rhythm. "You're going to be okay," I whisper. *Please tell me you're going to be okay.*

I turn and hurry for the exit, my own breath coming in short gasps. Sharp tears sting the corners of my eyes, blurring my vision, but I fight them back. As I reach for the gate, I hear a shout behind me. I turn to see a medic running my way. Now I'm in trouble.

"What are you doing?" she says, but I can't answer. She points to another exit at the front of the tent, and I realize my mistake. I was about to go out the way I came in, back through Tent Two, back into a group of healthy people. I shake my head and hurry toward the front exit. I don't turn back. I don't want to think about what could have happened if she hadn't stopped me. What my stupidity might have caused.

Chapter Twenty-Five

T HE WATER IN THE DECONTAMINATION shower pours over me, the sound almost deafening inside my suit. When I close my eyes, all I can see is Deb fighting to breathe. *You have to keep fighting*, I think. *You have to keep breathing, Deb. You have to get out of this terrible place.* I'm supposed to keep my chin up, or something, try to stay positive, stiff upper lip, keep up the old British spirit, or whatever, but instead I want to crawl into a dark hole and stay there until all this is over. Unfortunately, that's exactly what will happen to me if I don't stop messing around. I'm furious with myself for the risk I took coming here, not only to myself, but to the other people I could have harmed. What if the medic hadn't stopped me? What if I'd carried the virus back into Tent Two? What if people had died because of my stupidity? But all this is outweighed by my moment with Deb. I may have been an idiot, but at least I got to see my friend. I push down the hissing voice in my head that keeps adding *for the last time* and try to keep a sunny picture of Deb leaving for Elmington instead.

When the decon timer goes off, I tumble outside, feeling as if I'm fighting through treacle. The rain pours down, turning the grass beneath my feet into a greasy mess. From somewhere in the distance, the steady rumble of thunder growls like something big and ominous moving my way. I almost laugh at the idea. Nothing could be bigger and more ominous than this. But the thought of Bubble City turning into a quagmire scares me, all those medics trying to work with mud and water underfoot. I think about the rattle of damp breath in Deb's chest, and the worsening storm seems suddenly more dangerous.

Despite the torrents pouring around me, I don't want to go home. Maybe if I stay out in the rain, it will wash away the virus, wash away the tight knot of fear that sits inside my chest. It's wishful thinking, but it's all I have.

I turn toward the church, drawn in by a force beyond my own will. I stumble through the lych-gate and make my way down the mossy stone path toward the Dead Syddalls. The grass in the churchyard is taller than I've ever seen it before. Without the groundsman's constant mowing, lush green weeds push their heads up toward the sky, waiting for the chance to scatter their seeds, to spread from one small patch of fertile ground to the next. Away from the commotion of Bubble City, the silence of the churchyard presses softly around me. I can no longer escape death; it's everywhere—clawing, fighting, crying out for attention. But here, death seems peaceful and gentle, orderly. Here the dead disappear quietly back into the earth, the natural cycle of life turning as it should.

There are no new graves in the cemetery now. The tradition of saying goodbye, of gathering to lay loved ones to rest has been replaced. The dead leave our village in silence, in government-issued bags, in narrow plumes of smoke. There's no way to pay respects, to mark the passing, to let them know that someone cared. There's no way for the dead to be remembered. Everyone will be forgotten.

But when I reach the far end of the churchyard, where my

grandparents are buried, I find the grass trimmed and fresh flowers on both graves, their petaled heads drooping under the weight of the rain. I look down the row to see if maybe some good person has been and placed flowers on all the graves, but no, the flowers are only for my grandparents and Auntie Sandra. There's only one person in the village that would have done this. All this time I thought Dad was trying to clip my wings, to stop me from living my life, when in reality he was still feeling the pain of his loss and trying to protect himself. As I stare at the flowers, everything I once thought I knew about who I am and where I come from starts to unravel. I don't know if I have time now to put it back together again, but I have to try.

As I push through the long grass, a familiar gravestone looms in the dim light. Holding the tall stems aside, I crouch to see the inscription I've read so many times before. But this time the words jolt me: *EMMOTT CHARLOTTE SYDDALL, 1879-1961*. It's my great-great-grandma Syddall's grave, but the sight of my own name etched into the limestone loosens the heavy knot I've been carrying in my chest. I try to suck in courage, urging myself to be brave, chanting the mantras that I should be grateful, that I'm lucky to be healthy, lucky to be alive, that so many others have it worse than I do. They're all valid, but none of them ring true. I let go of the knot and gasp out a sob. I cry for Deb and for everything that's happened. And I cry for what is still to come.

I stumble back to the house, suddenly feeling cold inside my suit and needing the safety and comfort of home. Even though I've already deconned, I go through our agreed protocol, quietly stripping off my gloves, suit, and mask in the back garden and splashing through a tray of bleach water before taking off my shoes and creeping into the house. I use only one elbow to open the doors and head straight for the shower, where I strip off the rest of my clothes, drop them in the bottom of the tub, and shower off in the hottest water I can stand, hoping the noise doesn't wake Dad. It's one thing to stay protected from the possibility of disease, but now that I've taken myself into the heart of the illness, into Bubble City, I can't risk bringing the virus home. I'd never forgive myself if I put Dad at risk.

Once I'm clean and showered, I return Dad's badge and hide my suit behind the boot bin. I tiptoe into the kitchen, keeping my ears trained in case Dad catches me. But the house is silent. I ease open the kitchen door and poke my head in. There's an abandoned bowl of soup on the table. I strain to listen for evidence that Dad is up and about, but all is quiet. I don't feel like eating anything, but in the pit of my stomach is a deep hollow that's calling for something comforting. Even as I open a new can of soup and stick a bowl in the microwave to heat, I know soup isn't what I need to fill the empty spot. I'm not sure that hole will ever be filled again.

When the soup's ready, I carry my tray through to the living room, opening the door with my hip and going in backward so the door can't swing back and hit me. As I turn to maneuver myself around, I almost drop the tray anyway. On the couch, curled into a ball, a blanket draped over him, is Dad. My heart sinks. How long has he been there? Did he hear me leave or check in on me and find me missing? I'm going to be in a lot of trouble if he realizes I've been out.

He looks as if he's sleeping, so I try to sneak out without waking him, but with the tray in my hands, I can't open the door from this side. I look for a place to set it down, but as I do, I hear movement from the couch.

"Em?" Dad asks. "Is that you?"

"Sorry," I say. "I didn't mean to wake you."

He grunts. His eyes are open, but barely. "Where've you been?"

There doesn't seem to be any point in lying. My world has shrunk to the point where nothing I do can stay secret for very long. The village grapevine is no more than a shoot now, but one way or another Dad will hear or work out where I've been. I find this new need for honesty both painful and refreshing.

"I've been to Bubble City," I say. "To the tents. I went to see Deb."

Dad frowns. "At this hour?"

I tell him she's in the Care Ward, and I see him piece together the bits I've left out. "I just wanted to see her," I say. "It's horrible in there, Dad."

And then I can't stop talking. I tell Dad about the tents and about Deb in her bubble. I tell him about how she looked and about the suited medics caring for her. "It's like she's all alone in there. Nobody can touch her; no one can comfort her." My voice catches in my throat, and I wait for Dad's outrage to come. He won't let this continue. Dad will get this wrong righted. But he doesn't move.

Now that I look closer, I can see he's a bit pale. "Dad?" I set the tray on the floor and move in to get a closer look. "What's the matter?"

He holds his hand up, telling me not to come any closer. "It's nothing," he says. "I'm just tired."

A trickle of cold fear runs up my body. "Do you feel ill?" I ask.

He shakes his head. "I just need a bit of rest. I'll be fine."

"You don't look fine."

"I'm okay. Honestly."

I hesitate, wondering if he's telling me the truth. Given the stress he's put himself under, the constant running around to the villagers, he must be exhausted. Maybe he is just tired; it's the middle of the night, after all. But even as I convince myself he just needs some sleep, that dark hollow inside me opens a little bit wider, assuring me I am wrong.

"Em?" Dad asks as I reach for the door. I turn, waiting for the part where he flings in a last admonishment. He doesn't open his eyes, but behind his mask there's a hint of a smile on his face. "You did a good thing tonight," he says, and then he falls back asleep.

Chapter Twenty-Six

Tuesday, August 16

B Y MORNING, IT'S CLEAR TO me that Dad isn't "just tired." He's still not up by the time I finish breakfast, and when I poke my head around his bedroom door, he yells at me not to come in. In the glimpse I catch of his face, I can see he's pale and sweating. I can't leave him, so I grab my mask and gloves and venture in with a glass of water and a damp cloth.

Close up, I can see he looks terrible, and when I put the cloth to his forehead, he flinches as if he's been burned. I dab at his face as gently as I can, until he relaxes into the bed.

"Dad?"

He opens his eyes. "Don't touch me," he says. "Stay away."

"I'm protected, Dad. It's okay. Do you want me to get the medic?"

He only moves his head a hair, but I can tell he's saying no.

I know I should ignore him. I know that at the first sign of any symptoms, he should go to Bubble City. But if he has the virus, he'll be moved to the Care Ward. I can't let him go there. I can't let them take my dad to that place, so he can lie there alone, like Deb.

"I can look after you here," I say.

"No," he says. "I have to go in. Just let me rest a bit first."

He closes his eyes. A moment later, he is asleep again.

Downstairs I rummage through the supply box until I find more soup. In identical plain sachets, I find Broccoli and Stilton or Minestrone. I opt for the latter, as it sounds more like something you'd give a sick person. I fill the kettle and wait for the water to boil so I can turn the small pile of brown dust in the bottom of the bowl into nourishing soup for my dad.

He can't get sick. That can't happen to us. Dad's job in the village is to make sure everyone else is okay, and he can't do that if he's ill. I have to do everything I can to boost his immunity, to get him through this tiredness and back on his feet again. But even as I try to convince myself he'll be okay, the terrible reality wriggles into my brain like a serpent. I try to keep it back, but it finds the smallest gap in my defenses and worms its way in. My dad has the virus; I know it.

I catch my breath and shake the thought from my head. I can't give up on him. For once in my life, I need to be the best daughter I can be. I suit up, and when the soup's ready, I carry it upstairs along with a hot Lemsip. I know a cold powder won't stop this virus, but it might make Dad feel better.

I perch on the bed and, when he opens his eyes, I smile. "Soup's up," I say.

"I'm not hungry."

"I know, but have a bit anyway. It'll make you feel better."

His brow furrows, like he's about to assert his authority on the matter of the soup, but then it softens. The corners of his mouth turn up for an instant, not exactly a smile, but an acknowledgement of sorts. I help him sit up and prop pillows behind him to make him comfortable.

"Don't fuss," he says. "I'm fine."

"I will fuss if I choose, and you're not really in any shape to stop me."

The smile flutters again, and he takes the spoon from me. He takes a sip and lets it trickle down his throat.

"It's nice," he says.

"Well, I know it's not, but I appreciate the sentiment. Maybe I can raid the cellar and make some real minestrone."

He sips some more then hands me the spoon. A minute later, he slides down in the bed and closes his eyes. "Don't tell your mother," he whispers. "Not yet."

Personally, burdening Mum with this news is exactly what I want to do, but Dad and I are a team now, and I feel strongly about respecting his wishes. I promise him I'll tell her everything's okay, until it's time to tell her how *not* okay we are.

"Get some rest," I say. "I'll check on you later."

That night I get a text message from Mrs. Ashton. It's all proper and grammatically correct. It probably took her ages to type.

Dear Emmott, it reads. *I have been trying to reach your dad, but he hasn't responded. Is everything all right? Yours, Andrea Ashton.*

My heart sinks. The problem with being a rock for the village is that, when the rock becomes submerged, people notice. It's only a matter of time before people realize Dad is not out and about and piece together that something is wrong. I'm not ready to let him go—I might never be ready to let him go—so I have to keep him hidden as long as I can.

He's fine, I type back. *Phone problems. Can I give him a message?*

Ages later a response comes back. *Dear Emmott, Please*

thank your Dad for the veg. The smallest thing can give us hope in the goodness of mankind and for the possibility of the future. He is a good man and you are very much like him. Andrea.

I sink onto the bed and read it again until Mrs. Ashton's words start to stir something inside me. It seems ridiculous that a simple bag of carrots could prompt such a response in her, but after a while I start to realize it has little to do with the carrots themselves, although I'm sure they'll be enjoyed and appreciated. It's about the gesture. Dad's been right all along. It's about showing people that someone cares about what happens to them, that they're not going through this tunnel of hell completely alone, that the smallest things can make a difference. All this time I've fought against my dad, never understanding the thing that comes naturally to him, the thing that he's always understood and I haven't. But I keep getting stuck on the same fear. Being a saint might have kept my dad alive in his spirit, but I'm terrified that it could ultimately kill him. I'm afraid it might also kill me. I am not speaking in metaphors. The possibility of death has been all around me, but suddenly it's taken a few steps closer, and I am afraid.

Mrs. Ashton is wrong about me being like my dad. I'm not like him at all. My dad is a much better person, and that gives me little comfort in any way.

The next morning, I wake to the sound of someone calling my name.

"Dad," I gasp, clambering out of bed.

I fling open the door and flick on the light. There's a dark patch of moisture on Dad's pillow, and his hair has shrunk into tight, sodden curls. As I move toward him, he groans and thrashes his head from side to side.

"Liz," he murmurs. "Liz." After all that's happened, he's still calling for Mum. I feel a pang of guilt that I haven't told her yet that he's ill.

"It's me. Emmott," I say. "It's okay. I'm here."

"Emm… ," he says.

"I'm here, Dad."

His breathing is labored, and when he opens his eyes, they roll away from me.

"Go," he says. "Please, Em. Go."

"Go where, Dad? For the medic?"

His head lolls to one side.

"I'll go," I tell him. "I'll be back."

"No!" He grabs for my arm, but I'm out of reach.

"Dad…"

"Emmott," he says. His eyes range around my face until some inner force pulls them to mine. The ferocity of his gaze causes me to pull back. "You have to go."

"Go where, Dad? Where do you want me to go?"

"Away," he says. "London."

I don't understand what he's telling me at first, until I realize he doesn't mean leave his room; he means leave the village. "I can't, Dad."

"After," he says, his voice growing weaker. "After this. Go. Live." He forces a weak smile that rips out my heart and leaves a gaping ache where it used to be. "Proud of you," he whispers.

"I will, Dad," I say. "I promise. But not yet. I'm not leaving you alone."

"I can't leave *you* alone," he says.

In that instant, I see a flash of the future. Without Dad, I will be alone here, in the one place I vowed I would not die. And if I fall ill here, who will take care of me? I think about Deb and know what would happen to me. All these years Dad has worked to build our community, pulling everyone together for the good of the whole, and now it's every man for himself, and he knows it. Now the only person who will be there for me is me.

Dad drifts away again. I'm not sure if he even knows what he's just said to me. But I'm not going to run. I have to stay here and take care of him as best I can, for as long as I can.

That night, I'm suiting up again when the outside gate squeaks. For a brief instant I hope it's Aiden, before I remember how very, very bad that would be. He may have massaged a few rules for Dad and me, but I'm certain he wouldn't break this one. If he knows Dad is infected, he'll have to turn him in. I creep to the window and pull back the curtain just enough to peek out. I wait for the doorbell to ring, but then the gate squeaks again. I peer down in the dim light to see who it is. It's not Aiden; it's Mrs. Glover. Mrs. Glover with the reputation for getting her nose into everyone's business. *Bugger.* The last place I need her nose is in our business.

When I'm sure she's long gone, I creep down and open the front door to see if she's left a note or something. Even though she's known my family for years, it's no guarantee that she won't turn us in if she thinks we're a threat. It's not a fault of Mrs. Glover; it's the way things are now.

There is a note taped to the top of a paper bag. I pull both inside and close the door. Inside the bag is a bottle of cod liver oil and a small bag of what appears to be dried flowers. *This is my great-grandmother's cure-all tea*, the note reads. *It's worked for me so far, and I hope it works for you. Give your dad my best wishes, and let me know if there's anything I can do.*

In the silence of the house, all I can hear is my own breath moving slowly in and out, but what I feel is the slightest invisible sensation of knowing that someone else knows about my dad, and that someone else cares. I'm not alone, and knowing that helps me do what's necessary to keep my dad—and myself—alive.

When Dad shows no sign of improvement, I doubt my decision to keep him at home. In my brief daily calls and texts to Mum, I keep telling her we're okay, filling her in on other news from around the village instead. I rationalize that she's too far away to do anything and that telling her will only make her worry. But, if Dad doesn't get better soon, I'll have to tell her the truth. I don't relish that conversation, and so I cling to the hope that Dad will pull through.

Half a dozen times a day, I go through the procedure of donning my protective suit and taking care of him. When my supply of suits runs out, I develop a new protocol to wash them off in bleach solution and hang them up to dry on the shower rail. I know it's a risky venture, but when it comes to saner options, I have none.

Once I'm dressed, I rummage through the medicine cabinet, looking for anything that might help. I find vitamins and cough syrup, plus a half-used container of antibiotics. I gather them together and take them to Dad.

He looks afraid when I open the door. "It's okay, Dad," I tell him. "It's just me."

He forces a smile. I put my double-gloved hand on his forehead and brush his hair aside the way Mum used to when I was little. I know it won't feel the same to him with all the protective layers I have, but any touch has got to be better than total isolation. I prop him up and feed him more soup, then lay out the medicines for him to choose. I'm not sure he's alert enough to make this decision, but I'm too afraid to make it alone. When he points to them all, I know this is all a mistake. The one thing I know I must do is the very last thing I *want* to do.

"We should take you in," I say.

He shakes his head. "Not leaving you," he mumbles.

"You need to get proper medicine, Dad."

His face softens into a gentle smile. "No point. Just need you."

"I need you too, Dad," I tell him, and it feels like the most truth I've ever shared with him. In this giant mess of a village, we are all we have, and we just need to hold on as long as we can.

I give him the vitamins and an antibiotic and stay with him until he goes to sleep. I towel his face, and when he looks somewhat comfortable, I leave him alone and go to start the process of removing and decontaminating the suit. I hang it in the bathroom to dry and go downstairs to kill some time until I have to do it all again.

I drop the soiled cloths into the sink and run the water as hot as I can. I wash my hands, still in their rubber gloves, and scrub them with antibacterial soap, all the time watching the clock to make sure I wash for the prescribed time. The rhythm of my scrubbing causes my thoughts to churn. *I should let Mum know about Dad. But she's got enough on her plate, taking care of*

Alice. Plus, she might wig out and call the authorities to get help for Dad. But maybe that would be a good thing. I rub my hands harder, trying to scrub away my complicated responsibilities, but it doesn't work.

When I'm done, I boil water in the kettle and go through my new cleanup list, checking off every step to make sure I don't contaminate anything. But as I go through the monotony of cleaning, scrubbing, boiling, and bleaching, all I can think about is how much worse Dad seems today, and how the right thing to do is to tell Mum. And gnawing away under that is the knowledge that I shouldn't be trying to care for him alone, no matter what he wants, and no matter what I promised.

I'm just finishing the last step of the process when the doorbell rings. I slip my gloves off into the water and give my hands their final wash. I haven't been washing for the full thirty seconds when it rings again. Whoever is at the door seems determined to get my attention.

When my hands are clean, I dry them off, throwing the towel into the contaminated pile, and scurry to the door. Through the frosted panel, I can see the yellow mass of a suit. *They've found us out.* I curse under my breath and back away from the door. But there's no point in hiding; they know we're in here. All I can do is fake it and hope for the best. I shake my whole body, willing it to relax and look natural. I crack open the door. Aiden is standing there.

"Oh," I say, feeling my face flush with the memory of our last encounter and then burn with the shame of all the things I've done wrong since.

"You okay?" he asks.

"Of course," I say, trying to sound casual. "Why wouldn't I be?"

"I was wondering why you took so long to answer. I was getting worried."

"Bathroom," I say and force a quick smile. "Sorry."

Aiden's eyes narrow, and I'm sure he doesn't believe me, but I hold my smile, hoping he won't ask about my dad because I don't want to have to lie. It feels like a week before his eyes soften and he gets that sheepish look I've come to love. "I need to talk to you about something," he says. "Can I come in for a minute?"

Aiden glances over my shoulder and I catch myself leaning forward to block his view. Not that Dad is likely to get out of bed today, but if he calls for my help and Aiden hears, we're done. When I hesitate, he adds, "Please? It's important."

For a horrible moment I wonder if he's come to tell me he's been reassigned. "Are you leaving?"

"What?"

"You've been reassigned."

"What? No."

I can't believe how relieved I am. If he went, I don't know what I'd do. He's the only good thing left in this village, and if he left, it would be the last desolate straw.

But when I look up at Aiden, he has a look on his face that says that whatever he needs to tell me can't wait.

"Emmie?" he says, and the name startles me. He's never called me that before. No one has... no one except Dad. And suddenly I know why he's here. I search his eyes, and I find what he's come to tell me.

"It's about Deb."

Chapter Twenty-Seven

Saturday, August 20

I AM NUMB. I'M SUPPOSED TO cry, but I can't. It's as if the news Aiden brought is stuck against something in my brain, preventing it from reaching a place where it becomes real. My friend is gone. *Deb* is gone. No one will ever call me Salty again. When I need someone to give me practical advice, she won't be there. A whole class of new students at Oxford will note the empty chair, but they'll never know the brilliant woman who would have filled it. There are lives that might not be saved because Deb, the doctor, was not there to save them. Death begets death begets death. For the rest of my life, a piece of me will always be missing.

Aiden moves around our kitchen, making tea for me. He sets the steaming mug on the table, and I watch the curl of vapor swirl up and disappear. There will be no funeral for Deb. I won't get to say a proper goodbye to my best friend. I have no way to verify what Aiden has told me; all I can do his trust his word. I could go down to Bubble City and demand to see for myself, but I've already broken so many rules, and I know she won't be there anymore. The only bright spot is that I got to see her one last time, that she knew I was there. I'm glad I decided to do the wrong thing. All I can do now is sit here with this heavy cloak of nothingness draped over me, and wait—wait to see what happens next.

I don't have to wait long. In the next instant, there is a crash on the floor above us. I glance at Aiden, praying he didn't hear it, but by the way he looks at me, I know he has.

"What was that?" he asks.

I don't answer. I have a picture of Dad struggling to get out of bed, falling. I can see him, delirious, stumbling down the stairs and blowing our cover.

"We'd better go and have a look," Aiden says, turning toward the door.

"It's nothing," I shout, scrambling after him, but he's already at the stairs. I watch him go, knowing I am powerless to stop him.

A few moments later, he's back.

"What happened?" I ask, moving toward the stairs.

"Your dad knocked the lamp by his bed, that's all. But…" He moves toward the front door, pausing for just long enough to give me a sad, apologetic look that lets me know what he's about to do. It pierces to the very center of me, where it finds my growing collection of betrayals. "I'm really sorry about this," he says. "Honestly, I am."

And then he leaves. I lock and bolt the door behind him. I know he'll be back, but I'm not going to make it easy on him.

I take Dad a cup of Mrs. Glover's tea, my last attempt to do something useful. It smells of grass and spices, with a vague hint of compost, but the smell isn't totally unpleasant. Dad lifts his hand and lets it drop near the edge of the bed, inviting me to sit. I slide on, afraid to rest all my weight there and make him unsettled again.

"What's wrong?" I ask. I've heard some people get worse before they get better, and I remind myself of this as I look over his pale face. I can see Grandma Syddall in the shape of his cheeks and eyes, now that the boyish chubbiness of his face has sunk. His chin is my chin, a heart-shaped jawline with a smooth nub at the bottom. Alice has his nose, a bit too big for his face with a bulb on the end. I can't remember the last time I sat and looked closely at my dad's face, taking in the details and matching our similarities. When I was little, I would sit in his lap, whether he invited me or not, and press my finger on the bulb of his nose or wrap his curls around my little finger. When did I become too grown up to love my dad? When did I decide to pull away? When did everything he said and did start rubbing me the wrong way? If I could take back the last few years, I would. This time I wouldn't stop being his little girl.

"They're going to take me away, Emmie." His eyes range around my face, and I can see it's an effort for him to focus.

"No," I say. "I'm not going to let them."

"Protocol," he says. "I have to go."

"Then I'm going too."

"No. Stay. Don't go unless you have to."

"I'll be alone."

"It's better this way."

"For who?" I try to keep my voice even. "Not for you. Not for me, either."

"Emmie," he says. One word that tells me to step into line, to not make life difficult for him, to not make a nuisance of myself. This is why I'm not his little girl anymore. Little girls do as they're told. They never question; they never stand up for what they believe. Well, I'm not a little girl anymore. I'm not letting him go without a fight.

Within the hour, the doorbell rings. My whole body tightens with the knowledge that this is not a neighborly visit. I don't get up from the bed. I'll go and answer it, but I'm going on my time. It rings again. I glance at my dad, who gives the slightest inclination of his head. I lean in and run my gloved hand over his forehead, then trudge downstairs.

There are three suits at the door, two to transport Dad and the third perhaps because trouble is expected.

"Can I help you?" I ask.

"Looking for a John Syddall," says the first, fumbling with the paperwork through his gloves. "Is he your dad?"

I nod.

The man looks past me into the house, but I hold my ground. "Upstairs is he?" he asks.

"He's in his bed."

"Can we come in?"

I hesitate a second longer. "I'm sorry," I say. "I can't let you take him."

The two suits in front exchange a look, and the third steps forward.

"Emmott, is it?" he asks, peering at me through his mask. I nod. "I know this isn't easy for you, but you want your dad to get taken care of, don't you?"

"I'm taking care of him. Here. At home."

"On your own?"

"He's fine."

"I'm sure he is, but protocol—"

"I couldn't care less about protocol," I say. "I care about dignity, and I care about my dad being able to stay in his own house, not get shuttled off to some holding facility because it's convenient for you."

I see all three of them shift inside their suits. Their hesitation fortifies me, and I pull myself up straight, daring them to mess with me.

"Look, love," the heavy man says, his tone shifting to one I don't like, "we can do this the easy way or the hard way."

"Are you threatening me?"

"No, love. I'm trying *not* to threaten you if I can help it, but one way or another we are leaving here with your dad, and it would be easier for everyone—including him—if you let us do our jobs."

"Is there a problem?" asks a familiar voice.

I look up to see Aiden coming down the path.

"They're trying to take my dad," I say.

Aiden elbows his way to the front of the group, and the three men fall back under some unseen command.

"Can I come in for a minute?" he asks.

I look past him at the three men waiting for their chance to get past me and into my house.

"Just me," Aiden adds.

I step aside and he rustles in, closing the door behind him and turning the lock.

"You all right?" he says when we're alone.

"No," I tell him. "I'm not."

"Em, you have to let him go."

"You turned us in, didn't you?"

"I had to."

I shake my head. "What difference does it make to you if he's here or in a room full of other sick people?"

"We can't control who he comes into contact with if he stays here."

"Me," I say, my voice rising in exasperation. "He'll come into contact with me. I can control who sees him."

"But we can't control who you come into contact with. Can we?"

My face burns with humiliation. I don't know if he knows I went to Bubble City, but I know. I know I am not to be trusted. "I'm not sick," I whimper.

Inside his face mask, Aiden looks away. He doesn't need to say, "Not yet."

"We can't monitor everyone who promises to stay where we tell them. You can see how quickly we'd lose control."

Tears prickle the rims of my eyes, and I wish more than anything they wouldn't. I want to fight to keep my dad here, for him to have the right to stay in his own bed, but everything Aiden says makes sense, at least on a clinical, factual level. The good of the many outweigh the good of the few, or however the saying goes. I'd understand it better if Dad wasn't part of the few.

"I've been wearing a suit when I go in his room," I say, suddenly defiant again.

Aiden frowns. "Every time?"

I nod.

"How did you get more suits?" he asks.

I don't answer because I don't have an answer to that exact question.

"Emmott, for God's sake, please tell me you haven't been reusing them."

When I don't answer, he shakes his head with an exasperated sigh. "Emmott, there's a—"

"Protocol. I know," I snap.

"Em, your dad is really ill. The very best chance he has is to get proper medical care in an isolated environment."

I want to argue back. I want to tell him that I've seen inside

Bubble City, that I've seen my best friend go in there, and that I never saw her again. But my resolve to fight crumbles. As the pieces fall away, the truth behind my argument is revealed. It's a little girl's truth, a childish, selfish honesty that fills me with shame, but I cannot stop it tumbling from me. "If you take him away, I won't have anybody left."

But Aiden is already reaching for the door. He's seen the breach in my protective shield, and he's pushing through before I can close it again. "We'll make sure you're taken care of, Emmott," he says, "either here or in the Care Center. You won't be alone. I promise." He opens the door and nods to the waiting suits. They brush past me and tramp up the stairs of my house. I stand in the hallway—it's all I can do—and wait for these strangers to take my dad away.

When they bring Dad downstairs, I reach out and take his hand, touching his cool skin, even though I know I shouldn't. He watches me for a moment, his eyes scanning the visible parts of my face. "You're a good girl, Em," he says and squeezes my hand. I'm shocked how frail his grip feels, how weak my dad has become. I hold his hand as tightly as I can as I follow the procession out into the street. Then I let the suits load him into the waiting ambulance. He keeps his weary eyes on me every step of the way, his gaze unbroken until the doors of the ambulance close.

I watch them pull away until I can't watch any longer. Then I turn and run out into the village, hearing Aiden shout behind me. I don't stop. I make it to the war memorial before I realize I have nowhere to run. I can see the stitches of my life, so tightly knitted, unravel in front of my eyes.

Chapter Twenty-Eight

I CAN'T COUNT THE NUMBER OF times I've wished I could be alone. I couldn't wait to get away from the village and out from under the watch of my parents, to be free to be myself and do my own thing, without other people and their opinions getting in the way. I wished so hard for that, and now I've got it. Now I am completely alone.

I plop onto the wall by the war memorial and try to form a single coherent thought. Tears sting the rims of my eyes, but I blink them back. I am not going to feel sorry for myself. I am not going to cry. Despite my determination, an unwanted thought creeps its way into my head. *There is nothing here worth staying for and nowhere left to run.*

Once, after an argument with Dad, I tried to picture how he'd feel if I no longer existed. I imagined a noble Shakespearean suicide, a silent farewell to a world with nothing left to offer, my friends and relatives weeping for the waste of my precious life… caring too late to save me. But I knew I'd be afraid to chase death; too chicken to kick away the chair, step off the bridge, or swallow the pills.

But now, death is chasing me. It would be so easy to stop and let it catch me. The list of protocols is like a reverse recipe for my demise. All I'd have to do is switch the *dos* for *don'ts* and vice versa. *Don't* wear your mask; *don't* wash your hands frequently in hot, soapy water for at least thirty seconds; *don't* maintain at least two meters between other people. *Do* touch your face, eyes, and mouth; *do* go into restricted areas; *do* make unnecessary contact with people whose status is uncertain. It wouldn't be *choosing* death, would it? More like putting myself in the game and seeing if death chooses me.

I shake my head to clear these thoughts. Contracting the virus might be the only way out of this hole of hell, but it's not an option I'm prepared to take.

"Emmott?"

The voice startles me, and I'm reminded that, in the old world, I'd never have put myself in a position where someone could creep up behind me while I sat alone. Only in a place as dangerous as this could I feel so safe.

"You have to come back to the house," Aiden says.

I don't respond. I know he's right, but my body won't move, and my head is too muddled to force it.

"I'm ever so sorry." His muffled voice is not so much cutting the silence as swimming through it. "I didn't want to do this to you."

"But you did it anyway."

"Because I want him to have the best care he can."

"I could have given him that."

"But not the medicine that could save him."

"There is no medicine. That's the whole point. You have nothing to save him. All you can offer is a convenient place to keep him. You'd better go," I say, even though it's not really what I want him to do.

He hesitates long enough for me to know he's not going willingly. "I wanted to tell you that they're starting a vaccine trial," he says.

My heart flickers. "Will they give it to my dad?"

He shakes his head. "Not yet."

"They have to," I say. "If there's a chance it could help him, you have to try it."

"They won't take that risk until it's been tested. I've volunteered for the trial."

"What does that mean?"

"Well, mainly it means I won't get to see you for a while."

"Why not?"

"They'll keep us in isolation for at least three weeks, maybe longer."

"They're going to expose you to the virus?"

He nods.

I want to tell him he can't do it. He can't put himself at risk like that. Why would anyone do that?

"If this trial can stop the virus, it will be worth it."

"But you said yourself if you can make a difference to one person, you've done your job. You don't have to do this."

He looks away and shakes his head. "Maybe it will get you out of here quicker."

"You can't do this for me," I say.

"I'm not. I thought if I could save you, that would be enough, but it's not. I need to do this for everyone."

He sounds just like my dad, and for perhaps the first time, that doesn't sound like a bad thing. "I can save myself," I say without conviction.

"I hope so." He pushes up from the wall. "I'm really glad I got to know you, Emmott Syddall. Maybe someday soon you'll get to London. I'll pay you back all those cups of tea." A light springs into his eyes, and the filters on his respirator twitch upwards so I can tell he's smiling at me. I have no way to tell him how grateful I am and how precious that one kind smile is to me.

"I'd like that," I tell him, although I no longer know what "someday" would mean for me. Certainly not "back to normal" because normal no longer exists. But it would mean I'd be alive, that maybe I could piece my life back together again. And maybe it would mean I would see him again too.

He gives me one last look that is part joy, part fear, and maybe part love, and before I can tell him anything else, he turns and walks away.

When I get back to the house there is a large white X painted across my door. I am a marked woman now.

Chapter Twenty-Nine

WITH NOWHERE LEFT TO TURN, I ring Mum. I dial her number, pushing my emotions down as far as they will go, hoping not to freak her out. When she answers, I tell her about Dad. She doesn't say anything at first, and her silence stuns me. Does she really not care?

"I just thought you'd want to know," I say, ready to put down the phone.

"I'm glad you rang." Her voice is barely a whimper. "Your dad? Is he? How bad is he?"

I can't bring myself to lie any longer. "He didn't want to leave me. He should have gone in right away. Now, I don't know what's going to happen."

"Oh God," Mum cries, as if talking to herself now. "I should have been there. I should never have left him."

We're both silent because there's nothing either of can say to help the other. Finally, I hear Mum inhale, as if she's trying to compose herself. I try to do the same.

"Well," she says, her voice swinging upward, sounding as if Mum is zipping herself into a protective suit for what she's about to say. "I'm not going to ask if you're okay, Em, because I know you're not."

"No," I say. "I'm not. But I'm more worried about Dad at the moment."

"I wish I could be there."

"Yes, but you're not."

I hear her sharp intake of breath. It wasn't meant as a cruel dig, but I'm too tired to be kind.

"Em," Mum says, "you're going to have to get through this. You've been so brave."

"Brave?" A knot of fury begins to spin inside me. What does that even mean? That I'm stoic, or fearless? Bold, or controlled? I'm none of those.

"I didn't mean…"

"There is no bravery in what I'm doing, Mother." She has no clue. I'm not here because of some courageous decision, some act of self-sacrifice for the good of mankind. I'm just doing what I have no other option but to do. I'm getting up each day, getting dressed, remembering to eat (usually), remembering to follow protocol. I put one foot in front of the other and move forward as best I can. She has mistaken my held-up chin for bravery. It's up because I'm too scared to look down.

"I'm not brave, not at all," I tell her. "I'm afraid." It hurts to say that out loud, but I no longer want to try to pretend I'm strong. I'm afraid to stop, afraid to let go, to give in. "I'm afraid of dying," I say. "If I were truly brave, that's what I'd do. I'd stop pretending to be invincible, and I'd be brave enough to face death."

"Stop it, Emmott," she says, her voice shattering.

"You left me, Mum. You left Dad and me alone."

"I had no idea."

"You lied to me."

"About what?"

"About Mark. About Dad. About *everything*."

There is silence on Mum's end of the phone.

"All this time, you wanted your freedom—from the village, from the gossip, from this small, boring life. I get it, Mum. Believe me, I really get it. But now you've got what you wanted."

"I never wanted this, Em. Never."

"But you've got your freedom now, maybe more freedom than you ever imagined."

I regret my words but, as much as I want to, I don't put down the phone. I sit and I endure the silence from the other end of the line. Finally, Mum speaks.

"I've made some mistakes. A lot of them, and some big ones too. There are a million things I could have done differently, but you go through life, and every day you make hundreds of tiny decisions. Sometimes you never see the consequences, and most times you never get to examine what would have happened if you'd made a different choice. But now I have to pay for my mistakes. If I could do it over again, I wouldn't have left you alone. I wouldn't have gone away if I'd thought for one single second I might not see your dad again. But I made choices, and this is where they've landed me. This is where they've landed you. So I need you to know that I love you, Em. No matter what other poor choices I've made, I have always loved you. And I've always loved your dad."

"You have a funny way of showing it."

"Relationships are funny things. And family is the hardest of all. It doesn't come with any instructions, and you do the best you can. Unfortunately, sometimes it's not enough."

I pull away from the phone, as if I'm a balloon tethered to a spot on the ground, but with the longest string ever. I float up and up, away from everything I know, everything that has been solid and reliable in my life. Far below me are Deb, my best friend; Dad, my protector; and Mum, once my rock—all no longer in sight. Everything I need, everything I've ever counted on, is out of reach. I am trapped in every way imaginable. There is nothing left for me out in the real world. Everything I have now is contained within this village.

And even that is in terrible danger.

"We don't have a family anymore, Mum," I say. "We don't have anything."

For the next couple of days, I go through the motions of feeding myself and trying to stay healthy, but I lack conviction. I want to see Dad, but I'm on lockdown. I can walk out of my house just the same as before, but if I'm caught, I'll be escorted back. I almost wish they'd taken me too. At least that way I could check on Dad to make sure he's all right.

My new home aide drops by in the afternoon, leaving a box of fresh supplies. We exchange the requisite information. I tell him I'm fine, and he lets me know that Dad is about the same. I have no way to know if he's lying. He, on the other hand, gets my story by recording my temperature. It's a little higher than normal, but I tell him I've been upset. I'm not sure if he believes me, but he says he'll come back to check on me in the morning.

I don't know what to do with myself the rest of the day. I drag myself around the house like a Velcro pinball, clinging to the windows like an idiot, hoping that Aiden will come past. Just seeing him through the window would be like a dose of good medicine, enough to last me another day. But I know he won't come; he's in Bubble City now too.

The quiet in the house is overwhelming, leaving too much space for my dark thoughts about Dad and Deb to clamber in.

If I give myself over to them, I'm afraid I will never surface. Instead, I busy myself tidying the house and reordering the bookshelves, filing one shelf by height order, another by color, and a third alphabetically by author. Each mindless task takes me a small step closer to the brink of insanity.

Upstairs I pass the door to my parents' room, and the sight of the empty bed stops me. The expanse of rumpled, flowered sheet lies like my unknown future, with no certainty of *if* or *how* it will be used again. Will Dad come home? Will Mum? If they are both able to return, will they? If I'm able to leave someday, will I? Everything that was once only confusing and uncertain now hangs in indiscernible shreds.

I push around the door for the first time since Dad was taken away. I expect the room to feel different, given all that's happened here, but it doesn't. The room looks as if someone has spent the night in bed, got up this morning, and gone about his normal day. I push open the bathroom door, expecting to see a damp towel on the floor, whiskers in the sink, and a spray of toothpaste on the mirror.

But that's not what I see.

At first I'm startled by the shape of a figure standing in the bathroom, but as I jump back, I see it's not a person; it's a suit—one of Dad's discarded hazmat suits, turned inside out and hung from the shower rail to dry, as if he had been planning to use it again, the next time. Except there was no next time. Is this how he became infected, by breaking protocol? Perhaps he touched his face or lowered his mask when he shouldn't have. Who knows? I'm sure he's lying in his isolation unit now, running through every step he took in the days before he fell ill, and wondering what he did wrong. It's too late now. And I can't entertain the idea that it was from reusing his suit because

I broke that rule too. The thought washes through me, taking with it the last of my strength.

The next morning, I have to will myself out of bed and down the stairs to start another never-ending day. I put the kettle on first, then call the helpline number to check on Dad. All they can tell me is that he's "about the same." The nurse says he had a quiet night and promises again to call me if anything changes. I choose to believe that "about the same" is better than him getting worse, because the alternative is unimaginable.

As I put the phone back in the charger, I catch a glimpse of someone going through our gate. I can't be certain who is behind the mask, but from the color of her hair, it looks like Mrs. Glover. I dash to the front door, hoping to catch her, but I'm too late. She has already hurried off back down the street. I'm so desperate for human interaction that I almost step out of the doorway to run after her, but when I look down at where my feet would have landed, I am shocked to see a pile of bagged items on the doorstep. I go back inside to get my mask and gloves and carry everything inside, placing them in the sink. When I peer into the first bag, I find three oranges and a note. *We're thinking about you, Emmott. Take care of yourself. Your dad is in our thoughts and prayers.* It's signed from the Ashtons. The next bag holds another packet of Mrs. Glover's tea. *Please take care of yourself, Emmott*, reads the note. I rifle through the rest of the bags. Each one has a small gift aimed at keeping me healthy and well-fed, everything from tinctures and old wives' remedies to homemade jam and soup. Almost every bag contains a note of encouragement and a kind word about my dad. Every word fills me with gratitude. I can hardly believe that in the midst of the worst period in the lives of everyone in this village, these people have a moment to spare for me. They are my family now.

I'm suddenly overcome with the desire to take my suit and go out into the village, to pick up where Dad left off, to keep doing the good things he's been doing. I want to reciprocate, but I'm confined to isolation now. I promised Aiden and Dad I would keep myself safe. And as much as I want to help, I have a duty to keep others safe too, and that means staying away from them.

Before the sun goes down, I climb into bed and pull the covers around me. There's nothing else to do. Exhausted, my mind drifts to Aiden. I keep looking for him, hoping he'll turn up on my doorstep, vaccinated and healthy, but I haven't heard from him in days. The thought of what's gone unsaid is too much to bear, and the weight of exhaustion pulls my eyes closed.

I'm not sure how long I've been asleep when my phone vibrates with a text message. My first thought is that something has happened to Dad. My next is that it could be Aiden. I fumble in the semidarkness for my phone. But it's neither Dad nor Aiden; it's a text from Ro.

Sorry about your dad, it says. *I am out of quarantine.*

There is no good thing he could say to me about my dad. "Sorry" is all there is. But actions always speak louder than words, and he has so much more to be sorry for. Sorry I deceived you, sorry I manipulated you, sorry I ratted you out, thwarted your escape, forced you to stay. Oh, and sorry I told you I loved you, then as good as signed your death warrant.

A chamber of molten fury compresses inside me. I pull back my arm, aiming the phone at the far wall. But something stops me, an expression I'd overheard when the options for treating

Grandma Syddall's cancer had run out: "putting your affairs in order." I am not yet ready to surrender to my fate, but my options are fast running out, and I'd prefer my affairs to be settled.

Glad you're okay, I type back.

After a pause, he responds. *Sorry I let you down. Just wigged out*.

I hesitate, searching again for what I *should* say, over what I *want* to say. Finally, I say it. *You were right*. If I'd escaped, if I'd infected other people, if I'd been responsible for destroying other people's lives, I couldn't have lived with myself.

I wait for him to say something more, something reassuring, perhaps, *Maybe when all this is over...* So his response, when it comes, jars me.

Have a good life, Em, is all he says.

Have a good life! A good life. A life. Any life! How can life be "good?" How? The molten fury boils again, and this time I launch my whole body into the throw.

The phone clatters against the wall, and I am flooded with a sense of satisfaction at the sound of something breaking. No good news has come through that device, and I don't want to hear from anyone anymore.

But as I pull the covers back up and sink down into my bed, willing sleep to come again, a small, warm light ignites in me. If Ro has been released from his quarantine, is it possible the end is coming? Was Aiden right about this burning out in sixty-two days? We must be close to that by now. I should check the internet, see if my phone is still working, try to find out more news. I try to sit up, but the weight of sleep tugs me back down into the bed. As it pulls me deeper, I think, *I feel like I'm coming down with a cold*. And the last fully formed image I see is of Dad's suit, turned inside out, hanging up to dry.

Chapter Thirty

T HE NEXT MORNING, THE SUN flickers across my eyelids. But I can't open them. I feel as if I've been pinned to the bed by a ten-ton weight, my head fastened in a metal vise. My skin burns like someone's holding a million flames over me, but I don't have the strength to kick off my covers or even push them aside.

I know right away what's wrong. I'm sick.

Deep inside, a spark of panic flickers. *I can't be sick. I can't.* My mouth is hot and parched. I need water to douse the fear that swiftly catches hold of me. "Dad," I groan before I remember that he's not here. No one is here. The panic flares.

I pull one hand up from the mattress and reach for my phone. I need to call for my aide, someone who will help. My hand trails across my bedside table, exhausted fingers feeling for the cool plastic of my phone. It isn't there. An image surfaces of the night before, the text from Ro, the phone sailing through the air and ricocheting off the wall below the window. I can almost feel the broken phone taunting me from its resting place on the floor. I try to pull myself up, desperate now to reach my lifeline. Maybe it isn't broken. Maybe I can alert someone.

But when I try to move, my body is trapped under the ten-ton weight, its hold refusing to give.

I sink back into the bed as the exhaustion of the effort washes over me. Once again, I am trapped, a prisoner, this time in my own bed. Panic nibbles at my bones. How long will it take for someone to find me? Everyone has more pressing things to think about. I need water, but I realize: I'm not going to get it. I am helpless.

I close my eyes and try to conserve my energy. Maybe my home aide will come looking for me soon. Maybe someone will drop in to see if I'm okay. Maybe Mum will try to reach me on the home phone and raise the alarm. Maybe there's hope. Maybe.

Something rouses me from sleep, but I can't tell what. A noise maybe? I lie still and wait.

There it is again.

Is it in the house? I can't tell. It's close. Not in the room. Someone at the front door. It's someone knocking.

Hope propels me to open my mouth and call out, but my lips are gummed together, my tongue plastered to the ceiling of my mouth. I shout that I'm here, upstairs, but I don't hear my voice. I drift away again, unsure whether anyone has heard me or if I've even made a sound.

The next time I'm aware of anything, it's that the light in the room has dipped, reducing the furniture to gray silhouettes. My eyes ache, as if opening up is the last thing I could ask them to do. Night is coming. No one has been inside. If I don't get water soon, I will not make it through the night.

I'm too tired to be afraid anymore. I close my eyes and

feel the virus snaking through my body, overtaking me. I think about Dad, a silly thought that he'll be waiting for me. I wish I could have said goodbye to Mum and Alice. There is so much that needs to be said between Mum and me, and now we won't have a chance to say it. My body hurts all over, as if all my parts have been disconnected and each attached to an electric current. It sends an incessant series of jolts, but I have no way to pull away from the pain. There is only one way out now. A thought comes to my mind. *Scatter my ashes in the churchyard.* It's what I want. For my final resting place to be here in the village, among my family, the only place I have ever belonged. I think about Auntie Sandra. Maybe I'll get to meet her soon. The thought brings me peace.

Stop, I think.

I force my eyes open. I can't do this. I can't just give in. I can't die here, alone. I lie still for a moment, gathering my reserves. With all the effort I can muster, I roll out of bed and push shakily to my feet. I lurch like an unsteady toddler from one piece of furniture to the next, making my way to where my phone lies. There's a crack across the screen and a chip missing from one corner. I push the power button, willing it to life. Nothing. I have to get help. I steady myself against the wall and propel myself to the door.

I stumble down to the kitchen for the house phone, landing hard in one of the chairs. On the table is a cup of Mrs. Glover's tea, left from the night before. It's cold, and a thin film has settled on the surface, but I'm so thirsty, I don't care. I gulp down all that I can and rest my head on the table, waiting for my strength to return.

I must have drifted off, but when I wake up, I feel better—not good, but revived. I drink the last of the tea and push myself up from the table, testing my legs and finding them steady again. I doubt that the old lady's herbal concoction is fighting the virus, but something in it is boosting my strength, so I make another cup.

As I sip the hot tea and let its soothing warmth filter through my body, I know what I need to do. I don't want to be here alone, but I have no one left. My best, maybe my only, chance of survival is to let myself be helped. And I want to do that with whatever dignity I can scratch together.

Taking the marker Mum uses to label her frozen meals, I write my information across the front of my suit. *Emmott Syddall. Age 18. Infected.* I add a shaky cartoon rendition of my face. I struggle into the suit for the last time, sealing the joints as best I can and checking that my nose and mouth are covered. This time I'm not dressing to protect myself; I'm doing it to protect others.

I take a last look around the only home I've ever known. I don't know when I will see it again; I don't even know *if* I will see it again. I don't know how much of my family will come back, if they'll be able or even if they'll be allowed. Our future is more uncertain than it has ever been.

I step out into the early evening light, trying to focus on my mission. I pray my legs will have the strength to carry me to my destination.

It's eerie walking through the village, so many houses in darkness, the crosses painted over their doors. It's still and silent, the way I imagine it would have been when the first of my ancestors moved here almost four centuries ago. No sounds of modern technology, no cars or television, no bustle of daily life. Perhaps I will be the last of the Syddalls to live here.

Beyond the village, the last of the sun's rays graze the tops of the surrounding hills, bathing them in a dreamlike pink light. I wish I could feel the coolness of the grass again and smell the scents of acres of untouched countryside. I pause for a moment and lift my mask, sucking in one final deep breath of cool, fresh air. It fills my lungs and I hold it there, savoring the luxury just for a moment. Then I seal my mask to my face and turn my back to my freedom.

I'm only a few steps from Bubble City when my legs let me down. One buckles beneath me, and I stumble to regain my balance. Before I can, the other gives way, and I drift to the ground as if falling in slow motion through a cloud.

Chapter Thirty-One

I DRIFT IN AND OUT, BRIEF flickers of awareness bringing sounds to me. There's someone coming. *At last*. Hope ignites. I fight to keep my eyes open, afraid that if I blink, the person will go again. I try to call out, but I can't make any words form. I try, but I don't have the energy.

The figure moves toward me and reaches out a gloved hand. It blurs in front of me until it comes to rest on my arm, pressing the cool fabric of my suit against my hot skin. Through that gentle heat, I feel a prickle of electricity.

I force my eyes to focus on the face, trying to capture every detail before it fades again. Gray hair, glasses, a stern face, worried eyes. *Mrs. Glover?* But when I look again, I see I have it all wrong. Fair skin, freckles, kindness. *Aiden.* I try to focus on the kindness, but I don't know where to look.

"Emmott," Mrs. Glover says. "Emmott Syddall." The sound of my own name pulls me back. Fingers squeeze my arm, and the sensation draws me out of the clouds again. "I'll get help."

"Listen to me," the freckles say. "You have to fight this. I'm going to be here, but you have to fight."

I reach out to touch Aiden, but he's not there. My eyes can no longer find him. I try to smile at the thought that I can dream in clichés, but it's too much work. I see Mrs. Glover's face again before I close my eyes and let the darkness come.

There's a new light above me, falling across the floor, its edges reaching my feet but not the rest of me. I hear a noise that sounds almost like my name. Another dream. I hope it's Aiden again.

In my next flashes, there are hands on me, my name, voices. I can't respond, even if it were real, but I know I am in the hands of friends. Something cool touches my lips. Moisture. More voices. A sharp pain in my arm and sweet relief. In my dreams—*fever dreams*, I think—I see Aiden again, just like in my waking dreams. His helmet is off, and he's looking down at me. I recognize his tiger eyes, but his face isn't what I'd imagined. It's a lovely face. I'm glad I got to see it before I go. I lift up my hand to touch him. I'd like to touch him. It's a good dream, because in it, he takes my hand and lifts it to his cheek. I feel his skin. Warm. Electric. A pulse rushes into me. Love. It is. That's what it is. "You've been so kind to me," I want to tell him. "Thank you," too. I can't.

The pale ceiling seems to move toward me as if I'm being lifted. I look for Aiden again. There's something I need to tell him. Something important. But I can no longer see him. He has gone.

Chapter Thirty-Two

D ARKNESS.

Chapter Thirty-Three

Sunday, August 28

MY HAND RESTS ON MY stomach, its weight pressing on my physical body, but it's as if I'm touching something else that isn't me. My body is a shell, a box—like a coffin—and I am no more than a speck of light inside it. I no longer live within my body. I'm lost. It's not exactly how I feel. Small. Insignificant. That's it. I'm trapped inside this vast box, and I'm looking for a way toward somewhere safe.

My eyes ache in their sockets, and the soft parts of me pull away from the structural parts. My bones are laid out like a skeleton, unearthed by an archaeologist and arranged for display. There's nothing connecting them, holding them together, and there's nothing to make them move. The parts of me are separate, together in the same space, but not related to one another. I am disconnected.

My eyelids lay heavy over my eyes and it takes my concentrated effort to lift them. At first I see a slit of hazy gray. Light. I search for something solid to focus on, but there is nothing. Everything is a blur. The haze is suffocating, as if I've woken up in a cloud. My chest tightens, pressing me deeper into the clouds. I can't breathe. I don't know where I am.

There are sounds. Voices? A shadow moves in the distance.

Something passes across my face. Air? Beneath my fingers, I'm aware of a sensation, fabric, the coolness of a sheet. I don't know where I am, but I know I am alive. I close my eyes, secure in this knowledge.

The next time, my eyes open of their own accord. It's so bright.

White. Everywhere is white. I blink and colors unbend and appear from the brightness. Cream, green, brown, all muted. A draped ceiling. Lights. Blue bedding. A silver stand. A clear bag, tubes.

A face?

I look again. It *is* a face. A real face. Dark skin. Friendly eyes. The creases of a smile folding behind the edges of a simple paper mask.

"Welcome back, Emmott." The voice is pure and clear. Like an angel's voice, I think. I'm not imagining this. I'm here.

"Bit of ice?" the voice says. A woman's voice.

I try to move my head. It must have worked because she eases me up and places something cool on my lips. I open them and let the chill of an ice chip slide into my mouth. I press my tongue against it until it melts and cool liquid runs into my throat. Sweet relief. I open my mouth again, like a performing seal, and the angel drops in another chip.

"Rest now," she says, and moves away.

For once, I do as I'm told. I let my eyes fall closed and drift back to sleep.

The light has faded outside the tent, replaced by the glare of electric lights. There's another face I don't recognize. It's a smiling face, and it comes with a touch to my arm, hands on my body, gentle and caring, kind.

This time my surroundings spring into focus. The haze isn't cloud, it's plastic—sheets of it forming a square bubble around me. I'm not at home. *Bubble City*, I think. I shrink into the bed. Bubble City. Deb. Danger.

I look back at the face. It's a full face. No yellow suit. No respirator. No impenetrable barrier between us. I open my mouth to ask how, but I can't form any words. My mind flits to Aiden and the vaccine. Did it work? Am I here because of him?

And Dad? I try to ask, but I don't have the strength for any questions, only a handful of brief thoughts.

Dad is okay. Mum and Alice could be here soon. The quarantine will be lifted soon.

But Deb is dead. And Aiden will leave.

It's not the thought I want to sleep on, but I can't stop myself from drifting away again.

There is a new sensation in my arm now. It's not the same as the needles and the flow of medicine I'm accustomed to, and yet it's somehow familiar. I scrabble around in my memory, trying to name the feeling, but all I find is haze. I force my eyes open, the hazy bubble of plastic all around me filtering the light from the room beyond. I feel, rather than see, a dark shape beside me. It's the thing that's causing the sensation in my arm. I pull the bubble into focus, the layers of plastic becoming clear. The dark shape is a person, the nurse, standing by my side, her hand resting on my arm. There are no needles, just the warmth of her skin, a gossamer layer of glove between us, pressed against mine. It's the most wonderful sensation I've ever experienced.

"Morning, Emmott," she says. "How are we feeling today?"

I open my mouth to answer, but my parched lips feel as if they're glued together. I run my furred tongue over them and find my voice. It feels like weeks since I've used it. "'K," I say.

I'm aware of the smell of food—real food, not the fake stuff— and I realize I'm starving.

"You need to try to eat something today," she says. "We need to build up your strength so we can get you out of here."

"Elmington?" I rasp.

She nods and starts to rearrange me in the bed, her adept hands adjusting my body. She fiddles with a box on the side of my bed, and my upper body starts to rise. The pressure pulls away from my back as I'm tilted upwards, the fluids that have been pooling in me beginning to drain. I feel as if I've been freed from a heavy suit of armor. A light sparks in my brain, and then another, as I start to make connections again. If they're moving me to Elmington, I'm going to be okay.

I try to picture myself in the grounds of the big house, the sun on my face and the smell of fresh, clean air in my nose. And I try to imagine what it will be like to be free again. It's been so long, it's hard to conjure those feelings.

The nurse holds a small cup to my mouth, and the coolness of the rim sparks against my lips. She tilts it until water drips against my dry lips. It trickles into my mouth and rolls across my tongue. I swallow for what feels like the first time ever, as the cool rivulet trickles down my throat and caresses the inside of my stomach. I am alive.

My mind gathers together snippets of memory. They are vague at first, dark and painful, but bit-by-bit, I start to remember. I remember the pain; I remember the feel of Deb; I remember Aiden the last time I saw him. And I remember...

"Dad," I say. "Where's my dad?"

The nurse takes the cup away and makes a fuss of organizing the tray of food.

"Is he still here?" I ask again.

She turns back and rests her hand on my arm again. The sensation no longer feels wonderful. Through her touch she tells me everything I need to know. *I'm sorry* and *There was nothing we could do.* All the platitudes of bad news in one simple gesture.

"I'm sorry, Emmott," the nurse says, squeezing my hand. "Do you want me to stay with you for a while?"

I shake my head no. I want to see my dad. I want my mum to be here with me. I want my life to go back to normal, the way it used to be, back to when it was imperfect. I want to make sense of what she is telling me, that my dad is gone. That a person I've known since the first day of my life is no longer here. I can't grasp the idea that he no longer exists.

"I want to see him," I tell the nurse.

Her mask of professionalism slips for just a second, enough for me to see all the reasons why I can't see him, but then she gives the slightest shake of her head. "I'm sorry, Emmott, but he's already gone."

Rage struggles to gain traction. I want to prove her wrong. I want to get up and check every bubble in this place until I find him, because he has to be here. My dad would never leave me.

I push up from the bed, but the nurse puts her hand against my chest. It's a gentle movement, but it's more than I have the strength to fight against. And then another familiar sensation reaches my arm, and a river of warmth flows into me.

"This will help you rest," she says.

"I don't want to rest," I try to say, but I can't form the words. I want to feel pain. I want the fact that my dad is gone to hurt more than anything I've ever felt before. I want to feel my insides ripped out and cast aside so I can live with the hole that's left behind.

But instead, I feel the heat. As the bubble blurs back out of focus, I try to ask if anyone has talked to Mum. But finally, I feel nothing.

Chapter Thirty-Four

Thursday, September 1

M Y NURSE IS BACK AGAIN. The bearer of bad news, wielding her power over my pain. On or off. Feel or don't feel. She decides, not me. She seems to fight to find the appropriate expression for her face, one that's positive and encourages me to get better, but that also considers that I'm coming back to a life that will never be the same again. I turn my head away.

So many people are gone, so many more have lost their families and friends. My situation is nothing special. I'm just part of the tragedy, a statistic. I'm one of the lucky ones, I know. I survived, but I don't feel very lucky at the moment. For months to come, maybe years, the news reports will talk about "the victims" and "the hundreds who perished." Maybe they'll tell the story of the man who did all he could to shore up his community, or the man who risked his life to make sure his daughter wouldn't have to be alone, but they won't really *know* that man. They won't know my dad.

Every time a shadow passes the walls of my bubble, I wonder if it will be him. A part of me expects him to poke his head around the plastic sheeting and ask me if I want a cuppa any minute now. But death has become such an everyday occurrence that I know he has really gone.

I close my eyes and force my dad's face into my mind. For a second, I can't see him, and I panic, scrabbling through my memories, afraid in case I lose him. And then he's there, his moon face, red from the fresh air, his brow creased like sea waves—the way Alice would draw them. I see his cheerful smile, the one I always thought he kept for the villagers. Behind his glasses, his narrow eyes. They are kind eyes. How did I never notice this before?

"I have a bit of good news for you," the nurse says. "You've been cleared for Elmington. We'll move you today with any luck. We'll ring your mum to pick you up there."

I try to force a smile, but I can't get my head around the idea of leaving the village. Ironic since it was all I ever wanted. Beyond the cordon is a world that I no longer feel a part of. I remember reading about people serving long prison sentences, who become so used to the institution that they can't readjust to life on the outside. When I try to remember life as it was before the quarantine, I can no longer picture myself there. I can't imagine the freedom of walking out of this village and back out into the real world. I can't picture going to London and slipping into life, meeting new people and answering, "Where are you from?" I can't see striving for a foothold in life after this. How can I hold a conversation about art or politics or music or clothes when none of it could ever matter again? I feel like a pinball, waiting to be released from its launch, but I won't be free. All I'll be able to do is ping around, bouncing off obstacles, propelled this way and that, and ultimately ending up back where I started. Now that I've been a prisoner, the thought of freedom is terrifying.

The nurse touches my arm and gives me another practiced smile. "When all this is over . . ." Her voice trails away. I know she has nothing she can say to me. What she's been through must be way beyond her training. How can anyone prepare for this? And for the first time, I see her not as a nurse, but as a person with a home and a family she can't be with, and a life that's also been turned upside down.

"Thank you," I say. "Thank you for all you've done."

That afternoon, a birdlike orderly collects me from my room and packages me up for shipment. Chirping nonstop about the weather, Elmington, the latest royal baby, and news from Wimbledon, she hefts me into a wheelchair and drapes a clear plastic cape from my shoulders that stops just before it reaches the ground. I may be immune, but they still take precautions to avoid me carrying the virus out into the world. I try my best to keep a stiff upper lip, but I'm still caught out by the surprising feeling of being torn away from the only place I've ever called home.

As the orderly wheels me out to the decontamination showers, I take a last look at the Care Ward. Inside the individual bubbles are familiar faces in unfamiliar surroundings, neighbors I've known my whole life, people my dad tried to help and people who did what they could to help me, trapped in their sealed compartments. I feel guilty because I'm getting away.

I want to look away, but as I do, I catch sight of someone else familiar. I don't recognize the face at first—it's not anyone I know from the village—but something makes me ask the orderly to wait.

I stare into the enclosure, trying to work out what's so familiar. "Who's that?" I ask.

The orderly leans in and squints at the patient information tag tucked in a clear pocket above my head. "It's one of them Red Cross fellows, I think. The young one," she says.

It takes only an instant to piece together what I already know I've seen. Just a flash of skin, the shape of the edge of a cheekbone, and the sense of knowing that this is Aiden.

"Can I see him?"

"Sorry, love. Can't take you in there."

I understand, but I have to know if he's going to be okay. I can't leave here without knowing. "Okay, then I need to see Dr. Reynolds before I leave."

"There's an ambulance waiting for you," she counters.

"Please, I need to see her. It's important."

The orderly hesitates.

"Please. There's something she needs to know before she releases me."

It's a terrible lie, but it's enough to make the orderly decide not to take the risk. She parks my wheelchair and disappears outside. A moment later, she returns with Dr. Reynolds, who looks surprised and not especially happy to see me.

I get straight to the point. "What happened to Aiden?"

She glances at the orderly, then back at me. It only takes the tiniest flick of the doctor's head to let the orderly know she's dismissed.

When she's gone, Dr. Reynolds confirms what I've already worked out for myself. "Aiden didn't react well to the vaccine," she says. "He's stable at the moment, but we'll know more in the next twenty-four hours."

"But he's going to be okay. I mean, he's not going to…" I can barely bring myself to think the unthinkable, and there's no way I can say it. Death has become such a way of life around here that it almost doesn't seem real. "He shouldn't have done it."

Dr. Reynolds reaches out, as if she's going to take my hand. At the last second, she pulls back. One tiny gesture to remind me of what I am, perhaps not dangerous anymore, but an unknown quantity, a potential threat. "What Aiden did was incredibly brave. The trial was completely voluntary, and no one would have thought less of anyone who opted out. Look around here. We all had the chance to volunteer, but few of us did. A lot of people will be leaving here because of Aiden."

"But the vaccine made him ill."

"They made adjustments and tested it again. Our staff have been given the new version."

"So everyone can leave now?"

"Not quite," she says. "It's a bit more complicated than that. We'll administer the vaccine in phases, then observe for the incubation period. We don't want to move people out who might be infectious. It's going to take several weeks before the quarantine can be lifted." She goes on about decontamination and rehabilitation, but I'm no longer listening.

"Can I see Aiden?"

Dr. Reynolds stops talking and shakes her head. "I'm sorry, Emmott. Only medical and support staff can go into the units. When he wakes up, I'll let him know you were here. He'll be glad to know you've been relocated." She gives me another one of her practiced smiles, but it's not enough to convince me that Aiden will be okay. I'm tired of feeling helpless.

When the orderly wheels me outside, the daylight is shocking. I haven't seen the sun for so long, my eyes are no longer accustomed to its glare. It's a beautiful day in the village, the kind I've never fully appreciated until now. A light breeze rustles through the trees, making them sing a whispery song. A flock of birds wings overhead and disappears into the hills. No wonder the tourists loved it here.

As the orderly wheels me toward the waiting ambulance, I take a last glance down the street. At the bottom of the village, just before the "Welcome to Eyam" sign, the barricades and patrol are still in place, reminding me that our ordeal is not yet over, and our village is still far from idyllic. It may never be idyllic again. As I turn toward the village green, I spot the war memorial. I can recall easily the names of the former village residents, their family names familiar to me still. I wonder if they'll erect a new memorial to commemorate our latest battle. Every name would be familiar to me, my own family name the most familiar of all. If my dad were still here, he'd see to it that a memorial was created so no one would ever forget what happened here.

Against my chest rests the pendant Dad gave me for my birthday—the little gold woman on the swing. I'm free now to go back out into the world and do what I want to do, to pick up my life and move forward again. But in that moment, I know that I will do the one thing I swore I would never do. I will step into my father's shoes and make sure it gets done. *I will form the Memorial Committee*, I think, wondering if I could piece together volunteers from what's left of the villagers. No one will ever forget this, the price paid by so many. But then the thought of erecting a stone memorial—a cold, lifeless token of remembrance—seems so meaningless, and suddenly I know what I must do instead.

"Stop," I tell the orderly. I push up from my wheelchair, but she holds me back down. "I can't go," I say.

"It's all right, love," she says. "You'll be well looked after there."

"No." I push up from my wheelchair again, only this time I mean it, and the orderly doesn't have the coordination to maneuver the chair *and* hold me down. Two paramedics step toward me, but it's clear from their expressions that they're not sure what to do next.

"It's okay," I tell them. "I'm not going to run. I'm not going anywhere. I just need to talk to Dr. Reynolds again. That's all."

The paramedics glance at one another, then at the orderly, then at me. A nod from one of them, and the orderly wheels me around, parking me in the shade until Dr. Reynolds returns.

By the time she reappears, looking annoyed, I know exactly what I need to say, and I won't take "no" for an answer. I am my father's daughter.

Chapter Thirty-Five

Friday, September 2

M RS. GLOVER'S GATE GIVES A complaining squeak as I close it behind me and turn to give a last wave to the old woman peering through the gap between her door and the frame. She nods back, but just before I turn away, a rare smile creeps up behind her mask. It's a small, but satisfactory, victory.

In the street, I discard my gloves and mask, now more precautionary than life-saving, and check the next house call on my list. One more and I'm done for the day. The badge clipped to my shirt says that I am a volunteer Community Liaison. My name has been printed beneath in permanent marker, as official as I'm going to get. I have a whole new list of things I'm forbidden to do—administer food or medication to anyone, make skin contact—and strict protocol for entering and leaving people's homes. The mask and gloves are not for my protection anymore, but as a precaution to stop the last of the dying virus from hitching a ride on me as I move around the village. And to make my wary neighbors feel a little safer. I'm here to offer the one thing I have to give, something few others are able to offer—a little dose of familiarity.

Reynolds put up a good fight—I'll credit her with

that—but for every argument she presented, I countered with my defense. As a survivor, I am immune to infection. I am no longer harboring the virus, so I cannot infect others. My presence in the village, I argued, would help to reassure those remaining—those now vaccinated but waiting through the incubation period to get the all-clear, and those, like Mrs. Glover, who flat refuse to leave. I never thought I'd say it, but I respect her for that.

When my rounds are done, I head to Bubble City, scrubbing up and slipping into a papery protective suit, securing my mask and gloves. I can't help but think this is still all for show, but I go along with the rules, not wanting to rock any already unstable boats. This is the part of my duties that Reynolds most strongly opposed. It's also where I dug my heels in the deepest. I know this is a privilege, and I won't do anything to risk losing it.

There are only twelve patients left in the unit, according to the list I've procured. One of them is my best friend's dad. I am shocked to see how thin and pale Mr. Elliot appears, and my hand runs across my own knobby wrist, reminding me that we are all less than we were. Pulling a chair from one corner of the room, I move in beside him, my volunteer tag tapping against the side of the bed as I lean down and wait for him to sense me. He doesn't.

The list says that Mr. Elliot is stable. He will pull through. I don't know what else to say, so I tell him this: His wife and son are okay too, and I'm doing well and feeling like my old self again. It's not entirely true, but I want to tell him only good news. There'll be plenty of time for the bad. I tell him funny stories about Deb, remembering all our antics. I talk about my dad the same way, determined that no one lost to our village's tragedy will ever be forgotten. Mr. Elliot's eyelashes twitch, but he doesn't open his eyes or speak. I sit with him a while longer, chatting away as if it's just a normal day, until I run out of things to say. I promise to be back soon, and go through the process of taking off my gloves and scrubbing up for the next visit. I drop in on Mrs. Wainwright, who doesn't look well, and Mrs. Ashton, who manages to smile and pats my hand, offering me the comfort I'm supposed to be giving her. Eventually, I arrive at the big reason I fought so hard for permission to visit Bubble City.

I peer through the plastic sheeting of Aiden's pod, not quite ready to go in. Everything is familiar about the man in the bed, and yet nothing is recognizable. What's new is the shape of his body, the tone of his skin, the color of his hair. And the profile of his face. Out of his suit, Aiden is more slender than I'd imagined, his long limbs, previously inhibited by layers of protective armor, stretched out down the bed. His hair is short and spiky, lighter than I'd expected and with a reddish tint that looks like flecks of marmalade in the light. But I can't see his smile. Not yet. And from here, I can't see his eyes. It's this desire that finally draws me inside.

Moving across the temporary floor, I slide into the chair by his bed. My eyes take in every detail, committing them to memory while I can. I notice a scar on his chin and realize I might never get the chance to find out how he got it. We've done everything backward, and I'm afraid I might lose someone I know intimately and yet know so little about.

I reach out my hand, resting my fingers on his arm, touching his skin through this gossamer layer of glove. So close and yet so far away. My touch seems to spark against him, and

I'm afraid it will be too much for him, but I can't pull away. This is the thing I've wanted for so long now.

I rest my head next to his hand, holding my breath so as not to disturb him. And I wait.

When I open my eyes, my head is still on Aiden's hand, held there now by a dull stiffness in my neck. I must have fallen asleep. I'm pretty sure this isn't in my job description. I ease my head off the bed and look up. Aiden is awake.

He's looking back at me, his familiar eyes—his tiger eyes—surrounded by features that are still new to me. He smiles. I've only ever seen the smile in his eyes before, but without his respirator and hood, I can see him smiling at me with his whole face. It might be the most beautiful sight I've ever seen.

I want to be the first to speak, afraid that when I hear his voice—his real, unobstructed voice—I won't be able to respond.

"It's you," he says. He seemed so sure of himself behind his yellow armor, but now that he's exposed, I find his awkwardness endearing. I look away, thinking that it might help me find the courage to say something more profound.

Something moves into my field of vision, and his fingers curl into the palm of my hand. They're cool, but the sensation on my skin lasts only a moment before it's replaced by heat. He lifts my hand and holds it to his cheek, and I'm overcome by the sensation of his touch as it courses from his skin to mine, into my bloodstream and through my entire body. I've craved human contact, but I hadn't realized how starved I've been for this kind of touch. For his touch.

For weeks I've been untouchable and, although I've been

given the all clear, everyone remains cautious. If Aiden pulled away from me now, I'm not sure I could stand it.

But he doesn't pull away. He pulls me closer, and in one small, awkward move, I'm on my feet and leaning toward him. Instead of my hand, it's my cheek that's against his. I can feel his breath in my hair and the heat radiating from his body—a million sensations. His hair has a warm, sleepy scent, and his skin holds a vaguely plastic aroma left over from the suit. I'm aware of a slight prickle of stubble on his jawline and a whisper of eyelash against my ear. His breath begins to slow, and I'm sure I can feel his heart beating inside his chest. I know I can feel mine.

He runs his thumb over my temple, and when I finally pull away, he smiles. I reach out and touch the scar on his chin.

"Cricket ball," he says.

"Now I know something about you."

For a moment neither of us says another word. I find my eyes flitting around his face, taking in every lovely detail. He does the same to me. I haven't stood this close to another person for so long. It's odd that I've never noticed before how the air changes when you step into someone's personal space. Like when you put magnets too close together. Some pairs repel, and some attract. It's pretty clear to me which kind we are.

I glance back, but see no sign of anyone outside Aiden's pod. I have a small window of time alone with him, this close. I make a decision then. I peel off one glove and pull my mask down below my chin. Resting my hand against his cheek, I savor the brief moment of contact, his skin and mine. And then I lean in to kiss him. Maybe he'll pull back, but he might drift away again at any moment, and then I'll never know. I have to take the chance. I keep my eyes open and press my lips against his cheek. He seems to hesitate for a second, but then he turns my way. I stare into his tiger eyes, and he kisses me.

We are two tainted people, people no one will want to kiss for a long time, but we've found each other, in this unimaginable mess. My chest tightens, and I know I'm going to cry. I scrunch up my nose, trying to stop the tears from coming, but I'm helpless. Behind those tears is a wall of grief I've been holding back for weeks, and once they start, the dam will burst.

Aiden finally pulls away. "Thank you," he says. "That was so worth the wait."

He closes his eyes, and I can see he's drifted away again. I sit for a moment and watch him rest, then carefully pull my hand away and move toward the door, pulling up my mask and grabbing a fresh glove from the box, covering myself again. I have a protocol to follow—stripping down, scrubbing off, decontaminating, washing off his kiss—before I suit up again for my next shift. I don't have much to offer—a friendly face, a kind word, and a simple human touch, the smallest thing—but it's better than nothing. Dad would have been proud.

Author's Note

In 1665, a tailor in a small village in northern England ordered a bolt of cloth from London and inadvertently brought the bubonic plague to Eyam. As the disease began to claim its victims, members of the community made a courageous decision that changed the course of history. In an attempt to prevent the plague spreading to neighboring villages and towns, the people of Eyam elected to impose a quarantine on their village, cutting themselves off entirely from the outside world. All told, 260 people in Eyam sacrificed their lives and thus saved untold thousands. Emmott Syddall was one of those people. The story of her separation from her fiancé, Roland Torre, is depicted in a stained glass window in Eyam church.

In updating the story to the present day, I have taken many liberties with the setting, characterization, and events of Eyam's history. Although inspired by the true story, the Eyam and Emmott Syddall of *The Smallest Thing* are entirely fictional.

I hope you enjoyed reading *The Smallest Thing* as much as I enjoyed writing it. If so, please tell a friend. Word of mouth is still the best way to support your favorite authors, and I would be thrilled if you'd help me to spread the word about this book.

Write a review. Book reviews really do count. Even a few words posted on your favorite bookseller's website can help others discover a book. You can also copy and paste the same review to other book sites, such as Amazon.com, Barnes&Noble.com, and GoodReads.com. If you would consider posting a review for *The Smallest Thing*, I would greatly appreciate your time and effort.

Pass this book along to a friend. Or feel free to buy them their very own copy.

Share this book. Tweet, share, post, pin, text about this book. Your influence matters.

Stay in touch. You can connect with me at the following social media sites and on my website. Be sure to sign up for my newsletter to receive news of my upcoming books, get behind-the-scenes peeks into my stories, see what I'm reading, or just to say hello.

Website: LisaManterfield.com
Twitter: @lisamanterfield
Facebook: AuthorLisaManterfield
Instagram: @lmanterfield

Also by Lisa Manterfield

Kat Richardson isn't running away from grief; she's just hiding out in a gloomy Welsh university town until she's sure it's gone. Now, one year, nine months, and 27 days after the climbing death of her first love, Gabe, she thinks she's ready to venture out into the relationship world again. And Owen—a cake-baking, Super Ball-making chemistry student—appears to be a kind, funny, and very attractive option.

But the arrival of Kat's newly adopted niece, Mai, forces her home to northern England, where she runs headfirst into all the memories of Gabe she's tried to leave behind—and discovers that Mai stirs up an unnerving feeling of *déjà vu*. Before long, Kat's logical, scientific beliefs about life after death are in battle with what she *feels* to be true—that reincarnation is real and Gabe has come back to her through Mai. The question now, is *why*?

Taking on the topics of love, loss, and how we deal with

grief, *A Strange Companion* is a twisted love triangle among the living, the dead, and the reincarnated.

Acknowledgements

My heartfelt thanks to Steven Wolfson for his guidance and encouragement in writing this book, and for cajoling me into taking risks. I hold him solely responsible for the demise of one of my favorite characters. Gratitude also to Ami Cohen, Kate Stewart, Brauna Walsh, and Jeffrey Wolf for their enthusiasm about the early explorations of this story.

Jennie Nash, Sarahlyn Bruck, Kit Frick, and Eddy Bay lent their incredible talents to the vast improvement of this book. Kate Tilton kept me organized and took care of the important details.

My thanks to Rossitsa Atanassova for the gorgeous cover and to Glendon Haddix of Streetlight Graphics for the interior design.

I am grateful to Carollynn Bartosh, Rebecca Lacko, Kathleen Guthrie Woods, Maya Rushing Walker, and Sophia Walker for their feedback on early drafts, and for their encouragement to keep going.

My thanks to the people of Eyam for allowing me to rearrange and repopulate their village for the benefit of this story.

I am very fortunate to have a wonderful group of supportive friends and family to cheer me on when this writing thing gets tricky. And I have Jose. I'll never know how I got so lucky, but I am thankful every day.

About the Author

Lisa Manterfield is the award-winning author of *The Smallest Thing* and A *Strange Companion.* Her work has appeared in *The Saturday Evening Post, Los Angeles Times,* and *Psychology Today.* Originally from northern England, she now lives in Northern California with her husband and over-indulged cat. Learn more at LisaManterfield.com.

Lightning Source UK Ltd.
Milton Keynes UK
UKHW010908050522
402541UK00001B/240

9 780998 696928